Just Add Happiness

OTHER TITLES BY JULIE HATCHER

Not Quite by the Book

A NOVEL

JULIE HATCHER

This is a work of fiction. Names, characters, organizations, places, events, and incidents are either products of the author's imagination or are used fictitiously. Otherwise, any resemblance to actual persons, living or dead, is purely coincidental.

Published by Lake Union Publishing, Seattle
www.apub.com

EU product safety contact:
Amazon Media EU S. à r.l.
38, avenue John F. Kennedy, L-1855 Luxembourg
amazonpublishing-gpsr@amazon.com

ISBN-13: 9781662523472 (paperback)
ISBN-13: 9781662523489 (digital)

Cover design and illustration by Elizabeth Turner Stokes
Cover image: © Chinu_maru / Shutterstock

Printed in the United States of America

This book is dedicated to my poddy. Thank you for all the happiness you've added.

Chapter One

I checked my phone one last time as the first guests arrived for book club. My best friend, Alicia, had volunteered to handle the greetings, so I could stew a bit longer in my kitchen.

Book club night was my favorite of the month, but tonight it seemed my reckless mother, Trina, and my twenty-one-year-old daughter, Camilla, were in cahoots to give me an ulcer.

I wanted to scream.

Alicia returned to the kitchen, a bright smile on her petal-pink lips. She pushed a hank of stick-straight brown hair behind each ear and leaned against my counter. "Any luck? Did you hear from either one?"

"Nope." Mom didn't answer her phone, and my text chain with my daughter had cobwebs forming in the corners.

I tucked my cell phone into my pocket, then passed Alicia a tray of freshly plated blueberry chiffon tartlets. "I'm sure everything is fine."

She quirked a neatly sculpted brow. "Tell your face."

I frowned, then worked to relax my features. "Better?"

"Uh-huh." She rolled her eyes and lifted the tray. Alicia was a beautiful paradox. She was petite and curvy with a naturally doe-eyed expression, and her small, youthful appearance often gave strangers the idea she was a gentle, helpless soul. In truth, she had the mouth of a feral trucker and the attitude of an NFL linebacker.

I aspired to her personality, hating my often too timid and cautious nature. She could keep the curves, however; I had no use for them or any idea how to use them. Four inches taller than her five-foot-two frame, I was lean and narrow like a ballerina without the benefit of all the muscle and grace.

Alicia and I had met as freshmen at the University of Virginia. We'd been best friends for nearly thirty years since. Pretending with her didn't work, and I knew it, but it never stopped me from trying.

"Okay. I'm worried," I admitted. I worried incessantly about my mom and my daughter—their health, their happiness, and their general well-being. I did everything I could for both of them, and we had long-established routines. I visited Mom twice a month and traded text messages with Camilla daily, but for some infuriating reason, my mother wasn't home when I stopped by today, and Camilla hadn't responded to any of my texts since announcing a big trip with her longtime boyfriend, Jeff.

"My mom didn't answer the door today, and I can't get her on the phone. I thought she was out earlier, but now I'm wondering if she had a stroke in her living room, and I just shrugged, then drove away. Her place is a mess."

My mom was diabetic and had no business drinking, but I swore she was drunk half the time I visited. I could hear it in her voice. The hoarding was at an all-time high too. At this point, I suspected I was the only one cleaning her house, and I could only get over there a couple of times a month.

"What if she tripped and fell and can't get up?" The familiar heat of anxiety rose through my body like an inferno. I pulled my thick mass of brown hair over one shoulder and secured it with an elastic band.

"Your mom's sixty-five, not one hundred. I think she could've reached the phone to call for help if she fell."

I wasn't so sure.

"How about this?" Alicia offered. "If you're still worried after book club, I'll ride over with you and we can peek in her windows. I've got time, and it won't be the first time we've teamed up for a little surveillance."

I smiled. Alicia had climbed on my shoulders more than once in our twenties, catching cheating boys in a low-tech era. These days I'm sure there's an app for that. "I can't tonight," I admitted. "I don't know when Robert will be home, and you know how he is. He'll have a coronary if I even mention her." My husband had never liked my mother, and his level of unhappiness with her quadrupled every year. "If I'm not here when he gets home, I definitely don't want to be at Mom's place."

Alicia's eyes narrowed. She hated my husband and all his pedantic, patriarchal rules and nonsense. I didn't blame her. I hated him, too, but that was a problem for another night.

"It's just easier not to bring her up," I said. "He'll take the opportunity complain about what an awful human she is." I puffed out a breath. "She's not the greatest, but she's my mom."

My mother had spent my childhood shielding me from Dad's drinking and temper, instead of leaving him for both our sakes. Her vigilance kept her on edge, depressed, and exhausted. I'd felt more like a burden than her child for most of my formative years. She was so busy deflecting my dad's behavior that she never really got to know me. By the time I hit middle school, I resented her for what I'd endured at home and for dozens more reasons that I didn't even understand. Dad never hit me, but his presence and treatment of my mother had brutally murdered my innocence and stolen my childhood. He'd been dead for nearly eighteen years, but I was still mad at him.

Much to my dismay, after his death Mom spiraled instead of healing. She drank to numb her pain and refused to do anything that might bring her joy. Mom and I weren't friends, and we had very little in common, but we were eternally tethered by our shared trauma and DNA. So when she didn't respond, I worried.

"I wish I knew how to help her," I said. "In general," I clarified. "Assuming she's fine right now."

"Sometimes you can't fix things or help people," Alicia said. "And that's okay. If she's not ready or willing to make big changes, it's no one else's business, even if you really want it to be."

I made a vomit face. "I just want everyone to be safe, healthy, and happy. Is that too much to ask?"

Alicia studied me. "Have I told you lately that you're an incredible human? You tell me all the time, but sometimes I worry I don't tell you enough."

My gaze jumped to meet her eyes, and a sharp sting of emotion hit my chest. "Thank you. And you do."

She smiled. "I mean it. I know how hard you work to protect everyone and everything. You're a top-tier mom and the very best friend. A phenomenal baker. A better wife than Robert deserves, and a wonderful, kind, compassionate daughter. I get busy and forget to say so."

I rubbed the place above my aching heart with my palm. "Camilla was with Jeff last night when we talked, but I can't reach her now. Do you think she's okay?"

"Oh, please," Alicia said. "Jeff would protect her with his life. Plus, they're twenty-one and in love. They probably had a late night, rolled out of bed in the afternoon, and went out again."

"I'd be happy with a thumbs-up emoji. I don't need a whole diary entry. Proof of life shouldn't be too much to ask."

Alicia lowered the tray and leaned against the counter. "I get it. You see me worry about my boys, and they're all built like brick walls. I can't imagine having a daughter. The world is not kind to women her age. Or any age, really."

"You aren't helping."

"But she's with Jeff," Alicia added. "He'll keep the creeps and pervs of the world at bay. We still like Jeff, right?"

I nodded. Jeff was a nice kid, smart, and he adored my daughter, actively and with verve. That was part of the problem. "The last few texts she sent were about a big trip she's taking after finals." Until now, she and her boyfriend had been content spending summers at the lake or hiking through national parks. "Jeff invited her to the Maldives. They're staying in one of those huts on the water."

"Ooh," Alicia said, eyes alight. "Nice."

I opened my mouth to say it absolutely was not nice. That this was obviously his plan to woo her into a wedding engagement. That Camilla was the same age I'd been when I accepted Robert's proposal, and look where that had gotten me. But someone rapped on the kitchen door.

I spun to look at the clock above my stove. "Shoot. I lost track of time. Hold that thought." I hustled into the pantry and pulled a pastel-pink bakery box from the top shelf, then hurried to greet my caller.

"Hello," I cooed, brightening my smile as I opened the door I typically used for business transactions.

The scent of lilacs floated to me on the soft spring breeze, mixing with the aromatic notes of vanilla and chocolate rising from my box. Southern Virginia was beautiful any time of year, but spring was my favorite season. Blooming flowers always gave me hope for new beginnings, and I was in desperate need of exactly that.

A harried women in her thirties stood at the door, looking anxiously at me, then the box. "Bless you," she said, pushing fallen locks of hair away from her weary face. Her messy bun was hanging on by a thread, and she had two similar, but different, loafers on her feet.

"I couldn't have done this on my own," she said. "There just isn't time."

I nodded in full understanding. "The life of a mother is a twenty-four seven occupation."

She sagged visibly, and I fought the urge to hug her.

Kids screamed in the minivan behind her. "They never tell us they need treats for twenty classmates until the day before. Why do they do that? I work sixty hours a week and barely sleep as it is."

"That's why I'm here," I said. "I've been there. I get it."

She set a thin stack of cash on the box. Then we traded. I got the money. She got the pastries.

I loved baking, and I'd catered for Robert's law office for years, but more recently, I'd added a few small paying jobs on the side. The work provided cash that Robert didn't know about, and therefore couldn't control, and each job came exclusively through word of mouth, so he wouldn't catch me and complain. Everyone involved chose secrecy for personal reasons. My customers got to show up at events, or host them, with fancy desserts they pretended they'd baked themselves, and I saved the money so I could eventually hire a divorce lawyer. The business was a godsend for many working, frantic, sleep-deprived parents in the area, especially those feeling the pressure to do it all and make it seem easy. But it was an even bigger win for me.

I'd made cute pink business cards that featured only *The Invisible Baker* scripted in gold curlicue font and the number to an unregistered phone I bought at Target.

I closed the door as the visibly relieved mom returned to her minivan, then tucked the cash inside an old tampon box, hidden inside a tote for cleaning supplies in the utility closet.

Alicia waited at the expansive granite island. When I returned, the tray of tartlets was gone, presumably delivered to the sunroom while I handled business. "How much do you have now?" she asked, a knowing smile on her rosy lips.

"A few thousand." Finally enough to pay the retainer for the divorce lawyer I wanted.

She nodded with pride in her eyes. "That's a lot of baked goods."

I'd realized before Camilla's tenth birthday that my husband, Robert, was abusive, though I didn't have the word for it then. He never called me names, cheated, or raised a hand to me, none of the things my father had done to my mother, but Robert's small offenses had accumulated to the point of my continual misery, and I'd come to realize his behavior was intentional. Something I'd since learned was emotional abuse.

Robert grew steadily more awful over the years, and I'd hit rock bottom before I figured out the trouble was with him and not me. So, while he became colder and more controlling, moodier and more condescending, I crafted a plan to leave the moment Camilla went to college. I didn't want her caught up in the inevitable shit show of divorcing a narcissistic lawyer like Robert.

Somehow, more than a decade passed while I held everything together in our lives, my mom's, and Camilla's, and I'd finally saved enough money to hire a lawyer. It was three years later than I'd planned to escape, but I was good to go now, nonetheless.

"Feels kind of badass," I admitted.

Alicia's smile grew. "Rightfully so."

"I just wish I didn't have to sneak around like I'm selling meth instead of madeleines."

Alicia snorted. She lifted a vase of flowers I'd arranged for tonight. "I think this is it," she said. "Grab the wine. If you're finally getting a lawyer, we need to celebrate."

My phone rang, and we both froze. Mom's name centered the screen. "Oh, thank heavens."

Alicia waited while I answered, talked quickly to my mother, then disconnected and set the device to silent. "Apparently she was out with friends, and according to her, I don't need to know where she is every minute of every day," I reported. "I'm so glad she and I can have these talks."

Alicia rolled her eyes. "Well, at least that's one woman off your worry list."

For now, I thought. But her health was declining, and she'd stopped working, so she was behind on her property taxes. I feared she'd lose the house—which would be catastrophic. Robert and I could easily help with her finances, but he'd never agree to it, and he'd sooner burn our home down than allow her to move in with us. I didn't have enough hidden money to keep her in an apartment for more than a month or two. Not exactly a long-term fix. Dad left her enough money to get by, but lately she drank and shopped online as if that was her full-time job, blowing through her savings.

My husband was a selfish asshat, my mother a reclusive eccentric—who was lying through her nose about spending a day out with friends. She'd alienated everyone she knew except a longtime neighbor, Ilona. But like Alicia said, at least I knew she was okay for the moment.

"Now I just have to wait for my daughter to check in."

"Don't worry too much about Camilla," Alicia said. "She's smart like her mama. She knows her own heart and mind, and whatever decision she makes, if Jeff proposes, will be the right one for her."

I shrugged but couldn't bring myself to agree, because what if she was wrong? What would I do then?

"For what it's worth," she added, "there are good men in this world, Soph. I think Jeff is one of them. Your dad and husband are exceptions, not the rule."

"Maybe," I allowed. But in my experience, romantic love was the poison that turned nice men into monsters. "If I have to use my secret baking money to pay Mom's bills, it'll mean staying here another year, and I'm not sure I can make it that long."

"Let's hope it doesn't come to that," she said.

"Agreed. I'd probably kill Robert before Christmas in that scenario, but at least book club has taught me the best ways to cover up a murder."

Delight glinted in Alicia's eyes. "Now there's a crime I can get behind."

Chapter Two

I pulled two bottles of prosecco from the wine fridge, then raised them into the air. "Ready."

Alicia led the way through my formal dining room and living room to the sunroom overlooking the patio, gardens, and pool, where a half dozen women I'd met at various community events and classes sat chatting. Floor-to-ceiling windows provided abundant natural light, and the unobstructed views created a nice outdoor-living feel—without the heat and bugs.

I'd broadened my social circle a few years ago when I recognized that all my friends, Alicia aside, were handpicked by Robert. Wives of other partners at his firm, wives of his golf buddies, women from our country club. All people he'd met and vetted before introducing them to me. I decided he could keep them in the divorce. I wanted people of my own.

The book club ladies ranged in age from thirty-four, twelve years my junior, to somewhere over sixty. We lived very different lives in various parts of town, but we were united in two perfect ways: our love of books and our womanhood.

Sylvia was the first to notice me enter. She owned a small art gallery on the East Side and made more money in a day than I had in my lifetime. "There you are," she said, crossing long thin legs beneath her on the wide settee. "Everything looks incredible as always. I don't know how you find time to do all this. We were just discussing whether or not you really make these pastries on your own. If you have a baker, I need that name before my next gala."

"Thank you," I said, setting the wine on the table beside an elaborate charcuterie spread and several long-stemmed glasses. "It's all me. I took a few classes at the country club. They bring in first-class instructors, and the workshops are fabulous. Plus, I practice more than I should." I patted my stomach. "If you can't tell."

"We cannot," Sylvia said. "I bet Robert is counting his blessings for marrying you. You must be a hit at his office. Do you pop in with these to show off? I know I would if I made magic like this in the kitchen."

I struggled to keep my smile bright. I delivered sweets to the law firm weekly per Robert's request, but he pretended he had no idea every time I showed my face there. Sometimes he didn't make time to see me, though he told me exactly when to arrive and what to bring. He always had critique and commentary at the ready when he came home on those days. The pastry shells were too thick, tough, or underbaked. The recipe a little uninspired. Could have used more or less of this ingredient or that. Robert demanded perfection in all things, but he raised the bar continuously so that I'd never hit the goal. "I have plenty of time on my hands these days," I said. "Now that the nest is empty."

"Uh." Jeannie, the youngest of our members, scanned the space around us pointedly. "Sure, but it's one gigantic fucking nest."

I laughed and settled on the couch beside Alicia and Jeannie. "It's definitely more than the two of us need." Everyone loved our elaborate showcase of a home. Only Alicia and I knew the place was void of love and laughter beyond these meetings, or that every good and decent memory I made here was darkened by Robert's shadow. "But it feels so much cozier when you come over. Thank you for being here."

A soft round of *aww*s went through the little group. Then I picked up my copy of this month's book from the coffee table, thankful for a change in subject.

"Hey." Jeannie snapped her fingers. "That reminds me! I've been meaning to ask if you know about this secret baker that's helping parents get the hoity overachieving PTA moms off their backs at school functions and fundraisers."

Sylvia groaned. "I do not miss all that drama. It's not a competition, for heaven's sake."

"Everything is a competition in elementary school," Jeannie said. "Especially for the parents."

Alicia slid mischievous eyes in my direction before turning them to Jeannie. "No, but please give her my number. My three boys play five sports. All I do is show up to fundraisers and bake sales. The other moms can be so cruel to those of us who only have time to pick up something on the way."

I bit back the urge to tell them a related horror story, one that infuriated me still today. Years ago, I'd ridden with Alicia to drop off her oldest son for football practice, on our way to visit her middle son in the hospital, following an appendectomy. She'd cried at the sight of the cupcakes I'd baked for the nurses, because she'd forgotten to buy a dessert for her son's practice and we were already running late. I'd offered to run into the nearest grocer for her so she could wait with her youngest son in the car, but she told me the other moms would judge her either way. For forgetting. Or for buying, not baking. So she'd go empty-handed and at least gain a few extra minutes at the hospital before visiting hours ended.

As a stay-at-home mom of one child, I'd had no idea this kind of cruelty existed, or worse, that it was commonplace. Until then, Alicia had never said a word. I gave her the cupcakes I'd made for the nurses, and after that I'd baked for every event her busy family attended since then. Years passed before I first traded my baked goods for cash, but the Invisible Baker was born that night in Alicia's old minivan.

"No one will admit they've used her, only that they've heard the rumors," Jeannie said. "I hoped one of you had a hookup. I started buying from bakeries in neighboring towns, then transferring the goods into containers from home to pretend I made them. Nobody has time to make homemade treats anymore. We work, care for the home, carry the mental load, manage the kids, struggle through their homework, chauffeur them all over town for extracurriculars. It's impossible. But if you have the audacity to buy snacks instead of making them yourself, then half the other moms act like you've broken some code of conduct. It makes no sense, and besides that, putting anything I baked on the fundraising table would cause the health department to shut us down."

I laughed, a little too loudly, and Jeannie leaned forward to glare at me playfully.

"Oh, hush over there. Not everyone can bake like you."

I cleared my throat. "I thank the country club for all their lessons and my adult child for my free time to take those lessons. Sorry. Let us know if you have any luck finding out who this mystery baker is," I said. "Meanwhile, we should probably get started. What did everyone think of *Butterfly Mom*?"

Alicia lifted a small slice of Brie to her lips. "I enjoy living vicariously through youthful heroines, so this one was a heavy read for me."

"I don't know," Jeannie said. "I've been a youthful heroine. It's exhausting. I liked the meat offered here."

Butterfly Mom was about a single mom from the 1980s trying to juggle everything women do today with the added weight of living in a society hostile to her. Women in corporate America were treated as interlopers, secretaries, or coffee fetchers. Single motherhood was taboo, and being divorced was often the kiss of death in social communities, but the main character of this book persevered. "I admired her tenacity," I said. "It took incredible strength of character not to burn everything down."

Judy and Katie nodded from matching velvet armchairs.

I wasn't sure whom they were agreeing with.

"Did we all like Maisy Marple?" I asked. I found the main character relatable in the extreme. I'd set the book aside often as I read, needing time to absorb and process her heartbreaking trials and difficult decisions. I admired her strength, and in the end, she got the life she'd always wanted.

Sylvia shifted in her seat while the others passed an open bottle of wine around, filling glasses. "In my opinion, she wasn't very heroic or inspiring, and she waited too long to speak up and make a change for herself," she said, mile-long lashes flicking with her gaze.

"But she was so realistic," I said. No high-fantasy plots or fairy-tale romances in this read. Just one woman's plight to protect and raise her family. "I found her incredibly relatable. Just doing her best to make lemonade out of lemons."

"Really?" Madeline's sculpted brows pinched together. "I thought she lived in willful denial. She lied to everyone about how she was really doing. Her friends, her family—"

"Herself," Jeannie added.

I peered at Jeannie. "I didn't see her that way."

She shrugged. "It was frustrating, watching her toil unnecessarily, waiting for the stars to align before she chose happiness."

"You can't just choose happiness," I protested. "As a state of mind, maybe," I allowed, "but that wouldn't have changed her circumstances."

Murmurs settled in the corners of my sunroom, and a feeling of panic rushed into the following silence. I hated conflict, but I didn't understand how Sylvia and I had read the same story and taken away such different interpretations.

Sylvia pursed her lips and leaned in my direction, sharp gaze fixed on me. "Sophie," she said carefully. "She had to change her circumstances."

Alicia pressed her shoulder gently to mine in an invisible show of support while I wrestled with Sylvia's words. She'd spoken with such easy accusation, exactly like someone who'd never had to upend her entire world for personal reasons.

⁂

After the guests left, Alicia stayed to help me clean up. She packed leftover snacks into plastic containers and loaded glasses into the dishwasher.

I joined her, feeling prickly after the night's discussion. Why didn't the other women see the book's heroine as I did? Did they truly not understand that it took strength for Maisy to smile when she'd rather cry? Or that she was brave for showing up every day and doing what needed done? Heroines didn't have to lead armies to be heroic.

"Dinner smells delicious," Alicia said. She tipped her head toward my slow cooker. "What are you making?"

"Roast," I said. "Are you hungry? I can make you a plate. There's plenty."

"I'm waiting to see what the guys are doing."

I smiled. Alicia's "guys" included one doting husband and three wild teenage boys. Cameron Junior, or CJ for short, age eighteen, William, sixteen, and Quinn, fourteen. All high school varsity athletes, just as their parents had been.

An unexpected wave of longing to see my daughter hit like a tsunami.

"You want to talk about it?" Alicia asked.

I dragged my eyes to her, then shook my head.

"Okay. Then do you want to talk about why you're so attached to this book? You never press your opinion this hard. Don't get me wrong, it was refreshing to watch, and I loved it. But why?"

I bristled. "Maisy Marple was making the best of her situation. When did that stop being a good thing?"

"Uhm, she ate shit politely for four hundred and twenty-seven pages," Alicia countered. "It was hard to read at times. And since when do you choose stories about complacent women? This whole night has been like an episode of *The Twilight Zone*."

I collected the full containers, then ferried them into the pantry.

"You can't hide," she called.

"I'm not hiding." I returned to the island and poured a glass of merlot. I was, however, ready for a change of topic. "I'm still thinking about my mom. It's not as if she talks freely to me, but I can tell something's going on with her. I want to offer her help, but that will open up a can of worms here with Robert, and my hands are already full."

Alicia sighed. "I get it. She's your mother. It's natural to want to help. Robert would know that if he was human."

I cracked a smile. "Not Robo Robbie."

"Never Robo Robbie," she agreed. "But he'll get what's coming to him soon enough, and then you can do what you want for your mom and in any other aspect of your life." Her gaze landed on the slow cooker across the counter and she glared.

"It's easier to keep something warm for him than to listen to him complain about all the hours he works, and how the least I can do is make sure he comes home to a hot meal."

Alicia feigned strangling herself. Her hate for Robert was more passionate than mine.

I'd become neutral to him years ago, while Alicia continually wanted to hit him with her car.

"Why not put up a boundary on the way he speaks about your mother?" she asked. "You've got one foot out the door now, so it can't hurt to draw a line there. Then draw as many others as you can."

I shrugged, exhausted by the thought of trying to talk to him at all. "Or I could just pack up one day while he's at work and remove all traces I've ever existed before he comes home." I wondered how long it would take him to notice. I guessed at least a day if I left a meal in the slow cooker.

"Sure," she said. "That's another option."

A nonsensical panic rose through me, familiar and terrifying, as I thought of actually leaving him. Until now the concept had been surreal. As of tonight I finally had enough money for the attorney retainer. When I filed for divorce, he'd be livid. I'd be the villain. My name would be dragged through the mud around the neighborhood and in his professional life. Even at our country club.

I forced myself to breathe. My integrity was the only thing I had left that was truly mine.

"Your face is turning red," Alicia said. "What am I missing?"

I took a gulp of my wine, continuing to process. "I'm imagining the day I really do it."

"I will do cartwheels," she vowed. "When will you do it?"

"I don't know. I'm terrified." He wouldn't physically hurt me. Robert never did anything overtly. He was a sneaky, underhanded troll. Still—

I held the panic in my chest, dissecting it like a wriggling insect, and the epiphany hit so unexpectedly, I nearly laughed. "I think I'm afraid of him."

Alicia's expression went stern, and fire ignited in her eyes.

"Not like that," I quickly amended. "I think, mentally, all the years of walking on eggshells and not living up to his impossible standards have caused a glitch in my brain." Or perhaps my desperation to avoid being talked to as if I were something pulled from the bottom of his shoe caused my heightened anxiety, and presented itself as fear. Whatever the reason—"I know I have to do it, but everything in me is begging me not to upset him."

Alicia relaxed by a fraction, but her jaw clenched.

"You know what else?" I said, suddenly on a roll. "I'm terrified of leaving. I went from my parents' home to college to Robert. What if I leave the security that this life provides me, and I end up even more miserable? I already have incomprehensible amounts of guilt for staying this long and letting Camilla grow up in this weird, quietly toxic environment, but a little voice keeps warning me that this is the only way I can survive. By staying here. With Robert."

Alicia pulled me into a hug. "Pretty sure that's Robert's voice you're hearing, because you can do anything you choose and find real happiness wherever you want. I know that in my bones. I know it as well as I know I want to throw that slow cooker at his fancy new Benz."

Her phone rang, and she released me to look at the screen. "It's Cameron."

I turned away, taking the moment to regroup.

“Hey.” Alicia’s voice and the sound of jangling keys pulled my attention back to her. “Cameron’s meeting the boys after practice and taking them out for wings. They want me to go.”

I refreshed my smile. “Go. I’ll call you later and let you know if I hear from Camilla.”

Alicia nodded. “Call me if you need anything.” She put unnecessary emphasis on the final word. Alicia would come if I had a hangnail.

The thought brought a fresh surge of emotion as I watched her walk to her car. “Have fun! Enjoy the boys!” I called.

Then I slogged into the kitchen and turned off the slow cooker.

Chapter Three

I slid into bed at half past ten. The muffled sound of our garage door opening set me upright around eleven. Energy fluttered through me, and I hustled to the kitchen to pull out the roast and veggies I'd moved from the slow cooker to the fridge.

"Oh," Robert said, padding toward the island several moments later. His tie hung loose around his neck like a scarf. He carried his suit jacket and briefcase. "I didn't think you'd be up."

"I wasn't," I said, arranging his dinner on a plate before setting it inside the microwave. "I made a roast. I'll reheat you some."

"I'm not hungry," he said. "I had dinner at the club."

I blinked. "You weren't at work all this time?"

Robert's expression hardened. The pale-blue eyes I'd fallen in love with at nineteen now looked like those of the devil. "Yes, Sophie. I was at work, but I was there for fourteen hours. They let me out to eat. What did you think?"

I stiffened at his tone. "I thought you'd be hungry."

"I'm not."

The microwave dinged, and I retrieved the steaming meal.

"I wish you would've called," I said, equally angry with both of us. He was the absolute worst, but I was ridiculous for catering to a man I loathed. "Or sent a text."

"I was working," he said slowly. "What?" he asked when I didn't respond.

I shook my head and set the plate on the island. This was the last night I cared if he went to bed hungry. I never should've accepted the task as my responsibility. That was on me.

"What?" he repeated.

"Nothing. It's fine."

Robert released a laborious sigh and marched in my direction. His mussed hair and rumpled shirt gave the impression he'd been sleeping before his return home.

I wondered briefly if there was another woman. Oddly, I was never enough for him, though I'd started as the prize. A rebel, free of my hometown, my parents, and everyone who knew the old version of me, at least for a few short years. Happy, carefree, and uninterested in dating. I'd been a game for him to win.

He wanted me despite my lack of interest. Or maybe because of it. He chased me, pursuing tirelessly until I agreed to dinner. One yes had opened the door I couldn't close. He made a shameless spectacle of wooing me, and everyone except Alicia thought it was so cute. I wasn't sure what to make of it then. It was overwhelming to be so starkly visible and unapologetically wanted. I thought my luck had somehow changed. That, despite what I'd come to believe growing up, I was lovable, desirable, and worthy.

I heard rumors that he cheated on me in college, but I could never prove it. I'd had my suspicions over the years, but I lacked the backbone to confirm. Because what would I do if I was right? Leave? Robert was an attorney. He had money and influence. I had no work experience, no income, and a daughter I would've lost access to every other week. I couldn't imagine missing a single moment with her, and I feared he might try to poison her against me on the weeks she lived with him.

Then there was the porn. I'd once cried rivers over his need for those magazines when he had a loving wife in his bed. I'd crash dieted, though there wasn't anything wrong with my figure. I lost an unhealthy amount of weight, and I suspect I looked at the women in the photos more than he did, perpetually wondering how I could be more appealing.

Those were the years before I realized I wasn't the problem.

Back when I cared about him at all.

I stepped back as he drew near, thrown by the hostility flowing off him.

"Here," he said, lifting the fork I'd set out and stabbing a piece of tender meat. "I'm eating your dinner." He shoved the bite into his mouth and made a show of enjoying it. "Mmm. Thank you. I forgot to eat all day. What would I do without you?"

The fork clattered against the plate where he dropped it, and I stared as he strode away.

Resentment boiled in me, and I imagined throwing the used fork at his head. Instead, I followed him. "Have you spoken with Camilla?" I asked.

"No. Why?" He turned as he entered our bedroom, then went directly into his closet. "What's the problem now?"

I bristled but ignored his nonsensical statement. Camilla was always a delight. "Jeff invited her to the Maldives when school ends this year, and I think he might propose." I waited, but Robert didn't respond. "I think we need to have a talk with her before they leave."

Robert reappeared in sweatpants and a T-shirt. "I think you spend too much time worrying about what other people are doing. What I'm eating, when I get home, where our adult daughter goes on vacation. We aren't paying for that, are we?" he asked as an afterthought.

"No. And I don't care where she goes on vacation. I care that she might end up married before she finishes college. We need to encourage her to take things slowly and enjoy her life before settling down."

Robert grunted. "If she's happy, why interfere?"

"The wedding will cost you at least a hundred thousand dollars," I snapped, knowing that mentioning money would likely get his attention.

His expression turned bewildered. "It's our only daughter's wedding. Would you prefer a backyard barbecue?" He laughed at his terrible joke. "That sounds like something your parents would've suggested, actually."

As usual, I'm thrown by his response. Normally he made me believe saving money was all that mattered. It wasn't long ago he'd ranted and lectured me for buying a six-dollar box of Girl Scout cookies, as if I'd committed a capital offense, but tonight a one-hundred-thousand-dollar wedding was no big deal. I could never predict his reactions as much as I tried, and this was a prime example.

I shook off the mental whiplash and moved on. I wouldn't get any support for my concern for Camilla, so I provoked him. "Speaking of my parents," I said, "my mom worries me."

He scoffed. "Is that supposed to be news?"

I steadied myself with a hand against the bedroom doorframe. "I think she needs help."

"You think she needs money," he corrected, tossing the emphasis back to his usual point of view.

"Maybe."

"Your dad set her up nicely for their lifestyle. If she blows through the savings, that's not on us."

"I think her health is declining," I said. "She's not managing her diabetes."

He hooked headphones around the back of his neck and stared down at me, waiting for me to move.

"Where are you going?"

"I've had a long day, and I need to blow off some steam," he said. "I'm going to the treadmill, though I still don't see why it has to be all the way in the basement."

He'd let me choose the home gym location. I didn't understand why he'd asked me at the time, since the space was primarily intended for him. Over the years I'd come to understand his reasoning. He rarely worked out without first complaining that I set it up so far away and in such an inconvenient location. One more way to say I screwed up, or let him down. One more example of my ineptitude and incompetence.

I moved aside, and he brushed past me into the hallway.

"Don't give her any money," he said over one shoulder as he jogged down the steps.

I climbed back into bed and fell asleep to visions of Robert being shot off the back of the treadmill at high speed.

❧

In the morning, I left a note on the kitchen counter advising Robert that I'd gone to Pilates. On the off chance he came home while I was away, I didn't want him to call or question me. I didn't have the bandwidth to fight.

Mom lived in an older neighborhood two towns away. A twenty-five-minute drive into local history. Everything near the home I shared with Robert was new and shiny. Condominiums and gated communities surrounded by highways, upscale shopping and dining.

Harbor Heights, however, was the epitome of historic Virginia. Ancient oak trees lined uneven brick streets, their gnarled, reaching limbs entwined gently overhead. Morning sunlight filtered through the mossy, web-covered branches, creating a sparkling midday mosaic across the ground.

I smiled as I drove, appreciating the peacefulness and beauty. I'd loved growing up here, within walking distance of an active and community-centered downtown. Tidy brick homes with brightly colored doors and cheerful wreaths anchored green postage stamp yards. And ghosts of my childhood pedaled past me on tricycles, racing the boy next door.

Everything in sight was quaint, Southern, and charming.

Until I turned the corner, and Mom's place came into view. The once adorable cottage where I'd spent my first eighteen years was now the eyesore of the block, if not the entire street. A weathered gray porch and sun-bleached red door greeted neighbors and passersby. The home's chipped yellow paint and cracked white trim were the icing on a rotten cake. A ratty old wreath, the cherry on top.

I parked in the narrow gravel drive and stared at the overgrown lawn and crooked shutters blown loose by a recent storm. I felt ashamed for being ashamed that my mother lived here.

I sent up my usual fruitless prayer for a decent visit, then left my SUV in the driveway and trudged up the path.

Mom opened the front door before I reached the steps. "Where are you supposed to be this time?" she asked. Her gaze roamed disdainfully over my Lululemon leggings and tank top. "Yoga?"

"Pilates."

She sniffed and moved aside for me to enter.

I looked like my mom in most ways, willowy and fair skinned with little ski-slope noses and lightly freckled cheeks. But Mom had red hair. I had brown. Her eyes were narrow and close set, mine wide and round. As a child, I couldn't wait to grow up and be as beautiful as her. I'd never imagined she'd age like fruit.

The air inside her home was stale, the rooms crowded with an abundance of things. Unopened boxes from bouts of online retail therapy formed a wall near the entryway.

She closed the door, snuffing most of the light.

I blinked to adjust my eyes. Heavy drapes and endless piles blocked every window. "You didn't sound well the last time we spoke," I said. "I wanted to check on you."

"I'm fine." She crossed her arms, and the sweatshirt that fit her well not so long ago bagged dramatically in response.

When had I last visited? I tried to come every other week, but I'd missed our last visit when Robert ambushed me with guests. He liked to grill lunch on our new patio for prospective clients and pretend he was a family man. I played the role of traditional wife. After clearing the table of their meal, I'd presented them with a strawberry torte ringed in ladyfingers and tied at the center with a red ribbon. A woman in my flower-arranging class had commissioned the torte, but I'd cracked under the pressure to impress and served it to Robert and his guests instead. I spent the rest of my day making another torte to fulfill my order.

Mom coughed against a tight fist as she headed for the kitchen. The pallor of her skin and gauntness of her cheeks added further confirmation. She was far from fine.

I'd missed whatever she said but knew enough to follow.

We weaved along a narrow path between collections of old and new things, then stopped in the mostly uncluttered kitchen. She poured coffee into two mugs and passed one to me.

"How long have you had that cough?" I asked. Combined with her general appearance, I wondered if she'd somehow gotten pneumonia.

"Why?" she asked. "Afraid I'm contagious? Is that why you stayed away so long this time?"

My mind returned to the mental math I'd abandoned earlier. I hadn't seen Mom in nearly a month, and it irked her. "I'm sorry," I said, taking a seat at the table. "Different things kept coming up, and it's harder to get away than you'd think."

"That's because you married an asshole," she said. "Don't bother defending him. I know an asshole when I see one. Robert knows I see him clearly. It's the reason he never liked me." She lifted the lid on a nearby soup pot and removed a flask, then poured the contents into her coffee.

I bristled. When had she stopped bothering to pretend she didn't have a drinking problem? The child in me wondered when she decided I wasn't worth shielding from her ugly truths anymore.

Another round of coughing hit, and she covered her mouth with one hand while bracing the other against the table. Pain marred her pretty face with each sharp exhalation.

"Mom?" I reached for her, but she stepped away.

She lowered onto the chair across from me and breathed heavily for several minutes as I watched.

We didn't have the sort of relationship where we comforted one another. We didn't hug or share words of affirmation. So I sat helpless, wondering what I could do other than feel utterly useless as my mother struggled for air.

I moved to the sink and filled a glass with water, then returned to her side. "Drink this. I don't think whatever you put in your coffee is going to make you feel any better."

"You're wrong about that," she croaked.

I set the glass before her, and she ignored it, raising the mug to her lips instead.

I returned to my seat, frustrated and angry. "How long have you been sick?"

"I'm not sick. I'm old." She rose unsteadily and shuffled to the cluttered countertop, searching through the piles of things.

"You're not old," I argued.

"Then I'm just tired," she said.

Me too, I thought. For a moment I imagined saying it aloud. Maybe even discussing the things on my mind with her. She could give me some motherly advice for a change, and we could find some common ground. A little camaraderie.

I hated how much I longed for that sort of relationship and how little she wanted it.

Mom returned to the table looking paler than before. She placed a cigar box on the table and didn't take her eyes off the little container as she sat.

"What is that?" I asked.

What felt like unspoken fear filtered across the space between us and seized me.

I nearly leaped from my chair when she finally flipped open the lid.

A thousand miscellaneous buttons lay inside.

"Is everything okay?" I asked, unsure what to make of a box full of buttons.

She pushed her fingers into the contents, causing the little disks to slide and spill over one another. "I need to tell you something," she said. "I should've done it long ago, but as you are keenly aware, I'm a coward."

I frowned. "What are you talking about? I've never thought you were a coward." Mean? Yes. Odd? Of course. Pointedly determined to remain alone and miserable? Clearly. But I'd never considered her anything less than hardheaded and steadfast.

Her searching hand stilled inside the box. "Your dad is in France," she said. "Or he was. I don't know where he is now."

I folded my hands and silently questioned her mental health. Even drunk, she never forgot Dad was gone.

"Mom, Dad died when Camilla was three," I said, gently. "Maybe you should lie down. You've lost a lot of weight. I don't like the sound of your cough, and I think we should make an appointment with your doctor. Just to see that everything's okay." I mentally ran through my schedule for the rest of the week. I could coordinate the appointment, pick her up, and take her.

"Not necessary," she said. The words floated from her mouth like a sigh. "I don't want you to worry about me. I just want you to know he's out there."

"Dad is dead," I said flatly, shamelessly thankful for that truth. The echoes of his angry words, and her screams, permeated the ceilings and floors, the walls, and my heart.

I blamed Robert for my infrequent visits, but in truth, I hated coming. It was too hard to be here.

"He wasn't your father," she said.

Her words pulled me back to the moment, and I felt puzzled. "What do you mean?"

She freed an old photo from the button box, like a magician pulling a rabbit from a hat. Her gaze lost its focus, and she turned her attention to a nearby wall. "We were in college the first time he hit me," she said. "Carl, not Bastien."

Goose bumps rose on my arms. "Who's Bastien?"

"Bastien Allard. Sébastien, I suppose."

What were the early signs of dementia?

How could I get her the help she needed? What would that cost? How pissed would Robert be?

Could I get ahead of something this big and mitigate the fallout?

"We broke up," she continued. "Carl and me. He loved to yell, and he'd pushed me once or twice, but I told him if he ever hit me, that was where I'd draw the line." She set the photo before me. Her expression tightened with anger, and she wiped a tear from her eye. "I went to France for summer semester and time to heal. I racked up a ton of debt running wild for three months. Then I came home with you."

"I was born at a hospital ten minutes from here," I corrected. "I have an official copy of my birth certificate. Come on, Mama, let's go upstairs and rest."

She shook her head. "I was pregnant but didn't know for nearly a month after my return, and Carl had wooed me back to him by then."

My muscles tightened as what she said sunk in. She wasn't delirious or delusional. She was telling me that she'd been with someone else during a breakup with Dad. "Holy shit."

"I didn't have a way to contact Bastien back then, so he never knew about you. It was the nineteen seventies. Everything was casual," she said. "No cell phones. Long-distance calling cost a small fortune. No one around here could afford that. Letters took a month to reach a destination that far away. I didn't know his home address anyway."

My gaze dropped to the photograph with its curled corners and faded image. "I don't understand," I said. But that wasn't true. What she'd said was crystal clear, once I'd started listening. The tyrant who'd raised me wasn't my father.

"Why did you marry Dad, then?" I asked. A burst of unbidden anger broke through my lips, and my grip tightened on the photo. "Why would you marry a man who hit you—and kept hitting you for my entire life? Why would you do that?"

"He didn't hit me again until you were almost a year old," she said. "We made up when I got back from France, so I didn't see a point in mentioning Sébastien. Then I missed my period." She looked sheepish for a moment before lifting her chin. "I told him I was pregnant, and he proposed. He never questioned the timing of your birth. We just fell into step and carried on as if we'd never been apart."

My heart beat painfully as I absorbed this news. I wanted to scream or overturn the table. I wanted to cry. To demand a different childhood. But nothing seemed appropriate. Was any response to news like this appropriate?

"Mama, why?" I began again, more slowly this time, still unable to fathom her horrendous choice. "Why did you willingly live like that? Raise a child like that?"

Raise *me* like that?

"Those were different times," she said. Her dismissive tone indicated the conversation was over. She'd dropped the bomb in my lap. And that was that. "You can keep the photo if you'd like." Her frail body trembled as she finished the spiked coffee, then rose on unsteady legs for a refill.

My eyes traveled back to the faded image.

Mom was young and thin, wearing a bright smile and striped sweater with a denim miniskirt. Her long ponytails hung over her shoulders to her waist.

The man beside her was tall and narrow with a round baby face and mischievous eyes. His hair lifted on top, as if caught in a breeze, and he held on to my mother as if he'd won the greatest of prizes.

"Oh," Mom muttered, drawing my attention to her as she took a wobbly step backward from the countertop.

I was on my feet before I'd thought about it, arms reaching to catch her as she collapsed.

Chapter Four

Inside the walls of Wells Memorial Hospital, I felt like a child again in all the worst ways. I was rattled, worried, and afraid. Mom barely spoke a word after her fall, but she'd opened her eyes, and I took that as hope. Still, something dark twisted in my chest. A knowing I didn't want to accept.

She'd lost so much weight. Her complexion looked strange, almost yellowish, and based on our phone calls, it seemed like she was drunk by lunchtime these days. Historically, she waited until at least dinner. Then today she'd confessed something so huge, I still couldn't believe it was real.

The man who still starred in my nightmares, the monster who'd beaten my mother and caused me to hide in closets until the day I left home, the father who taught me to detach from life so it didn't hurt so much, wasn't really mine.

How was I supposed to process that?

Blasts of rage, shock, and betrayal stung my eyes and nose. How could she keep something like this from me? How could she let me believe I was made up of half his DNA? I hated parts of myself I'd never seen, because I believed they were there, passed on genetically and hiding as I had, waiting to come out.

I'd lived a lifetime afraid of my anger, determined to remain calm at all costs, and terrified of what might happen if I expressed those emotions. Afraid I was my father's daughter. That I'd ruin my relationships and make my daughter hate me.

None of it was real. She'd known, and she'd let me suffer. Eighteen years with him. And eighteen more since he'd died. Maybe she was the monster.

I pushed the thought aside, because I didn't know her at all, and that was also her choice.

Intuition told me she was sick, and she knew it. Worse, I suspected she was preparing to say goodbye.

I inhaled deeply through my nose, seeking peace and hating the ever-present scents of antiseptics and cleansers. The unique blend of smells that screamed *hospital, tragedy, trauma, death.* Would it kill them to add some of those diffusers to the air vents? Puffs of vanilla or lavender would go a long way to settle folks down. Why hadn't anyone ever done that?

Another ambulance pulled into the bay, and I let my head fall back against the wall behind my chair.

The emergency room's waiting area was packed with the ill and the injured, all waiting their turns behind an exam curtain. A dozen or more car-crash victims moved to the head of the line following a pileup on the highway that pushed patients with non-life-threatening issues down the queue. Once Mom was stabilized, she too would have to wait, but at least she'd made it behind a curtain before the first accident victims arrived.

I'd ridden with her to the ER, seated across from the EMT, afraid she would die. Now, when I could no longer be with her, or bear the stream of bloodied humans being transported from the wreck, I just wanted to escape.

I wished I hadn't left my SUV in Mom's driveway. The vehicle was my lifeboat. I used to sneak into the dark garage when Camilla was small just to sit inside my ride and cry. It'd been years since I managed actual tears, but my car was still a sanctuary. An escape hatch. Mine.

At one point in my life I felt as if I spent all my time on the verge of a breakdown and hiding that from my young daughter. I constantly looked for ways to explain away the tears in my eyes. Allergies. Yawns. Fatigue.

One day the tears dried up without me noticing, and I couldn't recall the last time I cried.

I still got in my car as often as possible, though, usually just to leave home. I went anywhere I could justify going, chasing the dopamine rush that came with driving away.

At the moment, shrapnel from the truth bomb Mom had dropped in her kitchen remained in my heart. The pieces pierced and sliced through me each time I thought of her secret. The weight of the photo in my shirt pocket was probably enough to kill me if the shrapnel didn't.

I supposed I was in the right place.

Someone nearby sobbed, and I scanned the standing room–only space. A mom rocked a baby on her hip at the desk, desperate to locate a loved one. All around me, others like her clung to one another, offering strength and comfort, whispering words of support.

I jumped every time someone in scrubs pushed through the door separating us from the curtained care units. My foot bobbed. My palms sweated. I considered calling Camilla but hated the thought of prematurely ruining her day. It was best to wait for news about her grandma's condition before getting in touch. Otherwise, I'd selfishly land her in my position. Maybe Mom would be completely fine.

Camilla had a good relationship with my mother, a much better one than I'd ever had. She was a fun grandma with enough boxes to build a fort in every room and treasures to unearth around every corner. She and Camilla picked flowers from her garden and dunked cookies into milk. They walked along the river and picnicked at the local park. I was grateful for all those things, but deeply envious too.

Mom had ignored me as a child, then seemed to hate me as an adult, but we never talked about it. This Frenchman, Sébastien, was a big missing piece of our puzzle. I wondered if she blamed me for her marriage to Dad and the abuse she endured at his hand. All these years she might've considered it my fault while I'd considered it hers.

"Oh, thank god!" A familiar voice reached through the chaos, and a moment later, Alicia came into view.

I'd texted her when the ambulance arrived, and we'd traded a few quick messages as the EMTs evaluated Mom and loaded her onto the gurney.

Alicia threaded her way through a line stretching to the door, then picked up speed down the aisle of metal-framed chairs in my direction. She crashed into me with a hug when I stood to greet her. "I'm so sorry, it took me forever to get here. I left the minute you called, but there's a huge wreck on the highway."

A woman seated across from us sobbed loudly at Alicia's statement.

"I think a lot of the victims are here," I said. My throat constricted as I imagined the possibility of Alicia getting in an accident on her way to meet me. "Thank you for coming."

"I will always come," she said, motioning me to sit. "Any news?"

"Not yet, and it's probably going to be a while. I think they treat the worst cases first, and she's got some competition today."

My best guess was that Mom's excessive drinking led to more sleeping and less eating since I'd last seen her. That would explain her weakness and the collapse.

I'd lost weight in the early days of my pregnancy, unable to keep any food down for days on end. I'd passed out more than once as a result, much to Robert's chagrin. Apparently, he found it incredibly unseemly to lie on the floor unconscious in public. It made sense that a lack of nutrition would have a similar effect on Mom.

Alicia rubbed my back. "Have you told Camilla?"

I shook my head. "I want to wait until I have some kind of news to share."

"Robert?"

I rolled my eyes. Robert had taught me long ago not to ask anything of him, and never to involve him in a crisis. He'd only make it worse for me. "No, but it doesn't seem like I'll make it home before dinner, so I'm hoping this is a night he works late." And I hoped that when I inevitably told him about what I'd gone through today, he wouldn't turn it into a fight.

Someone called my name, and I spotted a woman in blue scrubs in the distance. I raised my hand and moved in her direction. Alicia stayed close on my heels.

Fear for Mom's diagnosis replaced my initial gratitude for an update. If she'd already been seen and evaluated, she must be in worse condition than I thought.

The woman smiled softly as she swept her badge over the door sensor beside her. "The doctor is ready to see you. She's with your mother, who's resting comfortably."

"What's wrong with her?" Alicia asked, voicing the words I couldn't speak.

The woman looked to Alicia, then back to me, holding the door as we passed into the hospital. "I'll let the doctor fill you in."

Alicia took my hand and squeezed.

We arrived at a small room with lots of medical equipment and monitors. My mother slept in a bed with a stark-white blanket covering her thin, still frame, her skin contrastingly yellow. She seemed even smaller here than she had at her house.

An older woman with a tablet looked up upon our arrival, and the nurse moved to check the machines attached to Mom.

"I'm Dr. Bartlet," the woman said. Her gray hair was twisted into a tight bun at the nape of her neck. Clear blue eyes evaluated me. "I'm your mother's primary care physician. I keep an office at the hospital and see her semiregularly. How aware are you of your mother's health issues?"

I frowned. "I know she drinks too much and doesn't take care of herself," I said. "She had a cough today and looked ill before her collapse, but she said she was fine. And I know she has diabetes but doesn't manage it well."

The doctor motioned to the chair beside Mom's bed. "Maybe you should sit while we talk."

My limbs locked.

Alicia moved to stand behind the chair and patted the backrest. "Come on."

I forced my feet forward and took a seat. Whatever happened next, at least I'd have the facts. Then I could ask questions, sort my thoughts, and make a plan.

"Your mom developed type 2 diabetes several years back and was put on a diet to mitigate the associated risks," the doctor began.

I nodded. "She told me."

"She was given medication to combat the symptoms and progression, as well as counseled to exercise more and stop drinking entirely."

"I wasn't aware of any of that," I said, wanting to slip my hand over my mother's fingers and stroke her pale skin. But I couldn't take the rejection if she instinctively pulled away, so I folded my hands in my lap.

"Wait," I said. Something in Dr. Bartlet's statement gave me pause, and I mentally circled back. Mom first mentioned her diabetes a year or two ago, but the doctor said several. "How long ago?"

"Eleven years."

My jaw sank open.

Alicia muttered something behind me. I didn't understand her words, but the shock in her tone conveyed the sentiment.

"I had no idea," I whispered.

"I see." The doctor cleared her throat and waited for me to meet her gaze. When I did, she continued. "Trina developed high blood pressure and heart disease within a few years of the initial diagnosis. When her lifestyle didn't change, she fell into liver failure."

I grimaced, unable to properly process this news. "That can't be right," I said. "I see her a couple of times a month, and she's never mentioned any of this."

"Probably because she's chosen denial over action," Dr. Bartlet said. "Sometimes it's easier to put your head in the sand than to deal with major health issues and massive lifestyle overhauls. It's definitely not uncommon."

"And she's in liver failure," I said, repeating the nonsensical words.

She nodded.

"What can I do to help? What's the next step for her care?"

Dr. Bartlet inhaled slowly before she spoke again. "Trina is in end-stage liver failure now. We've discussed this at great length, and she understands that the only way to survive is via a transplant, for which her alcoholism makes her ineligible."

I winced at the word I'd thought a thousand times but never dared speak aloud. *Alcoholism.* My mom drank too much. But I'd never let myself think about it too long or hard. It was easier to think of her relationship with liquor as a personality flaw. Just one of many.

Alicia set her hand on my shoulder. "What if she gets sober?"

The doctor shook her head. "I don't think she has that kind of time."

My mouth opened and a small, strangled sound emerged.

"I'm sorry," the doctor said. "Truly. I wish I had better news."

"Will she be admitted today?" Alicia asked.

"Yes, for observation," Dr. Bartlet answered. "We'll give her fluids, regulate her blood sugar, then send her home with the usual instructions. Your mother's been in and out of this hospital a dozen times since her initial diagnosis, always under my care and treatment. She's tough, but she's not invincible, and I'm afraid her negligence has caught up with her."

My ears rang, and my mouth dried. "There has to be something I can do."

"It's Trina's choice," she said. "Her life to live or—" She broke eye contact for the first time, and in that instant, I saw past the thinly veiled facade. This woman cared for my mother. I supposed everyone in this profession cared for their patients on some level, but after more than a decade of appointments and medical interventions, I guessed she'd built a bond with my mom.

Yet my mother had never said a word to me. Not about Dr. Bartlet. Nor her terminal illness. Another reminder of where I stood on the scale of important things in her life.

"My best suggestion," Dr. Bartlet said, "is to get her some in-home care."

"Hospice?" I asked, but the voice didn't sound like my own. The room tilted slightly, and I wished that this was just another one of my nightmares.

"Hospice is one option," she said. "Any trained, attentive nurse would also be fine. Someone who can perform a quick daily check-in to chart her vitals and make sure she's eating. The amount of care and attention can be increased as needed. Do you have any other questions?"

I shook my head as my mind filled with words I couldn't speak. There wasn't enough time in the day to get half the answers I wanted, and the waiting room was full of other people in need of a doctor.

My mom was comfortable and stable. Too many others were not.

Dr. Bartlet took her leave.

"Shit," I whispered.

Alicia rounded the chair to crouch in front of me. "Are you okay?"

I nodded, still searching for my voice.

"I'm going to call Camilla," she said. "I'll give her the update and let her know you're . . . working through the blow."

The room was eerily quiet without Alicia in it. I stared at Mom and examined the machines standing along her headboard.

"Why didn't you tell me?" I whispered. *About your health. About my real dad.*

I supposed she didn't trust me with her secrets. And these were big ones, not easy to say aloud.

I hovered a hand over hers, longing to share my strength, to let her know I was here and she wasn't alone. But she wouldn't want my touch, so I held my own hand on my lap. If Mom was awake, she'd tell me to leave. The ache in my desperate heart grew.

"Why won't you let me know you?" I asked. *Why don't you want to know me?*

I pulled the photo of my biological father from my pocket and examined it closely. "How did you meet?" I asked. I wasn't sure whom I was asking, Mom or the photo. Both were equally unlikely to answer. "What did you have in common?" I continued. "Did you communicate in English?" Or was Mom also secretly fluent in French? "How long were you together?" *Were you in love?*

I had so many questions, and our time was limited now. I didn't have twenty more years to convince her I was worth her time. I had to make the days count.

My breath quickened, and my stomach churned. Heat licked across my chest and up my neck to my cheeks.

I could fix this. I couldn't stop it, but I could help. I could slow the process. I could clean Mom's house and fill her fridge with healthy foods. I could find her hidden flasks and bottles and dump them down the drain.

I'd hire a home health aide immediately and get them on standby.

Dad left her with excellent insurance coverage. I just had to take control.

My mother would not die drunk and alone. She deserved so much better than that. Even if she didn't think so.

Chapter Five

Four weeks later, I pulled into the parking lot at our country club, in no mood to spend time with my husband. Wednesday was our long-standing date night, wherein we fulfilled our obligation as club members to meet a monthly spend quota in the dining room. It also provided a grand opportunity for Robert to promote his family-man persona, publicly and to the desired crowd.

I checked the time as I crawled the lot in search of an available space. Robert hated tardiness, and I was sure to get a lecture on punctuality if a spot didn't open soon. The wind picked up as I circled. Strings of white bistro bulbs bobbed on tree limbs along the pavement's perimeter.

A storm was coming.

I really didn't want to get caught in it.

The taillights of a Porsche illuminated before me, and I hit my signal to claim the space. Victory curved my lips as I parked only a few yards from the building's front door.

I savored the small win before climbing out and hurrying into the clubhouse.

A group of men on their way out paused to let me pass. One held the door politely. Another offered an appreciative nod as I entered. On any other night, the small bit of attention might've buoyed me, but I was far too distracted tonight.

Mom was home from the hospital with round-the-clock care. I'd hired a nurse to look after her, but she hadn't spoken since the day she told me about my biological father. I couldn't help wondering if keeping that secret had been the only thing keeping her in motion. When I'd told Robert about her hospitalization, he made it clear that I was to utilize her existing health care to its fullest, because we weren't contributing any funds to the cause.

Unfortunately, her insurance didn't cover the amount of care she needed. So, I'd paid with my hidden savings. I blamed Robert for that.

And for the fact I had to start over on my quest to save up enough to leave this miserable marriage.

❧

In the dining room, the lights were slightly dimmed for the dinner crowd. Neat rows of round tables, dressed elegantly in white linens, centered the floor. The flames of votive candles flickered from the centerpieces, and soft classical music rose from a piano in the corner, a local pianist swaying with the tune.

A server led me over plush scarlet carpeting to our usual table. He clasped his hands behind his back while I sat. "Can I get you started with something to drink?"

"Just water for now," I said. "I'm meeting Mr. Bianco."

His gaze flickered over my shoulder, and he nodded. "I'll be back to check on you in a bit."

I opened a social media app on my phone when Robert didn't appear, and I marveled at the wonderful things everyone had going on. I tagged Camilla in a post for a female-only adventure cruise, encouraging her to get her girl-crew together and make youthful memories this summer. She spent too much time with Jeff. If she wasn't careful, she'd lose her best friends. Alicia had stubbornly stuck around after I'd made Robert the center of my world. Not everyone was as lucky as me.

Alicia had seen through Robert from the beginning. She called him out on his need to be in the spotlight, on his inability to focus on my needs after his initial push to make me his girlfriend. And he'd hated her in return for not being fooled. She'd seen his mean side for exactly what it was, while I'd wholeheartedly believed he was just joking, or I was just overthinking things.

Even my mother had hated him, but she hated everyone, and especially anyone that made me happy.

A group of women walked by my table, chatting quietly among themselves, and something pink caught my eye. A brunette I recognized from my flower-arranging classes passed a small business card to a redhead at her side, whispering in earnest. "I hear she's cheap and incredibly talented. Most importantly, she's discreet. She was trained in Paris but left the country after a major scandal."

I twisted on my seat, rubbernecking and openly gawking at their backs. That was my business card! I pressed my fingertips to my mouth, awed and delighted at the gossip about the Invisible Baker. I needed the sales. Mom's in-home caretaker wasn't cheap.

I needed to convince Robert to contribute to her care before the next payment.

I looked for the server and smiled politely. Maybe I did need a drink.

As if thinking of my husband had summoned him, the sound of his laughter reached my ears. According to my watch, he was more than fifteen minutes late. Given his obsession with timeliness, I hoped he had a good excuse.

I rested my hands on my lap, waiting to greet him. But he didn't come.

The waiter returned and I asked for a merlot. Then I scanned the room, puzzled. I was sure I'd heard Robert a moment prior, but where was he?

"Have you seen Mr. Bianco?" I asked the young man. "We were supposed to meet almost twenty minutes ago."

His eyes flickered over my shoulder again, toward the lounge attached to the dining room. "I believe he's with the men he golfed with earlier."

His words stung, and my jaw locked.

Robert wasn't running late. He was fifty feet away, drinking with friends, while I waited.

"Would you like me to tell him you've arrived?" the waiter offered.

"Please," I said.

Resentment sliced through me as I watched the server cross the room.

A moment later, a fresh round of raucous laughter reached my ears, and I imagined I was the butt of that joke.

When Robert arrived, his eyes were glossy from scotch, and his shirt was rumpled.

"How long have you been here?" I asked.

"I don't know." He looked at his watch. "Lunch."

"It's twenty after seven," I said. "Have you been drinking all this time?"

My words seemed to sober him and he scowled.

The server returned with an expectant smile.

"I think we need a minute," I began.

Robert spoke over me. "Chef's special. Medium rare. Garlic potatoes." When he realized I was talking, he said kindly to the waiter, "My apologies. I guess we need another moment."

The young man relaxed, charmed by my husband's smile. "Of course. Take your time. Would you like another scotch while you wait?"

Robert nodded, and the server disappeared.

Robert returned his focus to me, agitation on his face.

I wanted to ask him why he was so kind to everyone around us but so rude to me. The question would only start an argument, though, and I already had a topic sure to start that fire tonight.

Tension coiled in my throat at the thought.

The constant tiptoeing around him and preplanning everything I said was exhausting. Marriage shouldn't be like this. My life shouldn't be like this. I hadn't even told him my mother wasn't getting any better for fear he'd be furious about the cost of her care. It was ridiculous, and I knew it, but I couldn't make the nonsense stop.

Robert eyed me, as if reading my thoughts. "What's the problem?" He sucked his teeth, staring hard into my eyes until I looked away.

The server set my wine and Robert's glass of scotch onto our table, then hastened away. He probably felt the force field of tension around us.

Robert lifted his drink immediately.

"My mom's still ill," I said, taking the leap to get ahead of his simmering anger. If I wasn't direct, we'd wind up arguing about something completely different, and I'd have to wait for another week to ask him for money to help my mother. "She needs round-the-clock care, and her insurance doesn't cover that until it's considered end-of-life care." I paused to swallow the lump in my throat. "I'm her only child, and I can't exactly move in with her. I don't know what else to do." Robert didn't even like me to visit. "We have to figure this out."

His red face contorted into disgust. "You want me to spend my money on your mother because she drank her way through her trust?"

The couple at the table beside us cast sideways glances in our direction, and I flushed.

I lowered my voice, hoping Robert would follow suit. "I'm not asking for more than we have readily to give, and I'm willing to spend time over there helping, if I won't have to argue with you about it every time I come home. She's in liver failure, Robert," I pleaded. "It's been weeks without improvement."

He wiggled his short glass, rolling a giant sphere of ice inside. "And when she dies, we inherit her debts," he said dryly. "Seems to me like this is a lose-lose for us." He sloshed the amber liquid into his mouth, then set the glass on the table with a muted thud. "You don't need to spend more time there. That's not going to heal her. You can't control this like you try to control everything else with your lists and endless fussing."

I bit back my rage at his callousness and shoved it into a pit with all the other emotions I'd swallowed for years. I took a long drink of my wine before meeting Robert's eyes again. "I make lists and fuss so you have less to complain about," I said. "It's a countertactic."

Heat flashed in his eyes. Nothing was ever Robert's fault, and I knew I'd crossed a line by suggesting as much. "Is that right?"

"Yes."

My phone rang, interrupting our quiet standoff.

He muttered apologies to the neighboring tables as I pulled my phone from my handbag. I'd clearly embarrassed him.

"It's the nurse," I said, loudly enough for everyone listening to hear. "Hello?"

I rose and moved toward the exit, hoping for good news. Maybe Mom had finally spoken again. Maybe she'd told her nurse to fuck off and go home, and the woman was letting me know.

I had my clutch already tucked beneath one arm, ready to race across town to her.

"Mrs. Bianco, this is Rebecca."

"Where are you going?" Robert barked as I reached the clubhouse foyer.

"Hi, Becca," I said. "What's up?"

She sniffled, and I froze.

"Becca? Where are you?"

"We're at the hospital. Your mom . . . EMTs worked on her all the way to the ER, but—"

My world tilted and tunneled.

"I'm so sorry. Hold on. Dr. Bartlet is here."

"No," I growled, the word ripping through me.

"Sophie?" Dr. Bartlet's voice crossed the line to my ears. "I'm sorry to tell you that your mother went into cardiac arrest and passed away en route to the hospital. I made the call when she arrived."

Chapter Six

My mother's funeral was small and lackluster, a sad reflection of her life. She'd hidden in her little house, behind walls of unnecessary things, lost to an alcohol-induced haze. She'd broken ties with everyone. Stopped working. Stopped leaving home unless absolutely necessary. She didn't even know the neighbors anymore, save for one: Ilona Urban, who'd lived next door all my life.

Ilona was among the handful of mourners. A pair of funeral home employees sat in on the service as well, probably trying to make the room seem fuller.

Everyone wore black. I'd nearly worn athleisure; I was so accustomed to pretending I had Pilates on days I saw Mom.

Alicia, Camilla, and I sat in the front row, with me in the center. Jeff held Camilla's hand on my right. Cameron wrapped an arm around Alicia on my left.

Robert had to work.

Her funeral was preplanned, a small blessing in a time of chaos. My mom had set it all up after my father died, and she'd scrambled to make arrangements through the fog of loss and bereavement.

I appreciated her forethought but couldn't find the grief I should feel at a funeral. My heart and head were too full of unanswered questions and all the things left unsaid. Instead of sad, I felt hollow.

I dug my nails into the skin of my clasped hands as I imagined rising, walking to her body as the minister droned on about everlasting peace, and demanding she get up and fight! Make friends. Heal. Don't let Dad win! He took so many happy years from her life. It wasn't fair she'd hidden away for the rest of it.

My gaze rose to a slideshow of photos displayed on a screen behind the little podium. Images of Mom through the years. Some included me. Others had Dad. A few were taken with Camilla when she was young. Holidays. Barbecues. Days at the lake.

We looked so normal in photos. Like every other family.

The slides froze on an image of my mother in a chair, a young Camilla on her lap, and me at her side. We looked nearly identical there. Three versions of the same woman captured at different ages.

And a deep, icy chill slid through my bones.

My parents were consumed by their madness in my formative years. They completely neglected my needs more often than not, and I learned I was invisible before I learned to drive.

Then I married a man who continued that pattern. My fall from the pedestal that Robert put me on was slow, but steady. In the beginning, he'd convinced me I could do no wrong, and he worshipped me, so the first time he seemed unhappy with something I'd said or done, I worked hard to fix the problem. The adoration returned, and everything was great. For a while. Until I did something else to make him sulk, go silent, or rant. The cycle continued for years with shorter and shorter times of happiness in between, until soon there was only criticism alternating with silence.

The loud and clear message: I was a disappointment and a burden.

I easily believed I didn't matter, because that was all I knew.

I poured everything I had into Camilla so she'd never doubt her importance to me or this world, but she'd also seen my invisibility. I'd modeled it for her when we waited for Robert at dinnertime, then ate a cold meal without him after he didn't show. When I cheered alone from the sidelines at school events. When my Christmas stocking was empty. When no gifts waited for me under the tree. When I made my own birthday cake, and when Robert spoke to the air, asking things like, "Where's the remote?" or "Are there any snacks?" And every time, I stopped what I was doing to meet his needs, without even receiving eye contact for the effort.

It wasn't alcohol that poisoned my mother. It was a belief that she didn't deserve better.

I'd modeled my life on that example. Though I'd tried not to, I'd exposed my daughter to a dangerously toxic relationship as well.

Chairs shifted as people rose. Alicia squeezed my hand. "Come on," she said softly. "It's time to go."

And I knew no words had ever been truer.

In lieu of a proper wake, Alicia, Camilla, and I went to Mom's house after the cemetery. The men went home. I needed to figure out what to do with my childhood home and the myriad of things nearly lifting its rafters. She'd left it all to me in her will.

We picked up paper plates, plastic cups, pizza, and wine on our way there.

"Welcome to my humble abode," I said, unlocking the front door and letting myself inside. "I never dreamed I'd actually use this key again."

Alicia carried the bags over the threshold. "I'm surprised she never made you give it back."

Camilla stepped past me, eyes wide. "Wow. This is worse than I imagined, and it was pretty bad the last time I was here."

"Yep," I said. "It took me two days to make room for a hospital bed in the dining room when she came home in the spring. I scrubbed the kitchen and bathroom as well as I could, without throwing her stuff away, for the home health aides."

Stifling summer heat had made the air stale and stuffy. I raised the blinds and pulled back the drapes, then forced open the ancient windows to let in the breeze.

Dust motes formed clouds of silver confetti between us, fitting decor for this party.

"Is her air-conditioning broken?" Alicia asked as she looked for a place to set the grocery bags.

I checked the nearby thermostat, set to eighty, then lowered the temperature to something more reasonable and listened as the unit kicked on.

"Thank heavens," Alicia said.

"Mom?" Camilla's voice carried from the back of the house.

I moved in her direction, careful not to trip on boxes or bags. "Yes?"

"There's a table and chairs on the patio. Maybe we can eat outside under the umbrella," she said, peering through a rear window.

"That sounds perfect."

Several minutes later we toasted to my mother with plastic cups of red wine, but all I felt was tired.

Ilona appeared in the distance, trudging across the adjoined lawns to the patio. She was a decade older than my mother, somewhere in her mid-seventies, I guessed, but healthy and active, unlike my mom. She'd dyed her cropped gray hair pink. She'd changed out of her funeral clothes into jean shorts and a T-shirt. "I brought the mail," she said. "I've been keeping it." She set the stack of bills on the table. "Been feeding the cat too."

"What cat?" Camilla asked.

"Raisin."

I squinted at Ilona, backlit by the sun. "Who?"

"Trina's cat. She found him under the trailer when he was a kitten. He's indoor/outdoor, but he hasn't been to the vet or groomer in a long while, so I'd do that first, if I was you. He's sure to have fleas or worms or something by now."

I looked to the camper trailer, parked across the backyard. Mom purchased it years ago when the house started filling up with junk. She planned to live there while overhauling the cluttered house, but that never happened. Now the camper was full of junk too.

"Kitty, kitty, kitty," Ilona called. She clucked her tongue and made soft whistling sounds while scanning the yard.

"I didn't know she had a cat," I said. Why hadn't she mentioned it?

Oh, I don't know, my mind retorted. *The same reason she didn't mention my biological father?*

A dark, flat-faced cat peered around a nearby bush. Long, ratty hair snarled into mats at his ears. He watched with assessing eyes as we turned at once to stare at him.

"There he is," Ilona said. "This is Raisin."

Alicia wrinkled her nose as the feline lumbered closer. "What kind of cat is that?"

"We think he's a Himalayan mixed with a little Maine coon."

I looked to Ilona, smiling proudly at the filthy creature, and an unexpected bout of emotion clutched my throat. "He looks like something Mom would love."

Alicia and I laughed softly at the ridiculousness of my mom caring for anything when she wouldn't care for herself. Then again, based on the looks of Raisin, she hadn't taken very good care of him either.

Camilla lifted a chunk of greasy cheese from her pizza slice and offered it to the cat, who approached with caution.

"Well," Ilona said. "If you need anything, you know where to find me. I've got a soup on, and I don't want it to burn."

"Ilona," I said, rising as she turned to leave.

"Yeah?"

"I'm sorry for your loss," I said. She'd told me the same at the funeral home, but I hadn't known how to respond. Seeing the way she looked at Raisin reminded me that she loved Mom, and she was hurting too.

Ilona's eyes misted, and she nodded. "Take care," she said. "Call anytime."

When I returned my gaze to the patio, Raisin had joined the group, winding neatly around Camilla's legs.

Alicia smirked. "Looks like you inherited a cat as well."

The words hit with a slap and panic welled. “I can’t have a cat,” I said. “Robert hates animals.” He thought they were stinky and dirty. He said they’d make the house smell, and shed hair on everything. Additionally, pets were expensive and inconvenient, making it impossible to leave town without paying a sitter.

“I’ll take him,” Camilla said. Her offer interrupted my spiraling thoughts.

“What?” I blinked.

The cat perched on her lap now, purring loudly enough to hear across the table.

“I can take him. My roommates won’t mind.”

“What will Jeff say?” I asked. He didn’t live with her, but he was constantly at her side. “What about the hair?”

“A groomer will get that sorted,” she said, smiling at Raisin. “Jeff will think it’s nice I have something of Grandma’s to keep and love.” She glanced at her watch. “We can tell him when he gets here. He’s picking me up soon. I didn’t think you’d want to stay here long.”

I rubbed heavy hands against my face, pressure growing in my head and chest. “I don’t plan to stay long,” I agreed. “Figuring out what to do with all her stuff is a job for another day.”

Still, I hated to go home, where eggshells lined the floor, and an argument was sure to follow. Robert always managed to make me feel worse when I felt low. I could be pleasant or bland, but anything less than that and he’d lash out in petty, hurtful ways until I cracked. After I came home from the funeral, he would undoubtedly start a fight. Say something unkind about Mom, complain about her overdue property taxes, or the amount of time I’d need to spend here to prepare the home for sale. Sometimes the reasons for his verbal attacks were so opaque I couldn’t make sense enough of the connection to fight back. I just stood in the crosshairs while my bad day got infinitely worse.

“Mom?”

I dropped my hands onto my lap, brows furrowed, heartbroken as I looked to Alicia, then into my sweet daughter’s eyes. “I have to leave your father,” I said.

The moment of clarity was so strong, I couldn't keep it from her any longer. I'd known for years, had planned my escape over a hundred meals with Alicia and dozens of bottles of wine.

Camilla set Raisin on the ground and rounded the table to where I sat. Then she crouched and wrapped me in her arms. "I know, Mama," she said. "And I understand."

Robert didn't make a sport of ruining her days the way he ruined mine, but he was always a self-centered, moody authoritarian. He'd parented her with idle threats and grounding instead of love, on the rare occasions he'd bothered to parent her at all.

I pulled back to look at her, and part of me died as I read the sadness on her beautiful face. Any remaining piece of me that hoped I'd somehow shielded her from her dad's behavior hung its head in shame.

"I get it," she confirmed. "He's not good to you, and you deserve to be cherished." Her voice cracked as she pulled me back to her and held on so long I thought I might cry as well.

Camilla knew my marriage was bad, just as I'd known my parents' marriage was bad, and it gutted me that I'd continued the cycle.

Did she resent me for staying? Had she prayed to the moon and stars that I'd stand up and walk away years ago?

I couldn't ask. Couldn't move. Couldn't breathe.

"Cami," I said, suddenly frantic and desperate. "I don't ever want this for you."

She kissed my cheek, then returned to her seat. "Don't worry. I'm okay," she assured. "You will be too."

I nearly laughed at the thought. "I mean it. There's so much more to life than marriage."

Alicia uncrossed her legs and scooted forward to squeeze my hand on the tabletop. "We don't have to talk about this now. It's been a rough day."

I batted at my stinging eyes but took her advice and bit my tongue.

I thought only of how much I didn't want to be like my mom, and how much I hated that I was.

My life was far easier than hers in every possible way, but finances held me in place as well. *Finances, or fear?* I wondered. Maybe a little of both.

Camilla took Raisin, as promised, when Jeff arrived. He only smiled and petted the cat's head before setting him on the back seat of his sedan.

"He's such a nice guy," Alicia said, watching their car pull away.

"For how long?" I muttered, refilling my cup with wine.

Men were always nice at first, weren't they? No one had a second date with someone who treated her poorly or knocked her down on date number one.

"Hey," Alicia said. "Don't do that. There are good men in this world. My guys are all examples. There's one out there for you, too, if you ever decide to look again."

I released a long, labored sigh. "I think it's nice that you believe that. Right now, I just want out of the relationship I'm in, but I don't have the first clue about how to break it to him."

Alicia raised her cup to mine. "First you say, 'Robert, you're a cun—'"

"Stop!" I laughed, cutting her off. "I will not say that."

She shrugged and took a long drink.

"I spent all the money I saved on Mom's care," I said. "It'll take me years to save that much again."

"Oh, no. You are not doing that." Alicia set her wine aside and fixed me in a firm stare. "You talked to all those attorneys last year, and you had a favorite. Remember her?"

I nodded. "Jill."

"Call her," she said. "Let her remind you that regardless of what Robert says, everything the two of you have built together in twenty-two years of marriage belongs to you both. It's not his to parcel out as he deems fit. He can't keep it from you, and he can't take it away."

"He doesn't like to lose." And he hated any threat to his money. "Divorce can take a year or more. What if he won't leave the house while we go through the process? I can't live with him under those conditions. He'd make it his daily mission to torture me."

"So leave," she said. Her eyes brightened with mischief. "He doesn't have to be the one who moves out. I believe I recall you saying you wanted to pack your things while he was at work and be gone when he got home. Let's do that."

I felt my lips curve into a smile as hope flickered inside me. With Alicia's family's help, and Robert's long hours, I could pack up without him around to complain, berate, or stress me out. Then I'd only have to say the words and walk away.

I bit my lip, wanting desperately to believe it was possible. Leaving was a risk. Robert was an estate attorney. He was manipulative and greedy, with a network of other lawyers at his disposal. I was sure he could take me down if he wanted. My warped instincts told me to remain quiet and small and stay where I was. *Don't cause trouble.* It made sense to stay. The devil I knew was manageable. The devil I didn't know—everything outside my carefully cultivated life—was terrifying.

The ember of hope inside me wasn't ready to let this conversation go. "Where would I stay?" I asked. The words had barely left my mouth before I knew the answer.

Alicia raised her eyes to something over my shoulder.

And I followed her gaze to my newly inherited home.

Chapter Seven

It only took a few weeks to get everything into place. I completed the paperwork and signed the retainer for an attorney I hoped could outsmart my husband if he tried to be sneaky, then wrote a check she promised not to cash until the end of the week. In doing that, she gave me the gift of time. I just had to tell him I was leaving before he noticed ten grand had disappeared from our account.

Alicia and I had started packing the morning after Mom's funeral, and she took the boxes with her when she left. First I packed up my books, excess clothing, and personal items collected over the years. I didn't touch anything Robert used or might miss. As the big day grew closer, I was shocked that he didn't notice anything awry. Apparently he didn't notice anything about me or the house as long as it all appeared clean and pretty. He never said a word about the vanishing cake pans, mixing bowls, or cookie sheets. Didn't comment on the hundreds of novels suddenly nowhere to be seen, or the fact I lost seven pounds by directing my energy toward something that made me feel good instead of eating my feelings late into the night.

According to my attorney, the bank accounts would be divided in the end, as would any retirement or savings. We'd each keep our car, and any other assets were negotiable, so long as the split was equitable. That all seemed fair to me.

I used the local library's computer to set up a website and social media for the Invisible Baker, then routed payments to my newly established bank account through PayPal. With a little research and a hundred bucks, I even registered an LLC for the business. I figured that the money from the division of marital assets would keep me afloat for the next few years as my business grew. Until then, I had a brain, a talent for baking, and a plan.

I fell asleep each night astonished and hopeful. My freedom was one conversation away. I just had to tell Robert what he didn't see happening right before his eyes.

When the day came, I sat with my thoughts all evening, awaiting his return from work. My bravery wavered and faded with each passing hour, but it was too late to turn back. My SUV was packed, and my closet was empty.

The garage door opened around seven p.m.

My hands shook as I walked to the kitchen and leaned against the familiar granite countertop for moral and physical support. The house was still and quiet with only the evening sunlight streaming through the windows and the sound of chirping birds to fill the space. My phone, normally on the counter in its dock, playing music while I cooked, sat safely in my back pocket.

Robert strode inside, loosening his tie, eyes searching. "Hey," he said.

"Hi."

He set his laptop bag on the counter and frowned. "Why's it so quiet in here? Were you sleeping again? Where's dinner?" he asked, gaze darting around the room.

I never napped unless I was ill or had a migraine, both typically caused by him, but I didn't let his gibe distract me. Instead, I filed it away as further proof I'd made the right decision.

"Well?" he prodded when I didn't respond immediately.

"I didn't make dinner," I said. "And the house is quiet because I'm leaving."

He huffed a dismissive laugh. "Where are you going wearing that? Not the country club, I hope."

"No, not the club," I agreed. "I'm going to my mother's house, where I plan to stay."

His brow wrinkled with confusion and his lips parted. "What are you talking about?"

I laced the fingers of my shaking hands and willed my voice not to crack. "I'm leaving you, Robert," I said. "I'm not making dinner for you, or waiting up for you, or listening to you say unkind, underhanded things to me anymore. I've packed my things and hired an attorney who will file the motion for divorce this week. After that, you will be served. I left her business card on your desk. You can share that with whoever you choose to represent you in this matter."

He laughed. "You can't leave me," he said.

I produced car keys from my pocket as evidence and met his stare.

His lips curled back in disgust. "You don't have any money," he said. "You haven't worked since you married me. How do you expect to live?" A low, thunderous moan lurched from his lips before I could respond with any of my preplanned statements.

"Oh." He dragged the little word for several syllables. "Right. I see. You plan to take my money. You think you're going to get your hands on the savings and investments that I created and go set up shop somewhere else on my dime."

I rolled my eyes and collected my purse. "I'm done with this and you," I said as calmly as possible. "I'm tired of begging for your attention, taking your jabs, being treated as if I am somehow less when I am the one holding your precious lifestyle together. I lost my mother, and you couldn't be bothered to come to the funeral or even ask how I'm doing once since then. You bring nothing good to my life or this relationship, Robert," I said, sneering his name. "There's more to life than money, and you're about to learn that the hard way."

I squared my shoulders and blew past him, feeling invincible. I'd never spoken to him, or anyone, that way. And I liked not being a doormat.

I strode into the garage without another glance in his direction. "Goodbye, Robert. Have fun cooking, cleaning, and managing your own life, for a change."

❧

I arrived at my mom's house thirty minutes later. The cocktail of emotions splashing around in my head were of the Molotov variety.

I'd left Robert.

I told him I wanted out.

And I left.

Holy shit!

My open-mouthed smile remained maniacally wide as I pulled onto the gravel drive.

"Yay!" A big voice boomed from the backyard as I parked behind Cameron's pickup truck.

Alicia moved into view, clapping and whistling. Her husband popped the cork on a bottle of champagne.

I got out of the SUV and went directly to my best friend, who wrapped me in a hug.

"You did it," she whispered against my hair. "You fucking did it, and I am so amazingly proud of you."

I held on to her for a long time as fear and doubt crept in to eviscerate my joy.

"All right, all right," Cameron said.

Alicia wiped tears from her cheeks when we pulled apart, and Cameron handed us each a plastic cup of champagne.

"We're fancy around here," he said, raising his cup to ours in a toast. "May Soph's next forty years be filled with friends, family, and fun. May she also discover she is as capable and wonderful as the rest of us already know she is. Oh, and may ole Robo Robbie gain ten pounds a year while balding prematurely."

"Cheers!" Alicia called.

I laughed and drank, realizing I didn't care if Robert was fat or bald, happy or miserable. I just never wanted to share space with him again.

And I didn't want to fail.

Cameron was first to lower his cup, having tossed back the champagne like a shot. "The boys and I unloaded everything we could into the dining room and kitchen. The place is pretty packed now, but Alicia thought you might be able to stay in the trailer at night until you make headway on the house."

"And I'm off for the summer," Alicia reminded me. "Possibly the only perk of teaching teens at an underfunded public high school."

"She means aside from the opportunity to shape the minds of our country's future," Cameron said.

Alicia rolled her eyes and took another sip of champagne. "Yep. That too."

I gave the ramshackle house and overgrown lawn a long look. "Any chance you saw a mower around here?"

Cam lifted a finger to adjust the brim of his hat. "CJ will bring ours over on the trailer and take care of it for you in the morning. Then he'll come back on the weekends. Alicia already offered to pay him for it."

"No," I said.

She shook her head. "I've been giving the boys allowance for existing all their lives. They drive now. It's summer break. They can do this for you. Let them."

Tears burned and blurred my eyes without falling. I nodded.

"I mean it," she said. "I can be here to help as often as you want, and the guys will help when they can. Your mom's got three of anything you can think of in there. We'll hold on to the things you want. Take trash to the curb and everything else to some kind of donation center. We've got this."

"Sounds like a great plan."

"It's what I do," she said. "Now, what do you want to do first?" she asked. "Because you're fucking free."

I looked at the house again, then the backyard and trailer. I thought of Robert's rage, and a thousand possible repercussions for my absence.

Anything I'd accidentally left behind was surely in the trash by now. He'd see this as an act of war instead of a desperate bid for peace. The family-man persona he'd so carefully crafted would be shattered, forcing him to find a new mask. His second-favorite role was one of a victim. Tomorrow, he'd tell anyone who asked how blindsided he'd been and how gutted he was by my abandonment. That was if he played nice. Instead, he might confess that his happiness was all an act, because he'd been hiding the truth. That I'd been a terrible wife and mother. That's why he didn't always come out to see me when I brought desserts to the office. Maybe he'd say I was controlling. Maybe he'd label me an alcoholic like my mother. A cheater. Or someone who spent all his money on vanity and nonsense.

"Let's start with dinner," Alicia suggested when I didn't speak. She wrapped an arm around my shoulders and led me to the back patio, where smoke seeped from a grill. "Did you know we're tailgating tonight? I hired a private chef."

The table was set with place mats, plates, and silverware. A white cloth runner ran down the center with bowls of chips and pretzels beside covered trays of chunked fruits and sliced veggies. Cameron raised the lid on the grill and flipped shrimp and chicken kebabs.

"We should eat before the boys get back," Cam said. "Then it's every man and woman for themselves."

I laughed.

Tonight, we feast, I thought. *Because I have no idea what tomorrow holds.*

Hopefully not a famine.

I tossed and turned through the night in Mom's trailer. The space was cramped and smelled faintly of something unpleasant I couldn't name.

I was thankful for that last part. Strange scent aside, camping in the backyard felt unsafe, making my move into the house a priority.

At six thirty a.m., I dressed in leggings and a T-shirt with sneakers, then pulled my hair into a ponytail and drove to the nearest drive-through for iced coffee, mentally thanking Alicia for the gift card. I returned feeling awake and resolved.

The work ahead of me would be unpleasant, and dirty, so I'd planned ahead. I had purchased extra cleaning supplies with my grocery orders for weeks, then packed them with my things for the move. Alicia had set the boxes out for me before leaving after dinner.

Now I had to face the consequences of my actions and turn Mom's cluttered house into my new home.

I cued up some Taylor Swift and strode across the lawn driven by caffeine, adrenaline, and purpose. "Let the transformation begin."

I opened the windows and doors to circulate the cool morning air. Then I dragged things I didn't want, or couldn't use, onto the patio to deal with later. Unopened boxes of dishes, small appliances, and upright vacuums in triplicate. Plastic totes of VHS tapes and music CDs. Cases of unopened wine and canned goods.

Organizing the overflow as I went helped me track my progress, but I had to stop frequently to adjust the piles. I'd designated one side of the patio for items destined for charities, food banks, and shelters. Those organizations would properly distribute and put the items to good use. Everything on the other side was essentially trash. Items stacked on top of the table in the middle didn't fit into either category, so they stayed, temporarily, in limbo.

I scrubbed the dining room and kitchen floors on my hands and knees with a combination of hot water, dish detergent, baking soda, and white vinegar. My tried-and-true cleanser removed grease, buildup, and stains like nothing store bought could. The work tired my limbs and quieted my mind.

Sweat pooled between my breasts and shoulder blades as I continued to purge and scrub the walls, trim, and windows, whitening every stubborn grout line and bead of caulk. Slowly the dining room and kitchen, two rooms I'd cleaned as best I could before Mom returned from the hospital, looked like home again.

When I was sure I couldn't go on without food or a ten-hour nap, I steam cleaned the drapes and scoured her appliances inside and out. Then I opened the cupboards and groaned. Black magic was clearly at work there. How else could eighty-year-old cabinets remain on the walls while carrying such a load?

Hundreds of plates, cups, bowls, and mugs filled the top shelves. Bakeware, cookware, and small appliances filled the lower units. Every drawer was either stuck shut from excessive contents or impossible to close for the same reason.

Dirt, paint chips, and rust fell to the clean floors as I emptied and sorted.

"Goodness, Mom," I complained. "How did you live like this? Why?"

Why didn't I realize how bad things had gotten sooner? For her and her home.

I pushed the thought aside, knowing the answers. I hadn't looked too deeply because I didn't want to get caught up in her misery. I was already drowning in my own.

At least the floor was clean enough to sit on as I determined which items to return to the cupboards—right after I scrubbed and disinfected them as well.

I leaned my back against the stove and pulled a pile of mismatched dishes between parted legs. A strange sort of nostalgia stilled my mind. The bowl on top was part of a set I ate cereal from before school in the mornings as a child. Mom had a mug with the same maroon toile pattern. We bought the set from an estate sale on the edge of uptown during one of our few mother-daughter outings. She and Dad had broken our other dishes during an especially bad fight that week.

I ran my fingertip over the pattern, then across the chip on the bowl's scalloped edge.

She appeared in my mind's eye, sipping coffee as I ate breakfast before school. Every morning she woke me, then Dad, already jazzed up on caffeine and ready to tackle her day. I watched her wash dishes, fill a slow cooker with meat, and iron clothes on a board beside the sink, all while giving me a verbal rundown of things to remember. *Picture day Thursday. History test tomorrow. Stay late to help with the bake sale. Clean your room before you ask to run around with your friends.*

How had I forgotten the way she carried our mental load? She kept every appointment, commitment, and responsibility on her internal calendar. She sent cookies and cakes to the office with Dad when his boss, a coworker, or secretary had a birthday.

A knock at the open back door returned me to the present, and I dragged my body upright.

"Anyone home?" Ilona called. She poked her head inside as I dusted my hands against my pant legs. "You certainly got an early start. Just like your mother."

"Hi." I smiled at her familiar face. "It's a big job. I figured it was best to dive in."

She looked me over, then turned in a slow circle, whistling the sound of a falling missile. "Based on the amount of stuff already outside, I half expected the place to be empty. These are the same two rooms you cleaned before—"

"Yeah," I said. "But last time I just tidied enough to set up the hospital bed and make the nurses comfortable. I was on a tight timeline."

She pulled a canvas tote bag from her shoulder and set it on the stove. "Well, I came to help. I've got trash bags, rubber gloves, and some cleaning supplies in case you run out."

A few hours prior, I would've told her I had plenty of everything I'd need for a while. But after the work I'd done so far, I was grateful for the company and the extra supplies. "Thank you."

"Mm-hmm," she said. "Here." She pulled a small container from the bag and handed it to me. "Strawberry cream cheese Danish. Your favorite, if I recall."

My stomach growled at the sight of the pastry. "I love your Danishes," I said. "I would hug you, but I'm disgusting."

We moved to the table while I ate, and she unearthed two bottles of water, passing one to me.

"How are other things looking by light of day?" Ilona asked.

I knew, from her tone, she didn't mean the cluttered home. I shrugged. "I couldn't stay with him any longer," I said. "I blamed Mom for staying with my dad." The words came out before I thought better of them, and I looked away.

"She knew," Ilona said. "She carried a lot of guilt for the choices she made. She was trying to outrun her ghosts from the day I met her, but we can't hide from things we won't put down."

I wasn't sure which things she meant, but the sadness in her voice broke my heart. I set a hand on Ilona's arm and gave a gentle squeeze before I let her go. "She loved you, you know," I said. "I think you were her only friend for most of my adult life."

"She pushed people away," Ilona said. "I wasn't interested in leaving, and I live fifty feet away, so she was stuck with me. Plus, I've made my share of mistakes. I don't judge."

I turned my attention to the Danish and sank my teeth into the flaky crust. The soft, savory center melted against my tongue. "Amazing."

"It's your mom's recipe."

I licked crumbs from my lips as another memory of my mother resurfaced. "She loved to bake." She taught me to knead dough and how to proof it. We made everything from scratch, and she played music on the radio while we worked. "We danced in the kitchen," I whispered, only partially sure that was true.

"She cherished those memories," Ilona said, "even while complaining about your visits and calling you a stuck-up bitch."

"She never called me a stuck-up bitch," I said.

Ilona cringed. "Maybe not to your face."

A snort of shock turned to laughter, and I let it linger instead of cutting it off.

"There were two of us she couldn't push away," Ilona said.

I nodded. "I guess there were."

Chapter Eight

I missed Ilona when she left to run errands, but she promised to come back for lunch, and I'd offered to pay. Being here with her felt a little like having Mom back, specifically the kinder parts of Mom I'd temporarily forgotten.

The house was a time machine. Bits and pieces remained exactly as they were in my childhood, and with them came more memories. The way Mom fussed over my hair, dress, and shoes on prom night. Birthday parties with all my friends and a personalized cake. The hours she spent baking, only for a bunch of kids to demolish the work in minutes.

A treasure trove of my grandma's thimbles hidden inside a tea tin took me back to elementary school. I hadn't thought about my mom's mom in so long I barely recalled her features. We lost her when I was eight. Still, vague images of her at the kitchen table formed. She watched Mom cook and clean or brush my hair. And she critiqued.

I winced. I hadn't thought much of her commentary at the time, but as an adult woman today, I hated the memory for Mom's sake. Grandma adored me, but I wondered about her relationship with Mom. Did she know how poorly Dad treated her?

Did she know he wasn't my father?

I ran the back of one arm across my forehead and put the thimbles away.

Grandma was curt and expected everything to be done a certain way. The proper way. Her way. Would Mom have gone to her for advice about her pregnancy? Did Mom make the decision to pretend I was my dad's child on her own, or did Grandma help her hide the indiscretion, because it simply wasn't acceptable? Had she known and hated me for what I was in her eyes? An accident. Proof of her daughter's unwed exploits? The reason she married an abuser.

My heart ached at all the awful possibilities.

Mom said Dad didn't know I wasn't his daughter, but was it possible he guessed? She said he didn't hit her again for a year after she came home from France. Was that long enough for him to question why I looked nothing like him? Or why an allegedly premature baby weighed six and a half pounds? Did he hate us both because he knew the truth?

I'd spent my childhood counting the days until I could leave this house and get away from him, only to marry a man who treated me with the same simmering disdain. I hadn't really gone anywhere, and now I was back where I'd started.

I ordered delivery from a local sandwich shop. Then I closed the windows and pumped up the air-conditioning before the southern Virginia summer sun baked me into jerky.

I swept the floor again while I waited for the food, then carried a glass of iced water and stack of unopened bills into the dining room. I sat on the floor and sorted the bills into piles according to sender. Months of unpaid utilities made my stomach ache. The final notice regarding her property taxes didn't help.

Thirty days to pay or the home went up for a sheriff's auction.

I checked the date at the top of the letter and felt my heart seize. I had four days.

Fatigue, desperation, and hunger squeezed the air from my lungs. Why did I think I could do this? I didn't have any money. I didn't have time to bake and sell enough pastries to cover even half of Mom's debts. I had access to my marital accounts during the divorce, but there's no way I could get my hands on the amount it would take to set things in order. In all the years of our marriage, I'd stuck to a tightly constructed budget, spending only on necessities like groceries and gas. Robert paid the lease on my BMW, because everything was in his name, and all our utilities were autodrafted. With attached fees and penalties, Mom owed nearly ten thousand dollars. Robert would never let that much go without a fight. I needed a miracle.

I rolled onto my back and stared at the outdated pendant light. Unlike the kitchen, this room filled me with tension and dread. Long evenings waiting for Dad to come home. Wondering what to expect. A chocolate bar from the gas station, because he was happy? Or long laments over Mom's cooking until the meal went cold? Their arguments morphed into garbled screams in my head. The crash of thrown plates and clatter of overturned roast. Then Mama's tears.

My jaw locked, and I rolled onto my side, curling my knees to my chest, arms caged around them. I'd hated her for staying.

And yet I had stayed with Robert. Like my mother before me, I waited for my husband to come home too. I held my breath when the garage door went up. Braced for his mood. Endured his unkind words. All so my husband could treat me with the same hostility and neglect as my dad.

How would my biological father have treated me? Certainly not any worse.

For the first time in my life, I wasn't so sure I wouldn't have done exactly what Mom did, had I been in her place. She lived in a different time. In a different world. She didn't finish college. There weren't many job opportunities for single moms. *Divorce* was a dirty word to many, and if she left Dad, I wasn't sure what society would've made of her.

She'd needed so much help, but access to help didn't exist back then like it does now, especially not in the way of financial assistance and female advocacy. The awareness of marital abuse didn't exist, and women couldn't seek out the handful of available programs without fear of judgment or worse. Not to mention Dad never would've agreed to let her walk away.

I sat upright and scanned the clean room, now filled with my boxed belongings. I had six more rooms to empty before I could begin to unpack my new life. Three bedrooms and a bathroom upstairs, a living room and laundry room on this floor. I couldn't begin to think about all the closets, or what awaited me in the basement and attic. I'd save those projects for after I moved in.

The doorbell rang, and I forced myself onto my feet. Lunch had arrived, and Ilona would soon return. Good, because I wasn't doing well left alone with my thoughts.

I made my way to the front door and collected the bags from the porch, then sent a text to let Ilona know to come on over.

A stack of books on the windowsill caught my eye after I hit Send. Atop the pile sat a button box.

I set the lunch bags on a chair and opened the little box with greedy hands, plunging my fingers into the contents. The edge of something stiff scraped my skin. I pinched it between my thumb and forefinger, then pulled it free. Another photo of my mom and Bastien, my biological father.

My breath caught as I took them in, leaning casually against a fence backed in shrubbery. At a park, perhaps? Bastien wore a T-shirt with stripes and tan pants. Mom wore a cinched-waist dress and a smile as bright as the sun. She looked at the camera, but his eyes were on her.

I flipped the photo over, scanning Mom's faded script. *Sébastien Allard, summer abroad.*

My heart raced as I knelt and dumped the box's contents onto the floor. I spread the button pile with my palm. The little disks felt cool and smooth to my touch, brightly colored and cheerful against the worn brown carpet. I searched hungrily for something more. Another photo, or trinket, some additional clue about my origin.

There were only buttons.

I heard Ilona humming as she crossed the back patio and entered the house. Deeply rooted Southern manners insisted I rise and greet her, but I could only stare at the photo, buttons, and box scattered before me. Based on Mom and Bastien's clothing, the picture was taken on a different day than the photo Mom had given me. On the day she told me about my origin, and the man with one arm around her in this image. Was I already growing inside her then?

I'd obsessed over the first photo during the weeks I waited for Mom to talk again. I'd compiled questions and fabricated scenarios in my mind in which she told me every detail she could recall about the man she'd met in France. Since her death, I'd been so focused on leaving Robert that I hadn't had much time or energy to think about my biological father. Now, I wondered again what my life might've been if Mom had made a different decision. Could we have been safe and happy? Would she still be here today?

Ilona stopped a few feet from where I knelt on the living room floor. She didn't speak for a long moment, and neither did I.

Eventually she collected the bags of food from the chair and released a deep, audible sigh. "I see you found the buttons."

My gaze shot to her, the photograph still clutched in one hand. "You know?"

"Yep."

I jerked onto my feet. "How long have you known?"

"Longer than you," she said. "Before you ask, I didn't say anything because it wasn't my secret to tell."

I followed her to the kitchen and collapsed onto a chair at the table.

Ilona poured glasses of iced water and arranged our salads and sandwiches on plates. "I know it's a lot to take in," she said. "But she did what she thought she had to do to give you a good life. She wasn't sure she could find him again even if she wanted. She didn't have the money for another trip. She didn't want to move to France, away from everyone and everything she knew. She didn't believe he'd come to America for a girl he'd only known a short time, so she decided it was best never to say a word." Ilona pushed the glass of water in my direction. "That's all I know about it, so drink up, and try not to be too mad. She did the best she could with what she had."

I drank the water as she suggested, letting the coolness reduce my body temperature and my temper. Ilona was right. It was useless to be angry with someone who wasn't around to defend herself.

But that didn't mean I would let this go.

I struggled through my thoughts as I ate. If Mom had considered telling Bastien about me, then she must've had his address at one time. He was unlikely to live in the same place, but it was something to go on, assuming I could find the address. One look around this house proved she rarely threw anything away.

One way or another, I would find Bastien Allard and tell him he had a daughter.

I didn't need anything from him, but it would be nice to know if he wasn't the violent, unstable train wreck the man who raised me turned out to be. I'd tell him Mom passed recently and kept photos of him hidden. That I hadn't known until recently. I wasn't just being selfish in trying to track him down. I couldn't imagine a world where I didn't meet Camilla, or know she existed, until she was in her forties. Bastien deserved the truth. And he should have the chance to know me too.

Ilona's chair scraped over the linoleum as she rose from the table and carried her trash to the wastebasket. "How do you feel about yard sales?" she asked. "Might do wonders to get rid of some of this stuff. I can help if you want to get one going. Harvey, he's in the blue house on the corner," she clarified, "works at the paper. He'll put the ad in for us if we ask, and he's got two teenage daughters home for the summer. They can make posters and put them up around the neighborhood. Real nice girls. Always asking if I need anything."

It took a long moment for her words to register through the fog in my brain, another few seconds for what she said to make sense. I was so enraptured by the possibility of contacting my biological father that the sharp change in subject felt like being pulled up from the bottom of a swimming pool.

Part of me had completely forgotten she was there.

"Are you finished?" she asked, moving toward me, one arm outstretched.

I'd eaten my sandwich and salad, but I barely recalled doing so. "I might need to lie down."

Ilona's expression was patient, her smile sad as she cleared the table, then returned to stroke a gentle palm over my head. "I think that's a good idea."

❧

I searched Bastien's name online and on social media platforms until the lack of results left my mind as tired as my body. I fell asleep in the trailer, box fans propped in the windows. Then I dreamed of my mother.

I saw her in the kitchen, and I raged over the choices she'd made. Demanded answers and received none. My dad, Carl, was to blame for the emotionally toxic state of our home, but Mom let her fears keep her there. Keep *us* there. Fear of public opinion. Fear of his repercussions. Fear of trying to make it on her own. The fact that society put her in that position made me angrier and more breathless. Partly because I had the same worries before I left Robert.

My body jerked upright in alarm. Something had woken me. I didn't know what.

"Mom?" Camilla's voice pulled my eyes toward the door. "You in there?"

"Com—" I cleared my throat and tried again. The box fans were loud in the small space. "Coming!"

How long was she waiting?

A blast of air chilled my face as I passed the window. I ran a palm over my wet cheek in response. Had I been crying?

I pushed open the door and my heart melted.

Camilla smiled up at me. "Hey, Mama," she said. Her smile fell as she took me in. "Are you okay?"

I nodded, warmed by the sight of her precious face. "I think I cried in my sleep." A nervous chuckle bubbled out of me. I hadn't cried in so long, the tears seemed like progress, even if I wasn't awake when they came.

Interesting that I felt safer emoting in a trailer in my childhood backyard than I had in the McMansion Robert built inside a gated community, but it wasn't the time to dwell on that.

"Come in!" I frowned and laughed again. "Actually, I'll come out. What are you doing here? I'm so glad to see you!" I pulled her into a tight embrace, and she rocked me foot to foot.

"Just checking in," she said. "Looks like you made a lot of progress already." She stepped back and hooked a thumb over one shoulder, indicating the patio overflowing with Mom's stuff. "Anything I can do to help? I have a little time before yoga. I teach twice this evening."

"Evening?" I glanced at my watch. I'd slept longer than I realized. "Shoot. That nap cost me half the day."

She shook her head. "People experiencing emotional trauma require lots of sleep. It's part of the healing process."

I wrapped an arm around her shoulders and led her toward the house. "Can I get you something to drink?"

"Yes, but first, I have something for you. Give me just a sec." She broke free and jogged toward her Toyota. She pulled a tote bag from the floor of the back seat and hooked it over one shoulder, then hefted a pet carrier into her arms. "I picked up some groceries for you while I was at the store earlier. I dropped Raisin at the groomer and had some time to kill. Two errands, one cat."

I met her on the lawn and took the carrier, peering through the little gate. "Look at that blowout! This can't be the same creature. This is one of those diva pets from the national cat show."

"It's Raisin," she assured me. "The groomer had a couple of extra bandages on her fingers when I picked him up, but I still think this cat liked the attention."

I set Raisin's crate on the dining room floor and opened the gate. He lumbered out, stretching both front legs in a deep lunge before arching like a Halloween cat, then taking a seat. His dark, shaggy fur was neither black nor brown. Soft and shiny now, the tufts of hair stood out in all directions around his flat face and yellow eyes.

"You look so handsome," I cooed.

He bumped his head against my leg, then circled me slowly, tail up as if petting me as he passed.

"I thought you might like the company," Camilla said. "I hated thinking of you all alone here. I can't imagine losing you, then being left to sort your things. It's got to be so hard." Her voice trembled, and I hugged her tightly once again.

"I'm going to be okay," I promised. "I'm tougher than I look."

She released me slowly and offered a strained smile. "I'm not so sure about Dad."

I tensed. "Yeah?" A dozen awful scenarios flipped through my mind. Had he called her crying? Spewing slander? Something worse?

"I stopped by to check on him last night," she said. "He seemed confused, maybe in shock. He said he thought you were happy, and he never saw this coming. Also, apparently, he doesn't believe in divorce. He said marriage is supposed to be forever." She frowned and shook her head. "I listened while he talked, but if he really believed that, he would've been a better husband. He'd have at least tried to be your partner or friend. He didn't, and he can't really think you were happy when he barely spoke to you unless it was to complain."

Emotion wedged in my throat, stealing my words. Camilla had seen so much more than I wanted her to. She saw right past my forced smiles and pretenses. Just because she hadn't seen her parents fight like I had didn't mean she was any less aware of the toxicity. I hated that I'd let her witness this.

She deserved so much better.

"Are you okay?" she asked, frowning as I struggled to speak. "I can take the cat back if it's too much. I probably should've asked you first, but I'll need a cat sitter when Jeff and I leave for the Maldives."

"It's okay. Raisin can stay here." I stepped away with a forced smile. I tucked loose hairs behind my ears, hoping to look more casual than I felt. I'd nearly forgotten about her trip when my life fell apart. She and Jeff had rescheduled after Mom died. "When are you going?"

"August, the last two weeks before school starts. Jeff wanted me to have as much time as I need with you right now."

"Very thoughtful."

"He is," she agreed. "I'm not quite sure why you don't seem to believe it."

I dropped the act and lowered my shoulders. "I was your age when I got married. So was my mom. It didn't work out for either of us. I want so much better for you."

"I know you do," Camilla said. "But Jeff isn't Dad or Grandpa, and I'm not you or Grandma. My mama taught me about my very high worth, every single day, and she showed me how much she believed it with her actions. I see you, Mama," she said sweetly. "I saw you then, and I see you now. I hold everyone I meet to your standards. I will never accept anything less."

My eyes misted, and I smiled. "I did okay?"

"You were exactly the mother I needed."

And then the tears began to fall.

Chapter Nine

Camilla and I finished the kitchen and dining room before she left for yoga. Raisin stayed with me. If there was an upside to the out-of-control clutter at Mom's place, it was that she owned at least two of everything under the sun, including a carpet shampooer I used to steam and scrub the carpets and throw rugs. I found enough bottles of cleaning solution to do the same for every home below the Mason–Dixon line.

I accepted Ilona's offer to help with a yard sale via text message after dinner, and she said she'd let me know when the notice appeared in the paper.

I stopped working for the night when I found an unopened bottle of sauvignon blanc in a large vase with seven umbrellas. I carried the bottle with me to the trailer and finished half while searching online for Bastien Allard.

I came up empty yet again.

Raisin forced me awake in the morning, aggressively head bumping me until I thought we'd both suffer a concussion.

"Okay," I said. "Stop. I'm up."

He meowed and bit my toes where they hung outside the covers.

"Ow! Hey!" I burrowed beneath the blanket, wishing I'd switched to water after my first glass of wine.

Raisin bit my leg through the thin duvet.

"I'm up!"

I pushed onto my feet, wincing at the stiffness in my neck and back from the long day of scrubbing and moving things at the house. I reached for my toes, feeling every year of my age for the first time in a long while.

Raisin chewed my hair when gravity pulled it in his direction.

"No!" I swung upright and lost my balance momentarily, knocking my hip against the pop-up kitchen table. "Damn it!" A pathetic whimper crossed my lips as I straightened. "I can't live in this trailer."

I moved to the kitchenette's countertop and removed the pot from the ancient coffee maker, then stuck the vessel beneath the faucet. The cold-water knob turned easily, and water dripped slowly for several seconds before coming to a complete stop.

I tried the hot-water knob. Nothing. "This cannot be my life," I complained.

Raisin bit my calf.

"Stop." I pointed at the cat.

He sat and stared up at me.

I gathered my things and pushed open the trailer door. "Come on," I said. "I need coffee and a hot shower." After that I had to find a way to save this house. Time was running out, and I still hadn't made enough money to make a dent in the amount Mom owed.

Raisin trotted into the day, glancing over his shoulder every few feet to be sure I followed.

The morning air was dense and humid. A thick layer of fog clung to the grass like an apparition.

I picked up my pace, in no need of additional ghosts.

Inside, I fired up the single-cup coffee maker and set a mug beneath the drip. Then I went to the pantry in search of kibble.

"All right," I said. "Your turn."

Pellets fell to the floor as I carried the bag of cat food toward the bowls I'd chosen for Raisin.

"What on earth?" I turned the bag in my grip and found a hole near the bottom. "Shoot."

I groaned at the new mess on my clean floors, then set the bag beside the bowls. The cat food would go stale without a way to keep it fresh.

I rooted through the cabinets in search of freezer bags to protect the kibble.

Raisin scratched at the bag behind me, casting food onto the floor with every pass, by the sounds of it.

"I'm hurrying," I promised.

He appeared beside me, and my muscles stiffened at the sight of him, because the scratching didn't stop.

A slow turn in the direction of the bag revealed the reason.

A short scream wrenched through me at the sight of a small gray mouse. "Ah!"

I clambered onto the countertop and Raisin joined me. "What are you doing?" I asked. "Get him!" I pointed to the rodent eating his food, in case he hadn't noticed. "Attack! Or chase him away or something."

I'd never had a cat—neither Dad nor Robert tolerated pets—but I knew what cats did. Cats ate mice!

Raisin looked at the mouse, then back to me. And he nipped my arm.

"Hey!" I slapped a hand over the red spot near my elbow, then stretched to reach the broom propped against the wall. "Go away!" I called, waving the broom at our unwanted guest. When the critter didn't budge, I climbed down and whacked the floor a few times, hoping to scare the rodent away. I didn't have it in me to hurt him, but he couldn't stay.

The thumping worked, and the mouse ran off with a cheek full of kibble.

"Jeez!" I said, sweeping the loose kibble into a pile. "Why didn't you do anything?"

Raisin jumped onto the floor, walked to his still-empty bowl, and waited.

"Too good to eat food straight from the floor?" I guessed. "Won't chase mice. Only dines from a bowl. Maybe Mom should've named you Mr. Fancy Pants."

I lifted the food bag and gave it a closer look, unsure it was safe for Raisin's consumption after a mouse had been inside. "Hold on." I chucked the bag into the trash, along with the contents of my dustpan, then selected another bag from the pantry.

When I finished feeding Raisin, I put all the cat food into a big plastic bin and hoped mice wouldn't eat through my boxes of pasta and mac and cheese.

I added *get rid of mice* to my mental list of objectives. I couldn't bake here until the house was free of rodents, which meant no extra cash. A double whammy.

I missed baking, and I needed the money. I had only a few days left to get Mom's delinquent property taxes paid before the house was auctioned off. I hadn't found her bankbooks or any indication she had anything other than debt, so I had to make saving the house the day's priority.

I worked in the living room until dehydration set in and my vision blurred.

Definitely time for lunch.

I carried a plated BLT and handful of strawberries onto the patio, deeply grateful for the groceries Camilla delivered the day before. My backside had barely hit the seat before I caught sight of the open trailer door.

Had I not closed it securely behind me this morning?

I carried my sandwich to the potential crime scene, snacking as I walked, too exhausted to protest if I found someone mid-burgle. *Take it,* I thought. *Take it all so I don't have to figure out what to do with it.*

In fact, *take me.*

No one was inside, so I closed the door, checked it twice, then returned to my chair, plate, and strawberries.

I opened an internet browser on my phone as I ate and searched for ways to make fast money. My toenails needed fresh paint, which eliminated the possibility of selling feet pics, and without baking, I didn't have any salable skills.

A wave of grief and defeat hit hard enough to knock a weaker woman off her chair, but I didn't have time for a breakdown.

I lived in a compact warehouse of sorts. Surely there was a big-ticket item or two that I could sell for quick cash.

If not, I could always get a pedicure.

Chapter Ten

After lunch I found an unopened package of mousetraps in a decorative basket on the fireplace hearth. Apparently, Mom knew she had a problem, and cared enough to order supplies, but not enough to use them.

"Were you that depressed?" I asked the room. My eyes darted toward the popcorn ceiling, as if I might see her there. "What was it?" I asked, continuing the one-sided conversation. "How did you go from the woman I grew up with to this?" I waved the package around the room. "You used to fight back!"

Dad had been gone nearly two decades. Why hadn't she healed? Did she even try?

"Why couldn't we just be friends?" I asked.

A horrendous thought occurred for the second time, and my stomach rolled. Did she blame me for her abusive marriage? Just as I'd blamed her? She might not have married Dad, if she didn't have to hide her pregnancy.

Did she resent me?

The thought was gutting, and I felt the pain as it cut through my core.

My phone vibrated on the coffee table with a notification. My attorney's office had sent an email. I sat gingerly on the couch, careful not to smash a mouse or jam a knitting needle where it didn't belong. Then I opened the message.

Updates on my case, yada yada yada. The divorce paperwork was officially filed, and the courts had created a calendar of events on our behalf. *Please see attached.*

I opened the scanned document with excitement in my soul.

The only thing better than not living with my terrible husband was knowing soon we wouldn't be married at all.

According to the schedule, a temporary hearing would occur in two weeks, followed by two mandatory mediations in the next four months, a pretrial hearing thirty days later, and the trial the month after that. I did some quick mental math and determined I could be free from Robert's reign in just over six months. As long as everything went smoothly.

If we wound up in a legal battle, I had no doubt he'd drag it out as long as possible to punish me. I definitely didn't need that. I already had enough obstacles to overcome.

I acknowledged my receipt of the schedule, then added the events to my phone's calendar. According to the most recent chat with my attorney, the temporary hearing would be an in-and-out procedure because Camilla was an adult. For Robert and me, the court would determine how our expenses were handled until the divorce finalized. My attorney believed I would maintain access to our bank accounts to pay bills and living expenses throughout the process. I certainly hoped so.

I hadn't had a job since high school, and I didn't know where to begin looking for one. Thankfully, I had a little more time to figure that out. Assuming I didn't lose Mom's house.

The thought put me back to business. I needed to locate Mom's bankbooks, or paperwork that would lead me to her available cash. Additionally, I was on the lookout for anything of value I could return or sell for cash. And if I was really lucky, I'd come across Sébastien Allard's old mailing address. It's unlikely his parents were still alive, but if they were, they might still live in the same home. I could write and ask for a way to reach him.

Meanwhile, I called a local outreach center advertising free pickup on gently used furniture, before setting up the catch-and-release mousetraps.

Then I got back to work.

I didn't stop until I was certain I'd collapse and get buried under piles of Mom's things, only to be found months from now by trained spelunkers, probably hired by Alicia or Cami.

I carried a box I'd filled with treasures into the kitchen and cracked open a bottle of water from the fridge. Mom had sandwiched photo albums of my youth between books and magazines from decades past. I flipped through those quickly, then shook a few pieces of jewelry from the bottom of a bud vase—a diamond-and-ruby tennis bracelet with matching earrings. I set them aside to take somewhere for appraisal, then fanned the pages of a dozen notebooks filled with Mom's messy scrawl.

She hadn't let me get close to her in life. Maybe reading her written thoughts would help me know her in death.

I was halfway through a chicken salad sandwich and one of the old photo albums when a truck with the local donation center's logo rattled into the driveway. In the album, Mom had neatly arranged pictures of me blowing out candles on every birthday cake for eighteen years, along with a number of similar images from my twenties and a few of Camilla while she was still in diapers. My mother was many things, but nostalgic and sentimental weren't among the adjectives that came to mind.

Yet, the photos disagreed.

A pair of men donned work gloves as they approached the house.

Humiliation and embarrassment wobbled through me as I met them at the door. I wanted to distance myself from the chaos of this place, but shame made me bite my tongue. My mother had lifelong problems I didn't understand. I doubted the volunteers from the shelter would, either, and they probably didn't care. I swallowed the grief of my loss, and Mom's. Then I opened the door.

"Hi," I said, forcing hospitality into my tone. "Thank you for coming. Let me show you where I've set everything on the back patio. You can drive the truck alongside the house to shorten your path."

One of the men turned back for the truck. The other shook my hand. "I'm Albert, and we're grateful for every donation. Thank you so much for giving us a call."

My throat tightened. I nodded and led him to the patio.

By the time the sun set, the living room was scrubbed and empty, the carpet drying after my second pass with the steamer. I found a pearl necklace inside one of Mom's tchotchkes and a watch that I guessed was worth thousands. I had an appointment to see a jewelry appraiser in the morning. One way or another, I would pay off the property taxes and keep this house.

The air on the first floor smelled of cleansers and hope as I admired my work. I, however, smelled like a swamp monster. So I headed for the shower.

I dumped my things into the first-floor bathroom and started the water, then returned to the kitchen for a bottle of sweet tea from the fridge. I checked the mousetraps, both wishing I would and would not find mice in them. I didn't want the creatures in the house, but I had no idea what to do if I caught them.

Was I supposed to set them free outside? That seemed silly. Wouldn't they just walk right back in?

I returned to the bathroom a moment later and peeled sweaty clothes from my achy frame. I raked tangles from ratty hair and took one more drink of sweet tea before stepping under the impressive spray.

The shock hit my system like a baseball bat.

"Cold! Fuck!"

My feet slid on the wet tile floor as I bounced and leaped to safety. My heart pounded, and my skin pebbled. I gripped the sink's edge to steady myself, then cranked the hot water and flushed the toilet. A few moments later, the shower warmed to tepid.

I took the fastest shower possible, dried off, and left a voicemail on a local plumber's answering machine requesting he stop by to take a look at the situation as soon as possible. Then I trudged across the lawn to my bed inside the trailer, Mom's photo albums and notebooks tucked beneath one crooked arm.

Raisin stayed at the house.

The next few days followed a similar pattern, except Ilona began visiting after breakfast and staying through lunch. We marked items for the upcoming yard sale and reminisced about the days when I ran wild in the neighborhood.

The jewelry I found, along with a small check from a joint account with Robert, was enough to appease the county auditor and keep my property off the auction block. I still had to deal with the utility-shutoff notices, but I was counting my wins where I found them.

My phone buzzed, and I stilled to check the screen.

"That's not Robert, is it?" Alicia asked. She stopped by frequently, as promised, and helped any way she could. Her presence alone meant everything to me.

Ilona made a sour face.

"No." I shook my head. "He's pretending I don't exist. This looks like an order for the Invisible Baker." I had the calls forwarded from my other phone, now that I no longer had a reason to hide them. I opened the message and skimmed. "Someone wants to place an order for a coworker's birthday. Thirty-six mini vanilla layer cakes for the staff lounge."

My friends and I looked to Mom's newly cleaned kitchen.

"I can't bake here," I said. "I still haven't caught that mouse. Gives me the ick knowing it's still running free. That's a health code violation for sure, right?"

Alicia wrinkled her nose. "No luck with the traps?"

"No, but I also plugged in some things I found in the spare bedroom that claim to emit sounds to keep pests away. Maybe they worked?"

Alicia didn't look convinced. "Well, you can always use my kitchen, and I'm glad to help."

"Same offer," Ilona said. "But why not use your other kitchen?"

I glanced through the back window. "The trailer?"

"No," she said. "The one in that mini mansion of yours."

"Oh, sure," I said. "Robert would love that."

Alicia straightened. "It's still half your house, no matter what that butthead says. You moved out, but you're allowed to be there. Right? Is there something in the paperwork from your hearing that says you're not?"

"I don't think so, but I wasn't thinking about that. I never planned to go back."

"So bake while he's at work," she said. "No harm, no foul. He'll never know, and you can bake in the space you're most comfortable. Plus, you can get more done with the oversized double ovens than you can here or at my place."

"I bought my stove the year you were born," Ilona said.

I pinched my bottom lip between my teeth.

I could definitely use the money, and I usually got new orders when I baked for a group like this. Fixing the hot-water heater had already cost me four hundred dollars, and I suspected that was the tip of the iceberg where home repairs were concerned.

"When does she want the cakes?" Alicia asked.

I glanced back at the phone. "End of the week."

She smiled. "Easy peasy."

"Sounds good to me," Ilona agreed.

I inhaled deeply and released the breath slowly. I appreciated retaining access to our joint accounts, but writing checks or using our debit card meant providing a record for Robert. I'd moved out, but he still knew my every move: where I shopped, how much I spent, and when. And I hated it. Earning some cash would be wonderful.

"Well?" Ilona asked.

"I'm thinking," I said. "I can always take the buckets of coins I've found to the bank."

"Coins?" Ilona asked. "I love coins, and I have lots of rollers. I can help with that."

Alicia beamed. "Me too. And I can take any other jewelry or collectibles you have to the appraiser. Did you find more?"

I nearly laughed. In this house, there was always more.

"Come with me," I said.

I walked them to my parents' old bedroom, where everything with any cash value remained. "This is the last room I need to sort, and I'm keeping everything in here that I don't know what to do with. Coins are in the boxes on the dresser. Jewelry is in that case."

My friends dug in while I noodled on whether to bake at my old house.

"I'm going to do it," I said after another minute of thought. What did I have to lose? "Assuming Robert still works long hours, and he hasn't purged the pantry, I can accept the request and make the cakes this afternoon."

"Excellent," Alicia said. "We'll lock up if we leave before you get back."

"I'll feed Raisin," Ilona promised, glancing up from her coffee can of coins. "This is filled with half dollars, and there must be at least five hundred of them here!"

A smile broke on my face. "Good to know!"

Alicia waved, and I turned on a burst of energy and raced home.

❧

The massive fifty-two-hundred-square-foot home Robert and I commissioned so many years ago looked foreboding as I approached. I parked at the end of the block and entered through the utility door in the garage, thankful I hadn't returned all my keys.

Robert's car wasn't in the garage, so I let myself into the kitchen.

Everything was as I'd left it. Surprisingly so. Either Robert hadn't come home in a couple of weeks, or he'd started cleaning up after himself. The latter made me angry. If he could put dishes into the dishwasher and pick up his shoes and ties now, why hadn't he done it before?

To remind me I was his maid, I presumed.

I made a disgusted, throaty noise, as I got to work on the mini layer cakes. Everything remained equally undisturbed in the pantry.

Being back in the home where I'd raised our daughter and planned my escape felt strange, even after only a short time away. Maybe because I was the heart of this place, and without me it was just an expensive tomb. The energy had fizzled in my absence. Even the air felt different on my skin.

I couldn't help wondering if Robert came home more or less often without me here.

"There's not nearly enough time to go down that rabbit hole," I whispered as I tapped the screens to preheat the ovens. If he came home more often, it was better I didn't know. Especially with our temporary hearing next week. I wanted to do anything I could to avoid rocking the boat. Baking in the home I'd abandoned felt like asking for a fight, and Robert never fought fairly.

An hour later, I'd baked four sheet cakes using my favorite recipe and blessed double ovens. I rushed the cooling process as much as possible in our mostly empty Sub-Zero freezer while I whipped up the buttercream frosting.

I checked the time repeatedly as I tested the cakes' temperatures. When it was safe to cut out circles, I used a biscuit cutter, then arranged the disks onto parchment paper covering several large cookie sheets. I piped icing onto the cakes one at a time and topped them with a second round of cake. I repeated the process until all the cakes were stacked three disks tall and iced with decorative peaks. I dashed the tops with colored sugar crystals and added an edible purple flower before calling the project done.

"Not bad for a rush job," I said. Then I piped a little icing onto one of the leftover corners of my cake and gave it a taste test. I savored the flavors and textures on my tongue, then moved the extra cake and icing to containers and piled them into a canvas shopping bag. No sense in letting perfectly good cake and icing go to waste. Plus, I didn't want to leave any evidence of my work behind. I stole one last piece of cake before washing up the pans and dishes and putting it all away.

"One more thing."

I stepped back and snapped a photo. A little fodder for the Invisible Baker's Instagram account.

Chapter Eleven

I pulled into the lot outside Chez Margot, a French café on Main Street, after finishing my shopping the next day. I passed the little restaurant every time I visited my favorite riverside grocer, and I itched to finally get a look inside. Also, I was starving and in no mood to cook when I got home.

Twinkle lights wrapped support posts, and ivy climbed the redbrick exterior to a black-and-white-striped awning above the front door. The delectable scents of baking bread and fresh basil floated in the air, and my stomach growled in anticipation. If the food tasted half as good as it smelled, I'd never eat anywhere else again.

The interior decor continued the outside theme. Black accents, exposed bricks, and a plethora of plants made the space feel cheery and inviting. Chatter and laughter lifted on the air.

A framed photo of a gorgeous dark-haired couple hung near the hostess stand, an image of the restaurant in the background. The man's eyes were kind and the woman's smile enchanting. I'd never looked as happy or at ease in photos with Robert. I envied them both immediately.

Why did I spend two decades feeling insecure and uncertain with Robert when I could've been independent and free?

"Can I help you?" a man called, striding purposefully in my direction. His white dress shirt was unbuttoned at the collar, the sleeves rolled up to his elbows. A few wrinkles formed at the edges of his mouth and eyes as he smiled. He looked older than in the photo, but

I recognized him immediately. The platinum wedding band on his left hand shone in the light.

"I'm just picking up something for lunch," I said.

"Name?" he asked.

"Sophie, and you?"

He paused, then laughed.

It took a moment before I recognized my mistake.

"Oh, I am so sorry," I said. "You weren't asking my name to be friendly, and I'm not picking you up. I mean, I'm not picking up lunch. No. I am," I stammered. "Here for lunch. Not you—" I stopped talking and wrinkled my nose. *Dear lord,* I thought, utterly baffled. Was I this shaken by the presence of a handsome man? Or had hunger impacted my brain?

"You know what?" I turned, waved, then marched back the way I'd come in, so I could die in peace.

"Wait," he called. "Where are you going?"

I stopped just short of the exit and peered over my shoulder at him. "Oh, I'm going to walk into traffic now."

He burst into laughter and motioned me back. A dimple sank in one cheek as he grinned.

I immediately hated myself for finding another woman's husband so ridiculously attractive.

Maybe hunger really had addled my brain.

"I think we should start over," he said. "I'm Lucas."

A young woman in braids and a polo shirt with the restaurant's logo rounded the corner, then stopped short. Her eyes went wide at the sight of us, and she hurried in our direction. "I'm so sorry. I didn't hear anyone come in," she explained. "My apologies."

He waved her off, eyes fixed on me. "No, it's fine, Pam. Sophie and I were just talking. Will you take a bottle of merlot to the couple at table twelve? It's their anniversary."

"Of course." She offered a polite smile, then hurried away.

Lucas stretched out his hand. "It's nice to meet you."

I accepted the shake and fought a goofy smile. "I'm having a really weird day," I said. "I think I just need to eat."

"You came to the right place," he said. "This is my restaurant, and I happen to know everything on the menu is fantastic, because I'm frequently the chef."

A slight French accent tipped the words as he spoke, adding impossibly to his charm.

He released my hand after a little squeeze, then pulled a menu from behind the hostess stand. "Are you in the mood for anything specific?"

I bit my lip to stop myself from admitting I would gladly eat a week's worth of anything put in front of me. "I don't know," I said instead. "Maybe a salad."

"I thought you were hungry." He winked, and the strange sensation of sparks prickled through me. "Come with me," he said. "If you want to sit at the bar, I'll put together a sampler so you can find a new favorite."

He led me through the dining room, past red vinyl booths and herbs hung in planters on the walls. I marveled at the garden of ingredients just waiting to serve their life's purpose.

Lucas placed a glass of iced water on the bar before an empty high-backed chair. His wedding ring glinted in the light.

I climbed into the seat and looked at the menu, embarrassed by the odd feelings this benign conversation caused me, and the heat rushing across my cheeks in response. *We aren't flirting,* I assured myself. He was a polite business owner and, clearly, a proudly married man.

Maybe that was the appealing part. I deeply appreciated a man so happily in love. Was it possible that some men really do cherish their wives? Cameron did. Surely he wasn't the only one.

"See anything you like?" he asked.

I forced myself to meet his eyes and nodded. "Everything looks fantastic, but I don't know much about French food."

His eyebrows rose. "Is that right?"

I nodded, thinking of my French ancestry. I really should learn more. "I mean, I'm obviously a big fan of olive tapenade."

"Obviously." He crossed his arms.

"I also know my way around a bowl of French onion soup."

"We just call it onion soup," he teased.

"Noted." I returned my attention to the menu and concentrated on the unfamiliar dishes. Then I felt the drool form at the corners of my mouth. "You have crepes."

"Of course," Lucas said.

"I love crepes."

He caught my eye and pursed his lips. "Good to know."

An older couple called his name on their way to the register. He responded by asking about their family and a shared neighbor.

I hadn't visited a restaurant with such a comfortable community vibe since college. I gave the restaurant's dining room a more thorough inspection and soaked up the ambience. French loaves sat on tables with small pots of butter. Fleur-de-lis accents adorned the menus and place mats.

A random thought popped into mind, and I nearly rolled my eyes in response. Mom told me more than once that she'd named me Sophie after a French princess, Sophie Philippine Élisabeth Justine. The French often referred to her as Sophie of France. I'd assumed the inspiration came from Mom's trip to the country in the year I was born.

I never suspected how true that was.

The Chez Margot logo atop each page put a new question on my tongue. "Is Margot a family name?" I asked.

"It was my wife's name," he said. Lucas's wistful smile made it clear that he adored her. The past tense, however, gave me pause.

My gaze fell to his ring finger, and he caught me looking. "Oh. Is she—"

"Hit and run," he said. "It was seven years ago. Police suspect a drunk driver." He shrugged, but I could see the story cost him. He spun the ring with his thumb while he spoke. "She closed up late for me one night so I could catch up on paperwork. She didn't make it home."

My mouth opened, but words failed me. I couldn't imagine losing someone I loved so much I'd wear their wedding ring all these years later.

I couldn't imagine *being loved* that much.

"I'm sorry about your loss."

He smiled. "I feel her here with me most days. Usually critiquing my sauces." He pulled a bottle of wine from the shelf behind him and poured a few ounces into a glass, then passed it to me. "This was her favorite. How do you feel about Riesling?"

"Good." I accepted the glass, straight-faced, while recalling the way Alicia and I demolished ten-dollar bottles with screw-top lids. I knew less about quality wine than French food.

"This one is from Alsace, a favorite region of mine for Rieslings. You enjoy this. I'll get started on your lunch."

An hour and far too many food samples later, I was stuffed and ready for a nap. I delighted in the homey atmosphere and sense of belonging. No one questioned the cost of my meal or commented on the likely amount of calories. Pure heaven.

Lucas emerged from the kitchen, a dish towel hung over one shoulder, as I pushed the final plate away. "What's the verdict?"

"Someone will have to roll me home."

His dark eyes danced with amusement. "But what was your favorite?"

"The crepes," I admitted. "I wish I could make them like this, and believe me, I've tried. But they never come out quite right."

"So, you're a cook." His eyes narrowed. "I should have known."

I wagged a finger, feeling the effects of my second glass of wine. "No. Just a woman who loves crepes."

Lines gathered on his handsome face, and he reached beneath the high-polished bar. "Well, we can fix that." Lucas placed a flyer before me, then took the dirty plate away.

I turned the paper in my direction when he left. The flyer advertised community classes available at the restaurant. All were open to the public. *Authentic French cooking classes, wine tasting, crepe making.* I grinned. I supposed I was in luck.

"You can learn to cancan on Saturday nights," he said, reappearing with a handled to-go bag. "It's a lot of fun. Please say you can can."

I straightened my expression and shook my head at his terrible joke. "I'll see what I can do."

"No pressure," Lucas said.

I finished my glass of water, marveling at the local gem of a restaurant. "Did you grow up here?" I asked. I wasn't sure if I meant in the area or the country, but his accent suggested he wasn't raised here. Maybe he'd come for college.

"I came to America as an adolescent, then returned to France after high school for a culinary program. I considered going back again after Margot's death, but we built this place together, so I stayed."

"I think it's nice you still wear your wedding ring," I said. The words came out before I thought better of them. "It's clearly none of my business," I added, with a self-deprecating chuckle. "But nice."

His lips curved gently at the corners. "My family thinks it's too much, but the ring makes me feel connected to her somehow. I suppose I'll wear it until another woman wins my heart."

The young woman with the braids strode into view, phone in hand. "Lucas, Emily."

He dragged his eyes from me to her and nodded before turning back. "It was nice meeting you, Sophie."

"You too," I said. "Do I pay up front?"

"No, no. On the house," he said, already moving in the direction of the woman and phone.

"Wait," I squeaked, sliding onto my feet. "I can't let you do that."

"You can," he said. "Don't forget your bag."

I looked at the to-go order on the bar before me. *Sophie* was written in Sharpie near the top.

Lucas was nowhere to be seen as I left the building, but a peek inside the bag made me smile.

Crepes.

Chapter Twelve

I caught two mice in the coming weeks and released them both by the river. I didn't see another afterward, so I deemed the kitchen safe for baking and got busy. Mom had an arsenal of fabulous French recipes, and I tried them all. Now that I knew why she favored all things French, I wished I could know the man who inspired her as well. Unfortunately, every attempt I made to find him came up short.

Alicia and Ilona helped with the weekly yard sale while I worked on cookie orders Saturday morning. Nearly a month had passed since my big move, and we'd finally cleared the house of clutter. Unfortunately, a colony of bats in the attic kept me living in the trailer. Apparently, bats were a protected species and required a properly trained pest evacuator to remove and relocate them. Currently all my baking money went to the cause.

I snuck into my old house to bake large orders, where the newer double ovens saved precious time. I had the entry and exit process down to a science, and I liked the adrenaline rush more than I should.

Business boomed with the photos I shared regularly to social media and the generous number of contact cards included with every order. Summer break was in full swing, and it seemed everyone and their sister had a child's birthday party, wedding, or baby shower in need of pastries. Blessedly, I was fast becoming the go-to source, and I was slowly paying off Mom's bills without using a dime of money from my marital accounts. In fact, I tried not to think of my old life more than absolutely necessary.

The temporary hearing came and went without issue, costing me several nights' sleep for no good reason. The event itself was underwhelming, and I happily put it behind me. Another milestone completed on my path in the right direction.

Robert hadn't spoken to me or sent a single text message since the day I walked out, and he avoided eye contact at court. Alicia thought it was a miracle. I took it as a sign he was up to something, and I was afraid to guess what that might be.

The back screen door creaked open and slapped shut a moment before Alicia appeared. "Lunchtime," she said, marching to the fridge. She collected two bottles of water, then leaned against the appliance looking sweaty and exhausted. "I'm starving. Let's order delivery."

"Deal," I said. "Need a sugar pick-me-up?" I lifted a small pastry from the parchment paper before me and passed it her way.

"Good lord in heaven. Yes." She popped the mini sweet into her mouth immediately. A moment later, an appreciative moan fell from her lips.

Pride sizzled through me, drawing a smile on my face. "I hope Dr. Ford's baby shower guests will agree," I said. "She insisted on providing all the desserts as a way to show her new mother-in-law that she is equally domestic. As if running a successful private medical practice wasn't enough to impress her."

Alicia leaned against the counter, eyeballing the tidy rows of circular delights. "There will always be someone determined to think we aren't enough."

I passed her another treat. "Fact."

"I think as long as we know we're enough, who cares about the naysayers? They're obviously miserable. Happy people don't shit on other humans." She shoved the second treat into her mouth and let her eyelids flutter. "These are actually magical. What are they? When can I have more?"

"You are currently enjoying mini peach-and-berry croustades. I found the recipe in one of Mom's books. In the fall I'll make these with apples, orange blossom water, and cinnamon."

"Croustades are Danishes?" she guessed.

"Croustades get their names from the crusts," I said. "From what I've learned, they can be made from flaky or puff pastry like these, or from bread, potato, rice, or something else that's escaping me." I searched my brain. "Semolina, maybe." I hadn't spent any time looking into the savory versions. My sweet tooth demanded I make everything with sugar. "You can have more whenever you want. I think I owe you my perpetual servitude."

Alicia sucked a glob of filling from her thumb. "Excellent. How many orders have you filled this week?"

"Four, and I'm almost out of ingredients."

Hard to believe how quickly Mom's house went from practically uninhabitable to a place I felt comfortable baking. And as it turned out, I accomplished more in a single day, without the pressure of living with my bully, than I ever fathomed possible.

"I might have to raise my prices soon," I said. "I'm not clearing enough to make these more involved orders worthwhile. Basic cakes and cupcakes are one thing, but the specialized pastry doughs and fruits needed for the fancier stuff is killing my profits." I cringed at the thought of potential repercussions. "I like the harder recipes, so I don't want to take them off the table, but I also don't want to lose business if higher costs turn customers away."

"People know they get what they pay for," Alicia said. "Don't underestimate that. Plus, you provide a double service. Fabulous desserts and anonymity."

I smiled. "I'll update the website tonight."

"Attagirl. Now, what's for lunch?"

We ordered delivery, then arranged a picnic on the front lawn beneath a shade tree. We noshed and chatted as the occasional yard-sale shopper came and went.

Ilona wore a Velcro sun visor around her pixie-cut hair and a fanny pack from the early 1980s on her narrow waist. This was the last of the scheduled sales. Whatever didn't sell by closing would go to charity.

Ilona joined us, popped a grape into her mouth, and looked pensively in my direction. "Trailer door was open again this morning. I didn't see Raisin inside, so I shut it."

I rolled my eyes. "I can't keep it closed unless I lock it from the inside. I think the latch is busted."

Alicia raised her brows. "When do you move into the house?"

"Hopefully later this week, as long as the certified bat evacuation experts show up and get the job done as scheduled tomorrow."

Alicia laughed. "You really can't make this stuff up."

Wasn't that the truth. Who would have thought I'd leave a cushy life in a gated community to clean up decades of online shopping addiction and relocate a bunch of wildlife.

I returned my gaze to the tables full of Mom's collected treasures. "It's strange to see her things out here like this." Sorting the items had been easy. I could focus my mind on a daily goal. Selling it was different. Final somehow. "The dresses on rolling racks remind me of Sunday lunches. The vintage pumps and matching handbags make me think of long days by the waterfront, shopping and trying new cafés."

Ilona lifted another grape to her mouth, then dusted her palms. "Trina always looked so nice when we were young."

"She had to," I said, setting my chin on my knees. "Dad insisted." Just as Robert had. "Wives represent the husbands, you know? We can't go out into the world looking the way we feel or someone might realize how poorly we're treated at home."

Alicia set a palm on my back and rubbed gently.

I clenched my jaw. "I should've seen straight through Robert's nonsense when I met him," I said. "I had a lifetime of watching a fake man wear a fake smile and pretend to be something he wasn't. I, of all people, should've known exactly what Robert was."

A woman approached Mom's collection of blown glass vases, and I clamped my mouth shut.

My friends watched me carefully. "Sorry," I whispered. "I didn't mean to—"

Ilona frowned. "Don't apologize. You can say anything you want to us. I tried to tell your mom how important it was to voice her pain, but she kept it all inside. That's not good."

"Bitterness will grow roots in your heart," I said. A psychology professor wrote those words on the blackboard when I was in college. He said those same roots would eventually stop the organ from beating, like a python with its prey. He meant the lesson figuratively, but the grim analogy fit my mother's life well.

My throat grew thick as I stared at her picked-over items on the grass. "This stuff brought her some semblance of peace. Now it's just gathered on the lawn, priced at two dollars each, or best offer."

I felt Alicia's concerned stare on my cheek but couldn't bring myself to look at her. I wasn't good at vulnerability, and my tears formed frequently these days.

Ilona grunted. "Everyone's stuff ends up like this one day. Things don't matter once the person who loved them is gone."

The notion made Robert's obsession with money all the more laughable. We couldn't take anything with us when we left this earth, and no one was promised another day. He didn't have friends or hobbies. His only motivation to get up every morning was to work so he could earn more money and feel more important because of it. Whatever he chased was at the end of a rainbow. Utterly unreachable. He'd never be happy, and it made me a little sad for him.

Life was meant to be lived, and I wanted to live it.

I pulled my knees to my chest and wrapped my arms around them, unsteadied by a double wave of grief. For what was missing in my life. For the relationships I never had with my mom and husband. For the biological father I'd never know.

A tear slid over my cheek, and I wiped it away.

"This shouldn't have been her life," I whispered. "I've been looking through her old photo albums before bed. She was so beautiful and vibrant once. I remember her being smart and resilient. Dad stripped that all away, and she never recovered."

Everything could've been so different.

Ilona crossed her legs in the grass. She ran her palms over the blades and hummed softly. "Your mama wasn't really living. I think she was hiding, right to the very end. And you need to give yourself time. Your world is in upheaval. Your mama's gone. Your marriage is ending. Your daughter's grown. It's a whole lot for a person to sort out all at once. But you will. And your life will clean up nice, just like this place." She motioned to the house.

I'd power washed the stone last week and repainted the door and porch handrail. Cameron had repaired the broken shutters.

"Things will only look awful for a little while," Ilona continued. "As long as you keep working on it, life's going to look amazing real soon."

I met her eyes and found hope there. "Thank you for saying that."

She was right, of course. I'd taken the hardest step already. I thought of Sylvia from book club, telling me the novel's main character was supposed to make the necessary changes and choose happiness. That was my goal now, for my sake, Camilla's, and Mom's. Our family history of female misery ended with me. One way or another.

The changes I'd made in my life and this house already were incredible. Pride filled my soul. Whatever happened, I'd keep reaching for peace and joy.

I held on to my feelings of victory as we packed up the leftovers from the sale and moved the boxes into Cameron's truck. That night, as promised, I logged on to my website and raised all my prices.

When the moon made its appearance in the night sky, I slogged out to the trailer for what would hopefully be my last night of terrible rest. I sent messages to Alicia and Ilona, thanking them both for their help, then another to Camilla, letting her know how much I loved her.

My stomach growled, but I was far too tired to trek back across the lawn. So I pulled a spoon from the drawer and a jar of peanut butter from the shelf. I felt like a kid digging into the jar and stuffing a mouthful past my lips.

I stared through the parted curtains at the full moon overhead while bullfrogs and crickets played the evening score. "I miss you, Mom," I said. "What we had wasn't perfect, but I'd give anything to see you one more time. I should've taken better care of you instead of letting you push me away."

As with most nights, I fell asleep wishing the divorce was over, and praying tomorrow would come with good news of some kind on that front. Until I had the finalized paperwork in my hand, the feeling of dread would only grow.

I tossed and turned through the wee hours, cursing a beam of moonlight that shone onto my closed eyes. The threadbare blinds were useless. Something furry brushed against my foot and I pulled my leg beneath the blanket. "It's not time for breakfast," I moaned and buried my face against the pillow.

The cat rooted around my narrow bed until the peanut butter jar fell onto the ground and rolled to a stop. I'd been too lazy to put the snack away or brush my teeth. That second point could be a problem. Was I depressed? Or just exhausted? I didn't want to start down a path like Mom's. Owning a cat who never let me sleep certainly didn't help my mental health.

I listened as Raisin pawed and grunted at the jar. Hopefully peanut butter wouldn't make him sick. I couldn't afford a vet bill and didn't want to clean a disgusting mess.

My groggy mental wheels screeched to a stop, then reversed.

I'd left Raisin in the house tonight. Hadn't I?

I rolled onto my opposite side, eyes pinched shut, then carefully peeked over the bed's edge to the floor.

The dark fur shifted beneath the moonlight, and a shiny-eyed raccoon looked up at me.

"Ahhhh!" I launched upright, blanket gathered around my chest.

The creature reared back, tiny black hands raised in defense.

I sucked in a long, laborious breath, then screamed some more. "Get out! Get out! Get out!"

The raccoon made a grunting sound and moved toward the jar, as if I might want it.

The only thing I wanted was away from the trailer, the animal, and any fleas, ticks, or rabies it might be carrying.

I leaped past him on a bolt of adrenaline, blanket still clutched in my grip. I threw myself into the night with a gut-wrenching wail. The comforter tangled around my feet on the stairs, and I pitched forward, bouncing hard against the ground. A low *oof* wrenched from my core as the air left my lungs.

I opened my mouth to scream again but only managed a small wheeze.

Neighborhood dogs barked and porch lights flickered on. Bats circled in the sky above my chimney.

I rolled onto my hands and knees, picturing the animal on my heels as I bumbled toward Ilona's house.

Her back door swung open as I reached her patio. "What the—?"

I made a croaking sound, still unable to catch my breath, then tripped on her garden hose.

"Heavens!" Ilona crouched at my side, helping me upright as tears streamed down my dirty cheeks.

Across our joined lawns, the raccoon carried my peanut butter jar into the night.

Chapter Thirteen

I slept at Ilona's house that night, after showering the dirt and grass from my body. The water was hot, and her spare bedroom smelled of vanilla and lavender. My tired limbs melted into the cool sheets and didn't move until well after dawn.

When I made it downstairs to her kitchen the next morning, she brewed a pot of mint tea, and I made pancakes. It was the kind of morning I'd shared with Camilla a thousand times, and the quiet peace made me miss my mom.

At home, the bat abatement crew arrived as promised, and the process of thoroughly, professionally disinfecting the attic went off without a hitch. Which was perfect, because I was never sleeping in the trailer again. In fact, I sold the old eyesore on Craigslist within hours, and the new owner hauled it away sans fanfare. I hoped, for the buyer's sake, the raccoon wasn't hiding inside.

My life was looking better by the hour.

I held my breath as I checked my website for the Invisible Baker. Three fresh orders awaited me, despite the price increases, and my smile grew wide. I noodled on the best recipes to fulfill the requests, then grabbed my purse for a grocery run.

The sun shone bright in the afternoon sky, scorching the leather seats inside my SUV. I pumped the air-conditioning as I motored toward downtown.

I called Camilla, reminding her I loved her, and emphasizing the importance of packing sunscreen for her trip to the Maldives. I bit my tongue against the urge to say more. Like "Don't get engaged!" And "There's plenty of time to marry later. If he asks just say no."

I slowed at the light on the corner of First and Main, enjoying the view of our quaint riverfront town. Chez Margot beckoned me from across the intersection, with its delicious foods, welcoming atmosphere, and handsome owner. I found something about Lucas so wholesome and genuine. He crossed my mind more often than I liked, but always in pleasant ways. If his personality wasn't an act for the sake of his business, I supposed it was possible that not all men were completely awful. And Alicia hadn't found the only nonawful one.

At the moment, however, the only man I hoped to find was my biological father, and I wasn't having any luck with that. I'd searched through all of Mom's notebooks without finding any sign of his address. I still needed to sort and clean the closets and basement. Maybe I'd find another clue to his whereabouts in one of those locations. I'd found my share of half-empty liquor bottles in a dozen places they didn't belong; why not the address of my biological father in France?

The moment my divorce was final, and I had the freedom to use my half of the marital money as I pleased, I'd take a trip to the area of France Mom visited during college. If I happened across Sébastien Allard while I basked in the trip of the lifetime, all the better.

⁂

At the grocery store I piled a shopping basket high with everything I needed. A customer hosting a fiftieth wedding anniversary party had requested fresh, fruity, fun desserts. I had at least a dozen ideas for that event. Bourbon was the theme for the second event, a retirement dinner.

To say I couldn't wait to get started was a wild understatement. I made my way to the checkout with glee.

"Welcome back!" the cashier, whose name was Kathy, called upon my approach. "Baking again already?"

Kathy and I became acquainted during my first visit, when I wiped out her baking aisle and claimed it was for a friend's wedding reception. She'd made the sign of the cross over her chest and told me she wouldn't marry again for twelve flying monkeys. I didn't quite understand the expression, but I felt the gist of it in my marrow. We'd bonded over our youthful naivete and colossally failed marriages.

"Trying some new recipes," I said.

She snapped bright-green gum as I unpacked the basket. "What are you making this time?" She ran the items over her scanner and worked her lips into a grin.

"I haven't decided," I admitted. "But I'm leaning toward truffles, bacon brittle, and shortcakes. I have a new bottle of Maker's Mark at home and want to make the most of it." The high-quality whiskey-infused treats were sure to be a hit at the retirement party.

She sighed wistfully. "Can't go wrong with any of that. I'll have to let you know what they serve at my brother-in-law's house this weekend. He's retiring, and originally from Kentucky, so my sister themed the whole party around bourbon."

I stilled, feeling as if I'd stepped on a proverbial land mine. "Oh, yeah?"

"Mm-hmm." She bagged the last of my items and checked her screen.

I willed my face not to be as red as it felt. "Sounds like fun."

"I'm sure it will be," Kathy agreed. "Tammy throws one hell of a shindig, but she can't bake worth a dime. Knowing her, she'll put a bunch of store-bought cupcakes on one of her cookie trays again and tell everyone she worked all day on them. We'll be forced to pretend that we don't know the truth. Good manners and all that."

"Of course." My stomach knotted as I quickly reimagined my desserts for that event.

"Seventy-three twelve," she said.

I opened my wallet and spotted four twenties I'd received for an order of breakfast pastries. Paying cash was ideal, but it would leave me with less than ten dollars for lunch. "Let's do credit this time," I said, passing her my black card. If Robert scrutinized every charge and transaction, he wouldn't think much of a trip to a local grocer. He might, on the other hand, accuse me of wasteful spending if I charged another take-out order.

Kathy ran the card, and I mentally kicked myself for caring what Robert thought. I still needed to break my habit of managing his moods and navigating his nonsense.

Kathy's face pinched, and she returned the card. "Sorry, hon. It's declining."

I matched her pained expression. "What?"

"I tried it twice," she said, her Southern drawl softening the words. "Do you have another card?"

"That one doesn't have a limit," I told her. Robert had bragged about that fact at length, proud of himself for the credit approval. He used it everywhere we went, hoping others recognized it, and his importance by proxy.

A man got in line behind me, and Kathy raised a smile to him, before returning her patient eyes to me. "What do you want to do?"

I returned the card to my purse and placed my twenties into her hand. "This will cover it." I couldn't bring myself to try another card with a spectator. The only thing worse than Kathy seeing two cards declined would be sharing the experience with a complete stranger.

She finished the sale and tucked my receipt into the bag. Then she gave me too much change. "I gave you my employee discount," she whispered. "I divorced a rich son of a bitch once too."

My eyes misted as I reached for the bag. She recognized the fancy credit card. Wouldn't Robert be proud. "Thank you," I said, rushing to leave the scene of my humiliation.

"Don't mention it," she called after me. "Let me know how those truffles turn out!"

I climbed into my SUV like it was a getaway car, locked the doors, and screamed.

Chapter Fourteen

I called the credit card company when I got home, but they wouldn't give me any information. I was merely an authorized user on Robert's account. The representative suggested I reach out to him.

I left a message with my attorney instead.

Then I started baking.

I changed my plans for the retirement party to avoid Kathy realizing her sister-in-law was serving the same bourbon-based desserts I'd mentioned. I found plenty of alternatives, and I enjoyed the added challenge of finding the perfect replacements.

I sampled a little bourbon as I worked, having forgotten how much I liked whiskey. Why was wine the more socially acceptable choice of drink for women? I added that to my list of things the patriarchy stole, then vowed to take it back.

Soon, with the last of my cakes in the oven, I turned my attention to the mess, wiping most of it into the sink.

The drain gurgled, and the sink chugged but didn't empty. Instead of vanishing merrily into the pipes, the water backed up and accumulated.

My finger froze on the garbage disposal switch. "Do not break," I warned. I needed a working sink to finish my orders, and I didn't have any more money to spend on this house right now.

A bubble rose through the darkening water, and the sink's contents turned brown.

"Shit." I turned off the garbage disposal and searched for a mini plunger under the sink. I spotted a leak in the pipe and a small puddle already forming there. "Shit!"

I threw a dish towel on the puddle and shoved a plastic bowl under the leak. Then I grabbed the plunger and sank it into the murky water, aiming for the drain. "Please work," I prayed. Eyes closed, I gave the handle a few hard pumps.

To my delight, the water began to recede.

"Ha!" I left the plunger in the sink and backed away for a victory dance. I put my hands up and shook my hips in ways I hadn't in far too long. I laughed at the silliness, then doubled down and really let loose. "I am a confident, fast-thinking, independent woman," I sang. "I can do hard things. Nothing's going to stop me. Oh, yeah! Go, Soph—"

A sudden spray of sludge hit my calves through the open lower-cabinet doors.

I gasped, and the remaining water vanished from the sink. Before I could process what was happening, the leaking pipe burst, and filthy water rushed onto my floor.

"No!"

I lunged toward the mess, and my feet went up over my head. I landed on my backside with a thud, both feet sticking straight out before me. Grayish hunks of dough and bits of rotten food clung to the linoleum around me while my cute white shorts absorbed the putrid mess.

I slapped my hands against the ground in outrage and received a splash of the nasty water in return. Droplets stuck to my eyelashes and cheeks. My stomach churned, and I rose for a run to the restroom, arms pinwheeling as I went.

It was official. I hated this house.

The cleanup took significantly longer than expected, but I managed to get the desserts out of the oven on time and without another slip or fall. I dialed the plumber while the baked goods cooled on my newly disinfected countertop.

The receptionist answered with a bright and cheery greeting, but that all changed when I gave my name and address.

"Sorry," she said. "Services to this address are on hold."

"On hold? Why?" I asked. Nothing out of the ordinary happened when the technician repaired my shower and hot-water tank last month.

"Your payment didn't clear," she said. "We sent a letter to the address on file with the credit card, but we haven't gotten a response. You're on the do-not-service list until that changes."

My shoulders inched upward, recalling the credit card debacle at the market. "I'm so sorry. I didn't know there was a problem."

"We sent a notice to the address on file for the card," she repeated.

I pressed a palm to my forehead. "Sorry, that goes to another person." That other person was Robert. "If you send the notice to me, I can pay the bill," I said.

I had no idea how I'd do it, but I did a lot of impossible things these days. What was one more?

"Are you a renter?" she asked.

"No. This is my house. The credit card is my husband's, but I live here now." I curled my hand into a fist on my head, willing myself not to say more. The woman on the call didn't care about my situation. She just wanted to get paid. "I can write a check," I offered. "There was just a mix-up with the card."

"You have that check now?" she asked. "I can call the bank to confirm available funds, then get you on the schedule for your new issue. You can give the technician the check when he arrives."

"Perfect. Hang on just a minute." I hustled into the living room for my wallet and delivered the information she needed.

Soft taps from a keyboard crossed the line to my ears before a long, silent pause.

Robert would surely throw a fit about the amount of money spent on repairs for Mom's house, but what else could I do? *My house,* I thought, correcting the mistake I made too often. This was my place now. Mom left it to me. She trusted me with its care. And I was doing a bang-up job so far. *In fact,* I thought, *if she could see me, I think she'd be proud.*

"Nope." The woman on the phone made a low humming sound. "According to your bank, this account has insufficient funds."

"What?" I barked. "That's impossible. Let me give you the details again."

She repeated the numbers back to me and tried again.

"Sorry," she said. "Same results. We accept cash, if you want to stop into our local office. Then we can get you on the schedule again. Or just give us a call when you get the banking sorted, and we'll be happy to help. Thank you for choosing Premier Plumbers."

The line went dead, and I stared at my reflection in the kitchen window.

How was this happening?

It only took a nanosecond for the answer to emerge.

Robert.

I navigated to my banking app, and a negative balance appeared. My stomach roiled as I checked the amount remaining in savings. Someone had disabled the overdraft feature meant to stop checks from bouncing. "Son of a—" I turned the feature on, and funds began to transfer. I tried not to vomit as I took note of all the failed utility payments I'd made with blind faith and an empty account.

Suddenly the broken sink felt like a blessing. Otherwise, when would I have realized the money in these accounts was dwindling?

I should have known Robert was up to something. He'd been too quiet.

A shiver rocked down my spine as I let my mind wander to what else he might be up to.

The too-familiar feelings of fear and anxiety rushed in to replace every measure of peace and happiness I'd had moments before. The urge to put my head down and get my walls up snapped back into place like magnets.

My breaths slowed as the ugly thoughts rolled in.

Was breaking the cycle of unhealthy marriages really worth all this chaos? I wondered darkly. Odds were statistically in my favor to outlive him. If I'd waited it out instead of leaving, I might've enjoyed my twilight years alone and in comfort. Now I'd left him unattended and angry. That was a terrible combination.

"Fucking Robert," I seethed.

I opened the texting app to send him a piece of my mind, but the phone buzzed in my hand. My attorney's office was calling.

"Hello?"

"Sophie? This is Jill Gallagher returning your call."

"Oh, thank god," I said. "I think Robert removed me from his credit card, and he made some large withdrawals from the checking account I'm using to pay bills."

"Yes," she said, stalling my mini rant. "I'm aware, and I planned to schedule a meeting with you as soon as possible. Do you have some time to talk right now?"

"You knew?"

"I'm afraid so. I got wind of what was happening after the paperwork was filed. I reached out to opposing counsel for additional details, but he was slow to respond. I've been trying to get to the bottom of this all day. I hoped to have information for you before I called."

I waited, flabbergasted and confused. "What paperwork was filed?"

Jill paused. "Your husband filed for bankruptcy this morning."

If I hadn't been seated already, I might've knocked myself out hitting the floor. "That can't be right. He's a partner at a major law firm. We have money at three different banks, investments, retirement, savings—"

"Robert's attorney claims the losses were recent and significant due to a series of bad investments. He further claims that your husband canceled all credit cards in due diligence."

A low, guttural moan rolled up from my core.

"If there's a silver lining," she continued, "it's that all the accounts will be under scrutiny now. He won't be able to squander what's left in the joint accounts, and you still have access to those as well."

"What about the withdrawals made before the filing?" I asked. "Robert took several large sums of cash from the account I typically use."

"Cash is harder to trace, but he'll be asked about that. I'll make sure of it. When you get a chance, if you'll log in and send any available statements, that would be helpful as well."

"Doing that now," I said, downloading the files from my app. "I have a card for another bank I can use for now." Assuming he'd left any money in that one. "For the record," I said, "Robert would never run out of money, risk it all on any kind of investment, or file for bankruptcy. We had enough money to live comfortably for years without worry, and that doesn't include our investments. He's doing this intentionally. I'm certain of it."

"It's certainly not unheard of for a partner to hide money or assets during a divorce. Unfortunately, the proof is often hard to come by, unless you can afford a good forensic accountant. They aren't cheap, but you might consider it in this case."

"Let's do that," I said. "What will it cost? And do you have someone you can recommend?"

"I work with a great firm out of Norfolk. Costs vary, but I'd say you should be prepared to spend at least ten grand to get started. More if they find anything and really start to dig. We can get into this more during mediation prep."

I thought back to the dwindling balance in my savings account and knew it was now or never. "Send me the contact information."

"Will do," she said. "And Soph, a little unsolicited advice. I know Robert, professionally. I know his network and his type. This could get a lot worse real fast. If I was you, I'd get a job."

I thanked her for the advice and disconnected on a mushroom cloud of outrage and fear.

Without the money in those accounts, I'd lose my home. I couldn't afford to pay for more than my groceries with the money I made from baking. There'd be nothing left to pay my bills or property taxes. I wouldn't be able to buy more ingredients to keep baking, or to put gas in my car. I'd be stuck in this house like my mother, but without a choice.

Panic welled in me, and my cowardly inner voice taunted. *Told you we couldn't make it without him. Told you the punishment for leaving would be far worse than staying put. No one wins against Robert, and there's no going back now.*

I jumped when her text arrived moments later. I told my inner coward to shut up. Then I hired the forensic accountant.

With a little luck, Robert would take note of exactly where that money went and think twice before continuing this bankruptcy charade.

Chapter Fifteen

The next morning, I met a customer at a café and traded baked goods for cash. From there, I carried my iced coffee on a long walk down Main Street, enjoying the view. I ambled along a low brick wall, high above the flowing river. Couples placed locks on a section of fencing to represent their love. Others held hands, carried babies, and walked their dogs.

I admired the blue sky and vibrant flowers, felt the sun on my face, and the peace in my heart. This new life had tough spots, but I would never willingly return to how things were. I was proud of what I'd done so far to change my life and felt hopeful as I looked ahead.

I just had to figure out what to do about money.

The income I made from baking helped, and I loved the work, but it was a feast-or-famine situation. Five orders one day, none for the next week. Social media posts were raising awareness, and the engagement was great, but the newly raised prices weren't enough to make up for the inconsistent orders. I barely cleared minimum wage when I considered how much I had to spend on high-quality supplies.

These days, it was significantly easier to understand my mother's decision to stay with my father. I didn't agree with the way she'd lived, but I kicked myself internally for the harsh way I'd judged her. I'd previously assumed she could've just gotten a job to support herself and me, instead of marrying Dad or staying with him for so long. Nothing was that simple. Not now, and absolutely not then. Circumstances made things much easier for me than for her. I only had to make enough money to feed myself and keep the lights on at a home I'd inherited.

I should've had more compassion for my mother. The weight of my newly expanding emotions grew as I walked and thought of all the things I'd tell her today if I had the chance.

Now I was the one who needed a job. I had no idea where to begin. The only monetizable skill I had was baking. And maybe childcare, but I didn't particularly like other people's children, so nannying would be a last resort.

I supposed there were plenty of cluttered garages, basements, and closets in the area I could clean and organize for a fee. Could I complete enough projects every month to stay afloat? How did I find people willing to pay? I still hadn't finished all the closets at Mom's house. Some, I willfully ignored.

"What am I supposed to do?" I asked the universe, turning a palm and my gaze upward in a soft, exasperated plea.

The honk of a horn pulled my attention to the road, where a sedan narrowly missed a cyclist crossing the intersection.

On the corner, beside the frazzled biker, stood Chez Margot. In its window a small white sign held three neatly printed words.

Pastry Chef Needed

I crossed the street, drawn to the sign as if the universe put it there just for me. It certainly felt that way, and why not? I needed a job, and the restaurant needed a baker.

What would Lucas think if I appeared and applied? Would he remember me? Was it better or worse if he did?

I gave the sign a closer look when I reached the window. No further explanation was available. No small print suggesting I inquire within, or one of those QR codes that seemed to facilitate everything these days. Apparently, I had to ask for more information.

I squared my shoulders, pictured my emptying bank account and inherited money pit. Then I opened the door.

A dozen possible interview questions immediately flooded my head, and I wondered why I didn't take five minutes to prepare before entering. I added *overexcitable* to a growing list of things I was learning about myself. If only I knew my five greatest strengths and weaknesses, I'd have a far better chance at passing this interview. Did everyone who walked in get an interview?

I stepped inside and my chaotic mind quieted as I inhaled the delicious scents and tuned in to a soft accordion melody.

Hopefully no one asked where I saw myself in five years. "On the street, without this job" seemed like the wrong answer.

My gaze traveled the dining room. Was this a fair representation of restaurants in France? Had my mother eaten somewhere like this during the summer she met my father? Did he visit a place like this today?

An avalanche of more questions crowded my head. Where was Sébastien Allard? How could I find him? Would he want to meet me? Better yet, was I sure that was what I wanted?

An equally poignant thought presented itself unbidden. What if Sébastien was as big of a mess as my mother had been? Did I really want to know that?

"Ah! She returns!" a male voice bellowed.

I spun in search of the vaguely familiar sound and smiled when I met Lucas's eye. "You remember me."

"Of course I remember." He frowned. "I'm not as old as you think I am."

"I'm forty-six," I blurted, though he did not ask. "You can't be older than that."

"Can't I?" He clasped his hands and grinned. "Back for more crepes?"

My cheeks heated for reasons I couldn't imagine. "No, but thank you," I said. "For lunch that day, and the take-home crepes. They were perfection."

He tipped his head, interest brewing in his warm brown eyes. "What can I do for you today?"

I wrinkled my nose. "I'm here about the sign in the window."

His brows rose. "You know a French pastry chef?"

"I know an excellent baker," I said. "She's really good, a quick study, and probably wouldn't break your bank."

"Yeah?" He stepped closer, bumping into the welcome desk between us. "Is she looking for work? How can I get in touch?"

I extended my hand. "Nice to meet you, again."

"No." He dragged the word out for several amused syllables. "You?"

I nodded.

"You said you don't cook," he accused. He certainly had a good memory.

"I don't, at least, not well." I lifted one shoulder toward my ear. "I bake."

Lucas dropped forward, pressing both palms to the stand. "Tell me more."

I searched my brain for things I wanted him to know, and those I didn't. Then I told my overexcitable tongue not to say more than absolutely necessary. This job might be mine to lose.

"My mom was a novice baker. I grew up watching her. When I became a mother, I found joy in baking too."

He straightened and crossed his arms. "What do you know about French pastries?"

I smiled. "A little."

"Do you think you can manage the dessert list on our menu?"

"I'd love to try," I said, having no recollection of the desserts offered here.

Still, there were never more than four or five desserts on a menu. If I wasn't familiar with the processes, I could practice at home until I mastered them.

Lucas narrowed his eyes, considering me. "We talked about so many things. Your passion for baking never came up. Why?"

"It's not something I think about," I said. "It's become such a part of me it never occurs to mention it. It would be like telling someone my hair is brown."

He nodded. "All right. If you have a little time, why don't you show me what you've got?"

"What about the interview?" I asked. "Shouldn't we set a time for me to come back and answer questions?"

"This is the interview," he said. "I'm in a hurry to find a good pastry chef. I just hung the sign this morning, and here you are. I think that's fate. Don't you?"

"Mm-hmm."

"Great. Come." He waved his big hands, urging me to follow him.

We rounded the desk and crossed into the busy kitchen where everything was stainless steel and white, save the cement floor with its rough gray texture.

"This is where the magic happens," he said, hooking an apron over his head and passing another into my hands.

I chastised myself for the inappropriate thoughts his wording conjured, though Alicia would wholly approve.

Around us, men and women in matching aprons glanced curiously in our direction. Chefs turned strips of meat on a grill and checked the contents of their ovens. Others tossed salads and ladled soup into bowls. Waitstaff hurried through a swinging door to collect plated meals or place new orders with the kitchen.

"What do you know about soufflés?" Lucas asked, pulling my attention back to him. "They're a staple on every French restaurant's menu in this country. I try to switch up the options seasonally, but soufflés are always popular, as are sweet crepes, and crème brûlée. Paris-Brest, tarte tatin, and mille-feuille are regularly on rotation."

I focused on his words, pushing thoughts of his watching staff from my mind. I had only made soufflés in classes at the country club. My crème brûlée was decent, but I hadn't tried making either of the other desserts he mentioned.

"Ah, and chouquette," Lucas added. He looked heavenward and performed a chef's kiss. "Mémé made the best chouquette I've ever tasted. If you can touch her talents on that one, I'll be on your doorstep for dessert every night."

I laughed, and he clutched his heart, clearly still thinking fondly of his grandma's baking.

Lucas returned to business by pointing to a workstation with something already in progress. "The oven is preheated. The chocolate is melted and cooled. Now, I'll add the yolks here. You handle the egg whites there." He lifted a bowl into his arms and nodded toward a grand mixer. "Stiff peaks, then add the sugar and beat." He began his portion of the work. When I didn't move, he said, "Accélère!"

I didn't speak French, but the meaning was loud and clear. I turned to the mixer and got busy.

When I finished, he upturned a palm in the direction of the chocolate. "You know what comes next."

"I fold in the egg whites."

Lucas passed me a spatula, then stepped away, allowing me room to work.

I blended my portion of the recipe with his, careful not to lose volume. I moved the combined contents to a prepped baking dish without waiting for additional instruction.

"Nicely done."

"Thank you."

Lucas donned oven mitts and gently set the soufflé into the hot oven. "Do you have thirty minutes to stay and check your finished work?"

I fought the urge to smile and nodded soberly instead. "Yes, chef."

His kind eyes twinkled. "Well, then. Let's see what we can accomplish while we wait."

I had an idea or two. *Darn my newly dirty mind.*

The unexpected notion that I hadn't ever really been in love, or felt loved, romantically, hit like a hammer to the heart. My marriage had been a continuous power struggle, one which I'd continuously lost, and it had never been a partnership. Robert wasn't my best friend. He didn't help me or comfort me, and even when he said he wanted me, the words only applied to my body, never my mind.

No wonder I felt such attraction to Lucas. From what I had seen so far, he was a man who was kind for the sake of being kind, with no ulterior motive. Maybe he was part unicorn.

The tension in my shoulders eased as another thought registered. If I made a mistake, Lucas wouldn't yell at me.

"Have you made cannelés?" he asked, already pulling fresh pans and bowls onto the workstation.

I nodded with as much confidence as I could muster, knowing the full and true answer was *only once*. "Of course."

His cheek twitched with the hint of a smile, either pleased with my response or seeing straight through me. "Traditional cannelés have a crispy caramelized exterior and a soft custard center. They're tricky. We don't want to overcook the outside while getting the silky interior texture correct."

I recalled from class at the club that cannelés originated in the Bordeaux region of France. The pastries were small and cylinder-shaped with depressions at their tops. The ingredients list was very straightforward: eggs, milk, butter, sugar, flour, salt. Then a flavoring of some kind, usually vanilla. I preferred rum. Baking at a high temperature was key, as was keeping an eye on the process.

As I mentally ticked through the steps involved, Lucas gathered everything we needed from the refrigerator and nearby shelves.

"Anything else?" he asked, head tipped toward the workspace.

I scanned the materials. "Salt."

He produced a small container from his apron pocket. "Correct."

"When did you put that in there?"

He grinned. "What now?"

"Prep the batter, let it rest overnight," I said. "Pick up where we left off tomorrow." Would I be here tomorrow?

He waved a hand toward the workspace, and I stepped forward to begin.

I'd only worked with fresh vanilla a few times, but I put my chin up and sliced the dark beans down their centers, then scraped out their contents. The rest of the process came naturally, despite my limited experience with this particular recipe. I added ingredients to a pot on the nearby stove and adjusted the gas flame.

Lucas leaned closer, peering into the pot as I sank a wooden spoon inside and stirred. "Tell me more about your training."

I tidied up the space on autopilot. His word choice rattled my confidence. Baking lessons at the country club hardly counted as training. The bulk of my recipe research involved YouTube, and I'd honed my techniques through trial and error.

The urge to make my training sound like more than it was swelled in me, but I put it aside. I'd hidden so many truths over the years. About my feelings. My side hustle. My intent to leave my husband. But that wasn't who I was anymore, or at least it wasn't who I wanted to be. I didn't want to hide. "I took some classes and workshops at my old country club."

Lucas furrowed his brows, then turned a puzzled expression in my direction. "A country club?"

I carried the mixing bowls to the sink and started the water. "I suppose it's still my country club, at least until it's time for next year's dues." I glanced at Lucas as I rinsed the bowls. "Until very recently, I was a housewife with an overbearing husband who liked me to play a certain role."

"You're divorced?" he guessed.

"We're in the process. Not to be cliché, but it's complicated," I admitted. "I moved out in June. The lawyers are lawyering, but the process is slow." And might get even slower if Robert emptied the accounts to the point I couldn't pay my attorney. The thought jarred me, and I considered sticking my head under the water so I could scream. Surely, even Robert wouldn't do that.

"So, he used you and your skills to impress his guests," Lucas said.

"He treated me very well when others were watching."

Lucas's external smile fell, and emotion flashed in his eyes. "I'm sorry."

"I've had plenty of years to accept it. Now, my daughter, Camilla, is grown. She's a remarkable human with a big heart and good head on her shoulders. I'm proud of that, and I'm starting over the way I should have long ago." I dried my hands, feeling self-conscious. "Sorry. That was too much information."

I returned to the stove and extinguished the flame, then placed a lid on the pot. Before I said anything more to ruin my hands-on interview, I cracked eggs into a bowl, added sugar, then began to whisk.

Lucas moved a cup of flour in my direction, and I sifted it into my mixture.

We worked quietly together as the busy kitchen clanged and bustled around us.

When we finished, I dragged my gaze to meet his.

"Time's up," he said.

My heart sank. What did that mean? I tucked my proverbial tail and reached behind myself to untie the apron strings. "Well, thank you for—"

He opened the oven, and the rich scent of chocolate lifted into the air. "Ahh." He breathed the word, clearly impressed.

The soufflé was perfectly risen.

Pride filled my chest and split my lips into an open-mouthed smile.

Even if I didn't get the job, I'd made a gorgeous soufflé, and a popular local French chef bore witness.

"Exquisite," he said, moving the pan to the counter. "I'll finish up the filling for the cannelés and start on the dough tomorrow."

I nodded, honored to have had a hand in the process.

It was amazing, really. I'd walked in off the street, on a whim, and had the opportunity to make French desserts with a French restaurateur, chef, and baker. That sort of thing never happened in my previous life. Being spontaneous and brave proved far better than remaining small and unnoticed.

I added *brave* to a new list of ways to view myself.

"Same time?" he asked, removing his apron, then accepting mine when I passed it to him.

"As what?"

"To work," he clarified. "I'll add this hour to your first check. You did beautifully today, and if you're open to learning more, I'd love to show you."

I sucked in a sharp breath. "You're hiring me?"

"Let's call it a trial basis. We can finish the cannelés ahead of the lunch rush."

I forced my arms to my sides so I wouldn't hug him.

"I don't suppose you know someone who makes a decent éclair or macaron," he said, brow wrinkled as he looked at the empty bakery case. "My breakfast crowd likes sweets to go, and it'd be nice to contract with a local small business instead of buying from a wholesaler. I've considered hiring someone directly, but the added overhead makes that a no-go. Health care, training costs, insurance—" He rolled a hand in a circle between us. "It's a twenty-hour-a-week job all by itself."

I bit my lip, contemplating. "How many hours a week is the pastry-chef position?"

"Thirty," he said. "More around holidays, less when you need a break. Tell me in advance and we can prep and freeze inventory before you're away."

I smiled. "Very flexible."

He grinned.

"Have you heard of the Invisible Baker?" I asked, looking away as my cheeks heated under his gaze.

"No. Why?"

I examined the empty bakery display and wondered if I'd inadvertently hit the jackpot by walking into Chez Margot. "They have a social media account with photos of pastries like the ones you mentioned, and I think they're local."

"I'll check it out," he said. "You turned out to be exactly what I needed today."

Lucas held my eye contact a beat longer than necessary, and my toes curled inside my sneakers.

When he walked me to the door, he carefully peeled the sign from the front window. Chez Margot was no longer in the market for a pastry chef.

I'd fibbed a little about my baking company, but I'd added at least one new income stream to keep my life afloat. I couldn't be upset about that.

Now, I just couldn't mess it up.

Chapter Sixteen

I returned to Chez Margot just before it opened the next morning, dressed in dark pants and comfortable shoes, much like what the other employees wore in the kitchen. I coiled my hair into a tight bun and chose a basic white collared shirt. Simple. Classic. Professional.

Lucas spotted me outside as he unlocked the door. He wore a similar outfit to my own, but his hair was mussed and damp. "Punctual," he said. "I like that."

"I hope you'll also like this," I said, passing a bakery box into his hands.

He stepped aside to let me in, and I inhaled the clean scent of his shampoo and bodywash as I passed.

The restaurant was still and sleepy, the space quiet and dim.

"What is this?" he asked. He carried the box to the welcome desk and lifted the lid. "The Invisible Baker," he said, reading the business card taped inside.

"I thought about what you said and placed an order," I lied. After thinking it over for most of the night, I'd decided maintaining my anonymity was the best course of action. I feared Robert would demand a portion of my wages if he knew the Invisible Baker LLC existed, or he'd start an online smear campaign to ruin it. Maybe both. I wouldn't put anything past him, and we'd start mediation soon.

Plus, I didn't want to mess up my new job offer by asking for more than the job he'd offered me. First I'd prove myself to Lucas and become an integral part of his team. Then I'd confess that I was the Invisible Baker and see what happened. If he didn't want me to continue baking for the display case, there was a chance I'd get enough new business from the exposure to keep the company going in my spare time.

And if I was being honest, I wasn't ready to come out of my box just yet. The Invisible Baker was mine, and only mine, and no one could touch it. The company had been a life raft when I desperately needed one and became a beacon of hope for me. Telling anyone who didn't already know felt like poking a needle into my favorite balloon.

"I love pain au chocolat," he said, lifting a pastry for inspection. "For me?"

"For you," I agreed.

He bit into the flaky dough without hesitation. His eyelids fluttered closed, dark lashes casting shadows across his cheeks. "Magnifique."

I felt his compliment in my chest and fought the urge to thank him.

He offered the box to me, brows high.

"No, thank you." I'd had two with my morning coffee before packing his box.

"All right." He finished the pastry, then stowed the box beneath the counter. "To the kitchen. Right side goes in," he said, holding the door so it couldn't swing. "Left side is out. Always enter on the right."

"Got it."

"Tell me more about the Invisible Baker," he said. We moved to the workstation where we'd prepped the soufflé. "I didn't make it to the website last night."

I pursed my lips, considering my words. "According to their posts, the company bakes, anonymously, for people who want to impress others with their baking but don't actually want to bake, or don't have the time to."

He laughed, and the sound came from somewhere deep in his core. "Very clever. How did you get the pastries? A storefront?"

"They deliver," I said.

I realized belatedly that I was the delivery person.

"The pain au chocolat was incredible. If their other products are of equal quality, I'd be remiss not to ask for a quote."

I smiled and Lucas echoed my expression.

"With a little luck, we'll be the talk of the town this fall."

I hooked an apron over my head, unsure what he meant. "What's happening this fall?"

"I'm making changes," he said. "I want Chez Margot to be a casual bistro by day, and something more upscale and decadent at night. Black tie, refined menu, reservations only. The whole nine yards. First, I have to build clout so people will come."

"Those are big plans," I agreed. "The people will come, and it will be amazing."

He appraised me. "Let's hope. The dream begins with my new pastry chef. Decadence is all about the dessert."

"Oh, jeez." I laughed. "So, no pressure, then."

"None at all." He moved a clipboard from a hook on the wall to the counter. A list of prep steps was centered on the top page in bold. "First this," he said, tapping a fingertip to the print. "Then this." He fanned through the sheets of recipes. "The breakfast crowd is leisurely, except those on the hunt for coffee and sweets. They grab and go. The lunch crowd is always in a hurry. They dine in, then take desserts to go, sometimes by the dozens. So, every morning we bake in bulk. Make sense?"

"Got it."

Together, we prepped a half dozen pans of chouquettes, then lined them up for their turn in the ovens.

Around us, the kitchen slowly came to life. Lucas introduced me to each staff member as they arrived to begin their day. All were friendly. All were curious. I was an awkward mess. I was out of my element. They were at ease and clearly a family.

I did my best to concentrate on my work and look more confident than I felt. I failed, comically, and often. Jumping at the loud clang of pots and pans. Shivering at the scrape of metal spatulas on hot grills.

The sharp *chop!* of knives on cutting boards didn't help my anxiety, but I locked in on the tasks before me, and I persevered.

Soon the sweat on my brow made its way toward my eyes, and I paused to wipe the drops away. I plucked and fanned the material of my shirt, attempting to circulate the steamy kitchen air. A dozen voices morphed together as cooks and waitstaff interacted with one another, each hustling to keep up with demand. People zipped past my workstation in all directions as I pulled soufflés from the oven with shaky hands and a prayer.

The frantic pace of the lunch rush frayed my nerves. I'd never worked so steadily or for so long without a break. At home I had endless pleasant distractions, coffee and water breaks, doorbells and phone calls. In the kitchen of Chez Margot, there were only more orders.

"Time!" someone called. "Time!"

I looked up from my mixer to see a cook pointing frantically at the oven beside me. My timer featured a series of red digital zeros. "My soufflé!"

I abandoned the mixer and yanked open the door with a towel in my grip. A dark curl of heat rose from the dessert's puffy top, and panic washed through me. "Don't be burned. Don't be burned," I chanted, reaching for the tray. The tips of my fingers met with the rack in my haste, and I screamed as a perfectly rounded soufflé top sank like an overbrowned puddle. "Damnit!" I yelled, frustrated as I jerked away.

"Behind!" someone called, but it was too late.

I stepped backward into an incoming server. The young woman screamed and the tray in her hands went flying.

Our calamity rang through the kitchen, reverberating from the floor to rafters.

Meat bits and jus splattered over the tile and up our pant legs.

My ears rang, and my heart pounded. "I am so sorry," I gasped. "I burned my fingers, and I didn't mean to—"

The look on her face brought tears of humiliation to my eyes, but instead of accepting my apology, she walked back through the swinging doors.

I hurried after her. "I'm sorry!" I repeated.

"Whoa!" Lucas's voice reached my ears before he crossed the threshold to the kitchen. "What's happening and how can I help?"

The door swung sharply inward and connected with my face.

The force knocked me backward and rattled my brain. Shock and pain radiated through me, but words wouldn't form.

"Hey!" Lucas steadied me with a grip on my forearms. Then he pulled me against him as hot tears rolled over my cheeks. "It's okay. I've got you."

I wrestled free and ran.

I passed the server I'd collided with on my way to the ladies' room. She pushed a mop and bucket on wheels toward the crash site, but all I could think about was escape.

I dragged my shirtsleeve under each eye, struggling to pull myself together as I locked the restroom door. I couldn't afford to lose this job on day one. I liked working here and being a part of something bigger.

I hated that my instinct was always to hide.

Two soft thuds rattled the door a few moments later. "Sophie?" Lucas asked. "Are you okay?"

Leave me alone to die of humiliation, I thought dramatically, but I pulled myself together and unlocked the door.

Lucas held out a pile of clothing.

"What is that?"

"A uniform," he said. "I should have offered it when you got here. Then your clothes wouldn't be ruined right now."

My clothes? Who cared about those when I'd upturned someone's meal and flattened someone else's dessert?

"How's your burn?" he asked.

I followed his gaze to my hand. I'd nearly forgotten about my throbbing fingers. "Fine."

His smile was small and sad. "Why don't you change, then I'll treat the burn? It won't take long, and I think you'll feel better in fresh clothes."

I looked down at myself, stained with mashed potatoes and meat sauce. "Okay."

When I opened the door again, I found Lucas waiting outside.

He peeled himself away from the wall and gave me a thorough once-over. "Better."

My eyes were red and swollen from crying, but I nodded.

Lucas led me to a small employee lounge with a metal table, chairs, and a kitchenette. He opened a cabinet and removed a first aid kit.

I sat at the table and waited.

My neck and shoulders ached with tension. If Robert were here, he'd lose his shit and berate me for my lack of attention to detail. For not hearing the oven's timer, for not putting the oven mitt on properly, for backing into someone who was doing their job correctly, and for not using the swinging door in the way I was clearly instructed. On top of all that, I'd let my emotion get the best of me and left someone else to clean up my mess.

And I'd gotten hurt to boot.

Lucas approached with a mug of water. "Put your fingers in here to cool the burn."

I obeyed, unable to meet his eyes.

"That was a rough welcome to restaurant life." His tone was kind and a little playful, probably hoping I wouldn't cry again. "I'm sorry I wasn't there to help sooner," he said. "I should've been there to prevent the whole thing. I planned to stay by your side this week while you became acclimated, but the hostess's daughter missed the bus for preschool." He chuckled softly. "Not the first time. Won't be the last. Kenzie is an adorable typhoon in pigtails. Anyway, I was greeting guests when I heard the screaming."

I closed my eyes. "It was horrible. I tried to apologize but the server I ran into just left."

"Protocol," he said. "She wasn't injured, so her priority was to clean the floor before anyone else slipped or fell."

I thought of her pushing the mop and bucket toward the kitchen as I ran to the ladies' room.

"That was Kara. She told me what happened and wanted me to check on you," he said, drawing my gaze to his.

"Yeah?"

"Yeah. Everyone here has been where you are. The new member of a kitchen where everyone else seems to know exactly what to do."

My lips pressed into a remorseful smile. "Thank you."

Lucas arranged his first aid supplies on the table. He pulled out a chair beside me and took a seat. "The staff said you were killing it in there. John was impressed, and nothing impresses him."

"In the red chef's jacket?"

"Yep."

John yelled at everyone, like a tall, cooking drill sergeant, but they'd all obeyed without hesitation. The fact he hadn't screamed at me all day was the only thing holding me together when the orders came in at full force.

"John said you kept up through the busiest part of the hour, accommodating all requests from customers or staff, and remained absolutely unfazed by the chaos."

I nearly hooted in laughter. Clearly I still excelled at pretending things were great when they were not. I'd had many years of practice. I smiled at the ridiculousness anyway. "I was completely freaking out," I admitted. "Honestly, I'm surprised I didn't take out one of your servers sooner."

Lucas snorted. "You did well, Soph," he said. "Five stars. And for the record, we've all wiped out at least once in that kitchen, and some of us weren't on our first day when it happened."

I studied him, waiting for the inevitable *but* that never came. "You're not mad?"

"Mad?" He lifted my hand from the water and examined my red fingertips. "Why would I be mad? The customers can't stop raving about your desserts. Lunch hour is always busy, but we haven't sold this many desserts in—ever. It's incredible. Now we have to get this hand healed up so you can do it again tomorrow."

I blinked. "I can come back?"

His brow pinched as he dried my hand, then applied a bit of salve. His eyes moved to examine my face. "Did you hit your head? Of course we want you to come back. When word gets out about my new pastry chef, I'll need to make lunch by reservation only too."

I smiled at his use of the word *we*. No one was upset with me for the mess I caused? For the meal and dessert ruined? The added work to clean up both?

Could this level of acceptance be real?

Lucas worked a small tube-shaped sleeve over my burned fingers. "This will keep the tender skin from tearing or getting dirty while it heals."

"You're good at this," I said. I couldn't recall the last time I was on the receiving end of first aid treatment. Maybe when the nurses cared for me following Camilla's birth.

"I've done this about a thousand times," Lucas said, his expression going soft as he released me. "Margot burned her fingers at least once a week. She was a free spirit, creative, and always living in the next moment instead of the present one. I bought stock in this stuff during our marriage." He gathered his supplies with a smile.

I cradled my bandaged hand to my chest, feeling valued and important in ways I hadn't in a very long time. "Lucas," I said, my words barely more than a whisper. "Thank you."

"Don't thank me. Promise me you'll be back tomorrow."

I came back every morning for the rest of the week.

Lucas worked at my side, patient and attentive while I learned and mastered his recipes. He told stories of his life in France while we prepped batters and sauces. Then, later, as our cakes baked, he shared his feelings of overwhelming anxiety in the days before the restaurant first opened. I related, profoundly, to his joy and fear in every decision. Would it be the right one? Could he fix things if he failed? I'd felt exactly the same way since filing for divorce.

Somehow, in the loud, steamy kitchen, Lucas made me feel as if anything was possible. And if, at any point, I became unhappy with my circumstances, I had the power to change it all. I only had to believe I could and be brave enough to take the next step. Like telling my longtime bully I was leaving.

Lucas made it easy to be at ease. I especially appreciated the way he spoke about his late wife as though she might walk through the door at any minute. His bond with her was so honest and true, it was hard to remember why I'd ever expected him to behave like Robert.

And sometimes, when he spoke of his commitment to Margot, I wondered if perhaps romantic love wasn't always used as a tool for control. If maybe that was my trauma talking. Maybe my childhood experiences ruined my ability to have a healthy adult relationship.

Maybe instead of raising the bar on the kind of treatment I was willing to accept, I'd blindly followed my mom's example.

I sent up a prayer of protection for Camilla's tender heart. She loved Jeff completely, the way only a young, unjaded woman could. I didn't want that blind trust and devotion to be thrown in her face when she said "I do."

"What are you thinking?" Lucas asked, walking me to the door, as was his custom.

"I was thinking it's nice to hear you talk about Margot," I admitted. "I would have liked her, I think."

"She would've liked you," he said. "She preferred strong, independent women, especially those with a soft spot for the arts. Baking is clearly your art."

I smiled. "That's what I'm talking about. You say things like that, and it's just so—refreshing. It's too late for me, but I think Camilla is headed to the altar with her boyfriend, and I worry. I want so much better for her."

"Better than marriage or better than her boyfriend?"

"The first," I said. "Maybe both. Jeff seems fine, but the women in my family have a habit of making horrible decisions where love is concerned."

Lucas made a dismissive throaty sound. "Impossible."

I laughed. "I assure you, it is not."

"You're shifting the blame," he said. "You gave your heart to a man who didn't take care of it. That's not your fault. You loved. That is a brave thing. And look." He smiled. "You showed your daughter it's okay to walk away too. That's a great example, if you ask me. For what it's worth, I think you're both going to be just fine."

I certainly hoped he was right.

Chapter Seventeen

Two weeks later, I parked in the community lot downtown and watched the busy street for Alicia's arrival. Anticipation danced along my skin when she finally pulled into the space beside me.

Her dark hair swung around her chin as she climbed out and closed her door. "What's this?" she asked, scanning the area, then me. "Are you wearing a concert T-shirt from freshman year?"

I grinned. "Do you remember how much fun we had that night?"

"Barely. Where on earth did you find that?"

"It was with these jeans and a bunch of my old clothes marked for donation inside one of Mom's closets." To my delight, I'd also found my old shoes, stuffed animals, books, and posters. She'd kept everything folded neatly in boxes marked with my name. Some had small hearts drawn on the lids.

However she'd behaved outwardly, she'd still marked the passage of my life just as I marked Camilla's, and that knowledge was the boon I never knew I needed. Now, everywhere I looked, I found inarguable signs of my mother's love.

And her poor mental health.

Endless self-help books filled shelves in her closet. Books on healing after trauma, on grief recovery and surviving narcissistic parents. The latter reshaped my memories of Mom and Grandma together.

Mom needed help she never received, and she'd shielded me from her struggles the only way she could, by pushing me away. I'd shed gallons of tears over that realization.

Whatever else happened, I would keep choosing happiness. That was what Mom would've wanted, what Camilla should see modeled, and what I deserved.

Alicia's expression was dramatically blank when I met her gaze again. "You still fit into your jeans from college?"

I nodded, and she opened her car door as if she might climb in and leave.

"Wait!" I laughed. "Stop. The outfit is part of today's theme."

Curiosity glinted in her eyes, and she closed the car door. "There's a theme?"

No decent teacher could resist.

I rocked onto my toes, adrenaline pumping. "I'm embracing my lost youth," I announced. "Starting with things I missed out on by marrying too young and putting myself last all these years."

"Because you married a man who didn't allow you any joy," she added.

I rolled my eyes. "Yes, but I don't want to talk about him. This is about me."

Alicia's expression brightened. "I can get behind that. Any chance there's lunch in your plans? Because I'm starving."

"Absolutely. First we have to cross the street."

She turned her gaze to a tavern that catered to a demographic likely half our age. Neon beer signs hung in the windows beside flyers for live karaoke, local bands, and beer pong championships. "Interesting choice, but let's go."

"Not yet." I pointed to the smaller building next door. "I have an appointment there in five minutes."

"I don't understand." She jutted her chin forward. "You're pointing to a tattoo parlor."

"What do you think?"

She puffed out a disbelieving laugh. "I think I've birthed three gigantic, big-headed boys. My body is already covered in shiny silver warrior tattoos that amateurs like to call stretch marks. I don't need more body art, but I will hold your hand while you do you."

I linked my arm with hers and headed for the crosswalk. "I'm having my nose pierced."

"Oh, cute!" Alicia said. "I love that. I forgot how much you wanted one."

"Robert always said facial piercings, tattoos, and unnaturally colored hair are all signs of trashy people." People going nowhere. People with no financial future. People he didn't want to be associated with.

Alicia made a low throaty sound. "I know you're technically still married, but is it okay if I call him a cunt?"

I barked an explosive laugh. "You probably shouldn't call anyone that, but yeah, fine by me."

I steeled my nerves as I entered Impressive Ink. I wondered briefly if the piercing was a bad idea. Was I too old? Was it too out of character? What would people think?

"Change your mind already?" Alicia asked.

I internally guffawed at the direction my thoughts had gone. Further proof I needed this small act of defiance. "Just wondering if I should also get that lower-back tattoo I've always wanted."

"Definitely," Alicia agreed. "Maybe get a sleeve or two. I'm adventure deprived and living vicariously through you this summer."

The gentle buzz of a tattoo artist at work carried through the studio. A song I didn't recognize played on hidden speakers. A man at the front desk lifted his chin in greeting as I tapped my name into the screen at the welcome kiosk.

We walked the waiting room perimeter after I checked in. Hundreds of airbrushed images covered the walls. All were next-level artistry. I moved slowly, lightly mesmerized, as if touring a modern art museum.

"Fuck it," Alicia muttered, then headed back to the entry.

"Where are you going?" I asked, tracking her with my gaze.

She stopped at the front counter and spoke to the thirtysomething body builder with tattoo sleeves as divine as anything on the walls. "Can I get my belly button done?"

The man nodded, and I hustled to her side.

"What are you doing?" I whispered.

"Surprising Cameron. If you can get a stud in your nose, then I can have a hoop in my belly button."

A petite woman with inky-black hair met us at the counter and introduced herself as Iris. She led us to a table in back, then walked us verbally through our procedures. We took turns in the hot seat, holding hands through the scary parts, just as we had during each of our labors.

Before I knew it, my nose was numbed, the stud was placed, and we were on our way to the desk for payment.

Alicia passed the worker her credit card. "This one's on me," she said.

"No," I protested. "I can pay for this. It was my idea." And I'd gotten my first two paychecks from Chez Margot, which was nearly double my actual rate per hour, thanks to two large pastry orders for the Invisible Baker that Lucas had placed. I hadn't made much progress on the house recently, and I was losing sleep working double time to fill the Invisible Baker orders, but for the first time ever, I was earning decent money, and that felt wildly empowering.

She waved me off, nodding for the attendant to continue with her payment. "This was the first spontaneous thing I've done in ages. I love it. I also owe you for the inspiration," she added, motioning to her middle. "Cameron is going to flip."

I leaned forward and inspected myself in a small freestanding mirror on the counter. The difference in my appearance was minimal, but it felt astronomically huge. The shimmery rhinestone on my bright-red nostril felt like a declaration long overdue. I was free and worthy of joy, even if others didn't understand my choices.

"You look incredible," Alicia said.

The man behind the register slid his eyes my way as he passed her the receipt. His lips parted in a whisper of a smile. "That's what's up," he said.

Alicia tucked the paper into her purse. "See? That's what's up," she echoed.

I left the studio feeling infinitely lighter. Outside, the world seemed brighter.

"Are we—" Alicia paused dramatically, letting her mouth hang open for a long beat. "Are we total badasses?"

"Absolutely," I said.

"Makes sense," she agreed. "I think that hunk behind the counter was checking you out."

I frowned. "He was in his thirties."

"So?"

"So he's probably closer to Camilla's age than mine. Besides, men only look at younger women."

"Men look at all women," she argued. "Especially the hot ones."

I stopped outside the tavern. "Are you still hungry? Want to get a drink with lunch?"

"Big yes to all of that." Alicia opened the door, then peeked over her shoulder at me. "God, I love this day."

I squinted as my eyes adjusted to the dimly lit interior. The faint yeasty scent of beer met us at the threshold. Decades of grease, salt, and cigarette smoke permeated the walls. A thousand happy memories made at similar burger and beer joints back in college curled my lips into a smile.

We sat ourselves in a cracked vinyl booth, grinning like two Cheshire cats.

Alicia liberated a battered menu from behind the metal napkin dispenser and immediately perused the options.

I touched a fingertip to my new nose stud, confirming it was real.

A classic rock ballad played on the jukebox. Dartboards and pool tables filled the back corner where a handful of patrons bent over their cues. Old wooden table-and-chair sets peppered the dining area across from a heavily lacquered bar. Movie posters and album covers from the late nineteen hundreds hung on dark-paneled walls.

"I think we've entered a time machine," I said.

"This whole outing is a time machine," Alicia said, never taking her eyes off the menu.

A woman wearing a sleeveless black T-shirt and ripped jeans crossed the checkered tile floor in our direction. Her long gray hair swung in a thick braid that reached below her waist. "Can I get you something?" she asked without preamble.

Alicia peered at the woman over the top of her menu. "Two tallboys of your best local brew and a pair of whiskey shooters," Alicia said. "Jack Daniel's," she clarified.

The other woman nodded and left us.

I shook my head, amused.

"What?" Alicia asked. She passed me the menu. "When in Rome, right?"

I opened my bag and liberated a pink foam die the size of my fist. "I almost forgot. I made this for you."

She eyeballed the gift, then lifted it and read the sides. "One homework pass. One quiz answer. A minute of free time. A sticker. Trinket. Gumball." She laughed. "Why, thank you. I've always wanted—what is this?"

"It's for your classroom," I said. I found the die in Mom's stuff and thought of Alicia. It was blank when I found it, so I wrote on the sides. "Now you can tell your classes that when they are especially cooperative for you, someone can roll the die at the end of class, and they all get a prize."

We'd recently talked about the many ways her teenage students were like toddlers, including limited self-control, a penchant for games, and high reward motivation. The big die covered a lot of ground.

"You can get all this stuff pretty cheap at the dollar store or Target," I said.

She smiled. "They're going to love this."

I pulled a gift card from my purse and set it next to the big die. "I'd like to sponsor your first set of bribes."

Alicia took the card in her opposite hand and pressed both gifts to her chest. "You're the best. Thank you."

I blew her a kiss.

We finished our drinks quickly and placed our food orders. Then we requested another round. We ate onion rings and chicken fingers, french fries and sliders until time became meaningless, and our booth felt like a private island. A place where nothing outside the time machine could touch us.

"I haven't been day drunk in years," Alicia said, her words slightly slurred. "Except on vacation," she allowed. "But that's not the same, because the sun soaks up all the booze."

"No sun in here," I said, dragging crispy fries through a puddle of ketchup. Hopefully the carbs would absorb the alcohol.

"This is a good day," she said. "You seem happy."

"I am." I searched myself for signs of a lie but found none. I wasn't pretending anymore. I smiled.

"Have you heard from Robert?" she asked. "Any news on the divorce front?"

"Nope. We have mediation this week. That should be awesome," I deadpanned.

"Ew." Alicia wrinkled her nose. "It's too bad you ever have to see him again. I wonder what he's been up to while you've been creating a lovely little life for yourself?"

I had no idea, and I didn't want to think about it. "He's pretending we're broke, for starters," I said. "I'm glad he doesn't know he's the reason I'm working a million hours a week. I don't want him to have the satisfaction." I'd taken extra care to make the house and property shine from outside as soon as possible, just in case he drove by to judge me. I'd added fresh paint to the door and shutters, power washed the cement steps and walkway, planted flowers, hung a new wreath, and added a welcome mat, rocking chair, and planter to the porch.

"I hope your attorney obliterates him at mediation."

"No chance," I said. "Attorneys will not be present. Apparently, the court thinks couples that come to their own decisions and agreements are less likely to go back to court later." Unfortunately, I couldn't imagine Robert agreeing to any split of our money and assets, which was likely the reason he'd claimed bankruptcy.

"How are you feeling about that?" Alicia asked.

"Not great," I admitted. "But it puts me one step closer to divorce, and I love that for me."

She tipped her head, eyes narrowing. "You're being incredibly casual. I'm not sure if you're putting on a show, repressing your feelings, or truly don't care."

"I care." I sucked a dollop of ketchup off the side of my thumb. "But I mentally divorced Robert years ago. That's the only way I could put up with him intentionally ignoring me and dismissing my needs." Those things had become so normal that we'd barely interacted at all most days.

"Another reason I will always hate him," she said. "Withholding attention and affection is cruel. Abusers do it to wear away your self-esteem."

There was that word again, the one that crossed my mind more and more. *Abuser.*

"He didn't care what I wanted," I said. "Do you know that sometimes when I spoke, he circled a finger in the air to rush me along, so I'd get to my point?" I said.

Alicia stuck out her tongue in a mock gag.

"I was in charge of everything, but he was the boss. I mean it when I say the relationship has been over in my heart for a decade. The paperwork isn't finished, but I've been single for at least ten years."

She pointed at me, her head bobbing in agreement. Then she raised her hand and signaled to the bartender she wanted another round for us. "Speaking of bosses, how's Lucas?"

My heart fluttered nonsensically at the mention of his name. "Good. Funny. Stupid attractive."

She smiled. "What did he say when you told him you're the Invisible Baker?"

I pulled my lips into a low, dramatic frown. "I did not do that."

She gaped. "Sophie! Why?"

"I don't know. I'm not ready to out myself. The Invisible Baker has been a lifeline for me. Confessing I'm behind the name feels like letting it go. It won't be the same after that."

"What are you going to do? Work two jobs until you crack?"

"Basically, yes."

She laughed. "At least you have a plan, I guess. What else have I missed?"

I considered the question, then jolted at a brilliant thought I'd had earlier this week. "I have an idea about how to find Sébastien Allard."

Alicia stilled. "Your bio dad?"

I nodded, enthusiasm growing. "I ordered one of those DNA tests that tell you all about your ancestry. When the results come back, they tell you if you match with anyone else who's taken the test. Maybe he took one. Or one of his other children did, or his siblings or parents."

Her eyes widened. "That's brilliant."

The waitress delivered our new drinks and collected the empty food baskets. "Can I get you anything else?"

"Just the bill," I said, and the woman walked away.

"I want to be there when you take it," Alicia said. "And when you get the results." She pulled her phone from her bag and tapped the screen. "I'm texting the guys to pick us up. We're hammered. They can take our cars home too."

I erupted into laughter. I was day drunk in a dive bar with a nose piercing and my best friend. "This is so embarrassing! I don't want them to see me drunk. I changed their diapers."

"Me, too, so they better hurry. I have to pee, and I am not using this bathroom."

I cackled.

My life really was kind of lovely.

Chapter Eighteen

I shuffled through security at the courthouse, gazing at its high arched ceilings and historic marble floors. People in suits crowded the lobby, their strained expressions hurrying me along.

Mediation started in twenty minutes, and I arrived early to get settled before facing Robert, my nemesis.

My phone buzzed and I moved into a nearby corner to check the message from Camilla. She and Jeff had left for their trip yesterday, and I'd asked her to let me know when they arrived.

Camilla: Miss you Mom!

I smiled and typed an immediate response before she could disappear.

Me: Miss you too, sweet girl! Have an incredible time!

Camilla: I will! It's beautiful here

Camilla: You'd love this so much

Me: Thrilled for you! Soak in every moment

Don't rush into an engagement if the opportunity arises.

The small dots bounced on-screen, indicating Camilla was typing. I waited. The dots stopped, and my heart stopped with them.

Camilla: Sending pics and love

Camilla: Talk soon!

I rushed out a quick goodbye as images of Camilla, their immaculate bungalow, and the Indian Ocean popped into view.

My gaze lingered on each photo. Gratitude for my daughter's ability to travel like this and experience these things overwhelmed me, and my breath shuddered.

She looked so unequivocally happy.

The last picture was a selfie with Jeff at her side. She blew a kiss at the camera, but his eyes were fixed on her. The image reminded me of Mom's photo with Sébastien. They'd both experienced the kind of adoration I once dreamed of, and I envied them that.

I sighed as I tucked the phone away.

A few minutes later I spotted the door I was looking for. My reflection in the glass stared back, unimpressed. I'd chosen a cream-colored blouse and wide-legged black silk pants with matching pumps for the occasion. Small gold hoops adorned my earlobes, pearls lined my neck. From the outside I appeared poised. Inside I was Mentos in Coke.

I tapped my information into the kiosk screen and tried uselessly not to think of the shimmering rhinestone in my still-swollen nostril. Robert would see it as a sign I'd returned to white trash without him. Never mind that my parents had made a solid middle-class living.

I took a seat on a nearby bench and waited for Robert to arrive.

He appeared two minutes past our scheduled start time, wearing jeans and a polo shirt. He chatted with security, chummy and unhurried, then moved down the hall toward me.

I trembled immediately at his presence.

Thankfully, the mediator called us inside before he reached my bench. I took a seat at one end of a giant oval conference table, sure I'd throw up or pass out. I'd brought a list of things I wanted to address and notes for rebuttal to his inevitable pushback, but I wasn't prepared for my physical response to his nearness.

Logical or not, I feared him, and that made me angry. Which was a terrible distraction.

For three hours, we answered the mediator's questions, addressing one another only as needed across the massive table.

When I asked for an update on our dwindling bank balances, he accused me of divorcing him for his money. When I suggested he fire the gardener or cancel our country club membership to save money, he outwardly scoffed at my ignorance. According to Robert, the gardener was necessary to prepare the home for sale, and he needed the country club to continue conducting his business as usual. How could he afford to stop taking clients golfing at a time like this? He suggested I sell my mom's house. We were selling our marital home, after all. Why should I keep the property I inherited when we could divide the proceeds from both?

I bristled at his greed. "That's not fair, and you know it," I snapped. "We owe more on the marital home than it's worth, and Mom's place is paid for. Not to mention she left it to me in her will."

Robert feigned shock at my heated response.

The mediator pumped a palm up and down, cautioning me to remain calm. "It was just an idea, Sophie. That's why we're here," she said. "Let's keep brainstorming to find something you can agree upon."

At that moment I wondered if Robert had a connection to our mediator. I recalled his casual familiarity with the courthouse employees when he arrived. Divorcing a well-known attorney in a community as small as ours sucked.

I took a calming breath and fixed my attention on Robert for the first time, locking my gaze with his. "While we're discussing financials,"

I said flatly. "I'd like to know which investments you made that allegedly bankrupted us."

He chuckled and waved one hand dismissively. "I'd have to talk to my broker to get the exact stock names. Investment strategies are complex, and not at all a science," he added, implying I couldn't possibly keep up if he offered further explanation. He swept his gaze to the mediator, eyebrows lifted in a plea for understanding.

She nodded, charmed.

"Please do," I said, pulling their eyes back to me.

"What?" Robert asked.

"Do ask our broker," I clarified, heavy emphasis on *our*. The money wasn't his alone, and therefore, the person who moved it didn't work for him alone either. "I want to know which specific investments emptied our accounts. More specifically, I'd like to request documentation outlining the movement of funds and their loss."

"It's always about money with you," he said softly, though loud enough for the mediator to hear and make a note on her tablet.

I left frustrated and disappointed. When I reached the parking lot, he was waiting by my car, smiling.

I checked the area for witnesses or cameras before I approached, afraid I might need to document whatever came next.

"Have fun today?" he asked.

"Pardon," I said, edging past him to open my door.

"This is all your fault, you know." he said.

I dropped behind my wheel and closed the door. Then I covered my eyes with sunglasses to hide my fear.

Robert crouched, pointing his beady eyes through the glass at my side. "We had a good thing going, but you ruined it. Always wanting more," he said loudly and shook his head. "You won't even get spousal support now, babe. Then who will support your low-class lifestyle?" His gaze fixed on my nose piercing. "Better run and get your tattoos and hair dye fast, because the money's about to run out," he jeered. He straightened slowly and raised his hands wide at his side. "Wishing you all the best," he called.

I imagined hitting him with my car.

If he managed to fool the courts and get away with all our money, I'd be sunk. Everything I'd worked so hard to keep afloat would be gone in a matter of months. I'd already sold all of Mom's possessions with any significant value to pay off the property taxes, and I was working two jobs just to pay the utilities, buy food, and put gas in my car. I supposed I could sell the car, but I'd have to buy another to replace it, something older that would probably need repairs I couldn't afford.

My fingers tightened painfully around the steering wheel as I reversed away from the space, then left Robert fading in my rearview mirror.

I hadn't come this far to fail, and I couldn't let him have the satisfaction of believing he'd ruined me. My forensic accountants promised to be in touch if they found evidence to suggest we weren't really bankrupt. I hadn't heard a word from them yet, which wasn't good. There had to be a way to prove he was lying. But how?

❧

The next few weeks went by in a blur. I put off cleaning Mom's closets on the days I didn't work at the restaurant and instead decided to freshen up the decor. I painted the living room a bright cream and my bedroom a soft pink. I hung frilly curtains in all the windows and placed tchotchkes on shelves and stands. The house felt more like home each day, filled with a curated collection of things that made me feel like *me*.

I took a page from Chez Margot's playbook and added plants to every room. Potted herbs on my kitchen windowsill. Ferns and succulents in macramé plant holders elsewhere.

I worked through lunchtime at the restaurant most days.

Thanks to the growing popularity of the Invisible Baker, from dinnertime until eleven each night, I baked and then, exhausted, I slept deeply.

I had Lucas to thank for the abundance of orders, though he still didn't know I was the Invisible Baker. He only requested a few dozen pastries at first, but the number grew with demand. Soon customers waited at the doors for Chez Margot to open so they could get first dibs on macarons, éclairs, and pains au chocolat.

Lucas added signs to the display case, crediting the Invisible Baker. Orders for my small business quadrupled, and my social media following did too.

Deliveries were the trickiest part. I'd hired Alicia's sons for after-school deliveries when I couldn't do them myself—which was more and more often. I had no idea how I'd manage if business continued on this trajectory.

Tomorrow's problem, I thought.

Today was Saturday, and my day off.

I pulled into Alicia's driveway just after breakfast. Cameron and her sons played catch on the lawn outside their pretty blue-and-white cottage. She rose from the porch swing and moved gracefully in my direction, purse in hand.

Cameron broke away from the game to catch her around the middle and kiss her head before she reached my SUV. He opened my passenger door for her and waved. "Hey, Sophie. What's on the agenda this time? Should I arrange another drunken pickup or—"

"Shush," Alicia said. "We haven't decided yet. You're all on standby!" she hollered, projecting her voice in the direction of her watching teens.

They cracked up, and I smiled.

Cameron closed Alicia's door while she fastened her seat belt. "At least tell me if she's coming home altered again?" He worked his brows. "That was a surprise." He reached across Alicia, and gave me a high five.

"Hey! Stop that!" She shoved his arm back through the open window. "Fire up the grill when you get hungry," she said. "I don't know what else we're doing, but we're absolutely eating somewhere nice."

Cameron stepped away with a warm smile, then bent down for another peek inside. "Have fun," he said. "Let me know about that ride."

Alicia stuck out her tongue.

I leaned against my steering wheel to look at Cameron. "I'm going to be your favorite person after today."

He clutched his chest. "Are you going lingerie shopping? Say it's lingerie shopping." He pulled a wallet from his pocket and pretended to search his credit cards. "You know what?" He closed the wallet and extended the entire wallet as an offering. "Just take it all."

Their boys collapsed onto the grass one by one, grasping their throats and fake dying.

"Goodbye!" Alicia called. She waved the wallet away. "I love you. Don't text me."

I shifted into reverse, and sailed back down the drive.

Cameron, an engineer by trade and profession, volunteer coached T-ball teams when the boys were small, then peewee football and Little League. These days their three boys played five sports, and Cameron cheered from the stands at every game, during every season.

She really had married a good one. *High-quality men still exist,* I thought, and Lucas's image popped into mind.

I'd always thought Alicia lucked out with Cameron, but I was beginning to see she'd simply taken her time. She wasn't the kind to stick around to see if the chemistry picked up, or if a guy who bored her on the first date would be more fun on the second. If she didn't feel a connection, she moved on. She was down to do or try anything, but she was utterly inflexible when it came to her standards.

All these years later, that stance had gotten her everything I wanted.

"You look pretty today," she said, smiling as we motored away. "I especially love this hat." She tugged on the floppy brim. "It suits you."

I smiled. "I found it in one of the upstairs closets." I kept peeking behind the closed doors, only to get overwhelmed and change my mind about starting a new project when my hands were already so full.

"How's Camilla?" she asked.

"Excellent." I beamed. "Home from the Maldives and unengaged." I'd wanted to throw a party when she returned without a ring, but I kept my mouth shut and listened to the details of her trip with bone-deep relief.

Life just kept getting better.

"So where are we going today?" She steepled her fingers and touched them to her chin.

"How do you feel about a spa day?"

"Shut. Up." Alicia dropped her head against the headrest. "I deserve a spa day. Are we getting mani-pedis?"

"Yes. And Swedish massages," I said. "And a little of all their services, actually."

Alicia turned to me, lips parted in awe. "If Cameron dies first, I'm asking you to be my bride."

"Fine, but I expect a flash mob and a helicopter to take us into the sunset," I said.

"Of course."

I'd made six dozen assorted pastries in a single night for the spa, after another baker bailed before a big customer appreciation event. For that, I scored two full-service day passes in addition to a major payday. Who said baking wasn't the best job ever? Certainly not me. "Ever had a Brazilian wax?" I asked.

Alicia turned to stare, lips pursed. "Why?"

"It's on the schedule for after lunch."

"Absolutely the hell not," she said. "Do you know what they use for that procedure?"

"Wax," we said in near unison.

"Hot wax," she clarified.

"The wax is warm," I corrected. "It won't burn us, and the aestheticians are professionals. They've seen everything, and they don't care."

Alicia wrinkled her nose. "I will pass, but I mean it with love: Thank you."

I scowled. "Come on. Don't you want to feel smooth like a dolphin?"

"Not really, but it'll send Cam over the moon. Lord, that man will never leave me alone now."

I snorted a laugh and stepped on the gas when the light turned green. "You're welcome."

⁂

We arrived at Chez Margot around seven o'clock that night, having stopped for appetizers at the winery near the spa. As it turned out, a full day of pampering boosted our appetites, and I'd opted to stay for an additional haircut and style.

I spotted Lucas and Pam at the hostess stand as we approached the door.

"Thank god there's no line," Alicia whispered. "I need to sit down after that waxing. I feel exposed." She held her handbag in front of her, as if to hide her secret. "I can't believe I let you talk me into that."

"It wasn't that bad," I lied. It had hurt like hell, and I was horrified when I realized what a terrible job I'd been doing down there. The waxer had to go back multiple times to get the job done.

"I've never been so humbled," Alicia went on. "They made me turn over."

I flung the door open and let her inside before she said anything more.

"It was mortifying," she hissed. Her eyes went comically wide when I shushed her. "They took all I got."

"Stop." I laughed, drawing Lucas's attention our way.

Alicia tugged my arm. "I am dead serious. I was robbed."

Lucas's brows pinched as his gaze moved from Alicia to me. "Sophie, welcome." He pulled two menus from the stand with a smile. "Who is your friend?"

"Lucas, this is my best friend, Alicia. Alicia, my boss, Lucas."

Alicia shot me a coy smile. "Yeah he is."

I sank an elbow into her ribs.

She crossed her arms over her middle and chuckled. Then she pointed at the bakery's empty display case. "The Invisible Baker. Look at that, Sophie."

I shot her a warning look.

Lucas smiled. "We can't keep their pastries in stock. Apparently, it's a whole thing online. No one has a clue who owns the company. There's lots of speculation. Whoever is behind the brand, they're helping me reach my financial goals to make this a black-tie dinner venue."

I couldn't meet her eye. She'd told me repeatedly that I needed to come clean to Lucas, even if I kept the secret from everyone else.

Every day that I didn't confess made it a little harder to deliver the news. I wasn't sure he'd understand. He didn't know what I'd been through, and what I was still going through. Alicia had witnessed everything, but she still didn't understand my hesitation.

Personal reasons aside, I felt like a criminal when I thought of the lengths I'd gone to keep my name separate from the bakery. I took orders only online. The payments went to my LLC's bank account. The contact page had a custom email address.

Why would I do all that if I didn't have something to hide?

I still found it difficult to believe I didn't need to be invisible anymore.

Lucas led us to our table, then pulled out our chairs and waited while we sat.

I squirmed under his careful appraisal.

"You changed your hair," he said finally. "It's lovely."

"Highlights," I said, pushing a swath of soft waves behind one ear. The stylist had added blond and platinum strands through my naturally mousy locks, successfully covering and blending my grays. She cut layers and sideswept bangs, then used her blow-dryer to add volume. "We had a spa day."

The effects of the experience left me feeling young and dramatic. I couldn't wait to do it again.

Lucas's attention moved to my hands, probably clocking the professional French manicure, before returning to my eyes. "Special occasion?"

"Celebrating our badassery," Alicia chimed in.

He smiled. "In that case, I'll get the wine." Lucas patted the table, then strode away.

"He likes you," she said. "I told Cam already. He agrees."

"Cam has never even met him," I told her. "Neither had you, until now."

Alicia arched a brow. "But I listen, and I hear it in how you talk about him. You know what else? You don't just think he's hot. You like him too."

My face heated. "So?"

Her jaw dropped. "I knew it!"

I shook my head at her and busied myself with the menu. "Doesn't matter. He's my boss, and I'm technically still married. Plus, he's in love with his wife."

"His wife would want him to be happy," she said.

"Oh sure." I guffawed. "Would you want Cam to move on if you died first?"

Her expression turned feral. "If I die first, he's to climb into the coffin after me and close the lid. No exceptions. No excuses."

"Very healthy."

She looked back at her menu. "Death will not us part, that's all I'm saying."

I laughed.

"This isn't about me, anyway," she said. "Robert shouldn't be a stumbling block either. I'm not convinced the two of you were ever truly married," she said. "Legal precedence aside. You were strangers who shared a house."

She wasn't wrong. I'd been so busy trying to be what he wanted, in the early years, that I was never really myself. Then I was so focused on achieving the white-picket-fence dream that I overlooked and forgave all the awful things about him that should've sent me packing.

"And have you seen Lucas?" Alicia continued. She fanned her face with the menu. "Soph, that man is fine."

"He's my boss."

Lucas returned with two wine flights. Each board carried five glasses, arranged from white to dark red. "These all come from the same region and vineyard in the South of France," he said. "A white, two rosés, a sweet red blend, and a full-bodied cabernet sauvignon. Take your time with the menu, and I'll be right back with some water and a basket of bread."

I watched him walk away.

Alicia folded her hands on the table and leveled me with a knowing stare.

Two hours later, I was stuffed with French bread, beef bourguignon, and wine. The restaurant was quiet, and Alicia had excused herself to the ladies' room so long ago I wondered if she'd secretly walked home.

"How was everything?" Lucas asked, rubbing his palms together as he returned to check on us.

"Good. Thank you. I think we're calling it a night when Alicia gets back."

He nodded. "That's too bad."

I didn't disagree.

"Have you heard from Camilla?" he asked. "She's home from her trip now, yes?"

I stared, stunned for no good reason. I found his attention to the details, especially regarding things that mattered to me, intoxicating. His genuine interest and concern tugged at something deep in my heart. "She's good."

"No engagement?"

I shook my head.

"Do you think she's disappointed?"

The question took me aback. I hadn't given this concern a single thought, but I wondered if she was disappointed. Her longtime boyfriend had taken her on a major romantic vacation. She must've expected a proposal as much as I had. How did she feel when it didn't come? "I don't know," I admitted.

Lucas slid onto Alicia's chair and watched me. "How are you holding up? You seem tired when you come in most mornings." He lifted a palm. "Your work is magnificent, but your energy is low sometimes. I don't want to cross a line, but I wonder—"

"What?" I asked, when he didn't continue.

"About your divorce," he said. His tone was soft and his expression sheepish. "How are you really doing?"

I briefly considered refreshing my smile, offering a canned response, and telling him I was fine. Instead, I finished the wine in my glass and sighed. "Not great," I said frankly. "My husband is a bad guy. He was emotionally abusive, manipulative, and neglectful for the entirety of our marriage. I'm not convinced he ever loved me, or that I'm lovable, and I haven't loved him in a very long time. To me, the divorce feels like a formality, but he's turned it into a quiet war. We were arguably wealthy six months ago, but today I live in the home I grew up in, and he's filed for bankruptcy."

Alicia appeared, cell phone to her ear, a wide smile on her face, and I knew she was talking with Cameron.

I stood, a little wobbly from the wine. "I should go," I said, knowing I'd overshared, and blaming the wine.

I wanted him to know everything I'd told him, because Alicia was right. I had feelings for Lucas that an employee shouldn't have for her boss. So it was best for both of us if he saw me clearly as the train wreck I was.

"Hey." Lucas rose and cleared the space between us in one long stride. His voice was low and gravelly.

Alicia stopped short, several feet away.

Lucas moved so close, I felt the heat of his body on mine.

I arched my back for a better look into his soulful eyes. "Yeah?"

"You aren't unlovable." Each word reverberated in my core.

He took the bill from our table and put it in his shirt pocket, then turned to Alicia. "It was nice meeting you," he said. "I hope you'll both have a nice night."

He held my gaze a moment longer, then walked away.

Chapter Nineteen

My DNA test arrived more quickly than anticipated, and I opened it with eager hands.

I read the instructions twice before collecting my sample and returning it to the mailbox with silent prayers. Did I have family out there? I'd wished for siblings and cousins as a child. Wanted big family reunions and holiday get-togethers with family crowded around the table. But Mom and Dad were only children, and their parents had passed while I was young. If not for Camilla, I'd be afloat, genetically speaking, and I didn't realize how much I wanted an anchor until the possibility became real.

Camilla texted consistently following her return from the Maldives and visited often on her way to the yoga studio. It wasn't until a text arrived as I clocked in at Chez Margot that I grew concerned.

Camilla: Dinner at the club?

I grimaced at the four seemingly innocuous words. My last visit to the country club didn't end well, and I didn't want a repeat. I couldn't think of a good reason for Camilla to request a meeting at the club, unless this was a family affair and she'd chosen neutral ground. I steeled my nerves and drummed up enough faux enthusiasm to respond appropriately.

Me: Of course!

My suspicions were confirmed that night, when I got out of my car and spotted Robert at the valet with a new Mercedes. I'd arrived early to settle myself for whatever came next. Apparently he had a similar idea, except he'd probably wanted to hide the car.

"What was that?" I asked. Irritation sharpened my tone, and Robert smirked in response.

He watched with amusement as the young man in a crimson vest and matching tie drove the car away. "What do you mean?"

"I mean, you're claiming bankruptcy. How the hell did you get a new car?"

"Language," he chided. "Swearing is for the uneducated. Next time, search deep for some big-girl words."

A wave of nausea washed over me. I wanted to scream. To punch his smug face. Or turn and leave. Camilla's request was the only thing keeping me there.

I turned on wooden legs and marched toward the door.

Robert followed. "The firm leases new cars for the partners every year," he said. "You know that. It's just one more benefit of an advanced degree."

"Funny," I said, ducking inside as an outgoing guest held the door. "I recall writing all your law school papers." He'd bullied me into finishing the bulk of his graduate work while I stayed home with Camilla in the early years, treating me like a loafer, insisting that helping with his class assignments was the least I could do to pull my weight. "Maybe I should have the new car."

Robert caught up to me easily. Heat blazed in his eyes as he nervously flashed his plastic smile at passersby. "Watch it, Soph. You're playing a game you can't win. You can, however, make it worse for yourself."

Fear trickled down my spine, and I picked up my pace.

A dining room hostess noticed our approach and smiled. She led us to a table for four near the back, and I chose a seat facing the door.

I wanted to see Camilla's face the moment she arrived. I was sure I'd know what this was about if I could just get a look at her. Was she quitting school? Moving to the Maldives? Did she get an incredible job offer? As long as she wasn't getting married, I could get through this night.

A server arrived within seconds to take our drink orders. I ordered a glass of chardonnay and Robert asked for scotch. Alone again, he warned me to watch my alcohol consumption, reminding me that my mother drank herself to death.

I imagined tossing the wine in his face when it arrived and wished I'd ordered merlot so it would stain.

Thankfully, Camilla and Jeff arrived before the drinks.

Robert rose to greet them. A cheek kiss for Camilla. A handshake for Jeff.

My gaze zeroed in on her ring finger before she reached my side of the table. A fat round diamond winked and glinted, and my stomach heaved.

She hadn't gotten engaged in the Maldives. I'd seen her photos and had lunch with her multiple times since the trip. There wasn't any sign of a ring.

Until now.

"Mom," she said, bending forward to hug me where I sat. "It's so good to see you. You look amazing!"

Jeff moved into view when she released me. "Nice to see you again, Mrs. B—" He stopped mid-sentence, looking as if he'd swallowed a bee. "Uhm." He looked to Camilla for assistance.

She visibly cringed.

Robert barked a laugh. "You can still call her Mrs. Bianco," he said. "That's her name."

"Call me Sophie," I corrected, interrupting Robert for a change. "From the looks of that ring, we're going to be family."

Jeff beamed. "We are," he said. "I still can't believe it's real. I promise I will do everything I can to make Camilla happy every single day of our life together."

I slanted my eyes at Robert, then forced a bright smile for my daughter and soon-to-be son-in-law. "I love hearing that," I said. "In truth, I was on the fence about taking back my maiden name, but seeing as how Camilla's name might also change soon, I think the timing is perfect."

Camilla took the seat beside me with a gasp. "Oh, Mama, I love that. I think Grandma would be so happy."

I swallowed an unexpected lump in my throat as I let the thought sink in. Could I do something to make my mom proud? I certainly hoped so. But seeing my daughter's delight was just as good. Maybe even better.

I felt Robert's heated gaze on my cheek as I chatted with the happy couple, but I didn't look his way. Robert Bianco's hold on me was weakening each day, and that truth had never been so evident.

I walked alone to my car after dinner, eyes upturned to the stars.

"She's getting married, Mom," I whispered. "I think you'd agree that she's the best part of us, so let's hope she does a better job choosing than we did."

Raisin met me at the door when I returned. I fed him a half can of his favorite pâté, then changed into my pajamas.

I baked until my level of distraction surpassed my progress. Then I climbed the steps to my mom's old bedroom. Gone were the clutter and chaos, replaced by open space, lacy curtains, and braided area rugs. A small bookcase anchored one wall. Nightstands with lamps bookended the bed. The space was technically mine, but it was also still hers. Standing in the doorway, I could see her at the mirror, checking her hair or putting on jewelry. She'd remained beautiful and steadfast in the face of absolute hell.

I aspired to be half as strong.

I couldn't recall when I first started blaming her for Dad's mistreatment, but I was deeply sorry for that now. I leaned against the doorjamb for support. Arms crossed and emotions high, I felt her presence in the room and clung to it. "I'm so sorry, Mama," I whispered. "I should've been a better daughter. And when I grew up, I should've been a better friend."

Raisin trotted past me and headed for the windowsill, where he kept tabs on the world below. Moonlight beamed through the gauzy curtains and illuminated the closet door.

I moved into the light and opened the door.

Mom's walk-in closet was stuffed to capacity with things I'd tucked aside to go through later and boxes of items that had been there long before that. Clearing and sorting the space would take days, but something edged me forward anyway.

I started with a hatbox, worn and frayed along its edge. The weight of it suggested I'd find more than a hat inside. I carried it to the bed and reluctantly removed the lid, and found piles of photos and paperwork. I nearly returned the box to the closet, too tired and weary to start sorting, but the corner of an old report card caught my eye.

I crawled onto the bed and lifted a stack of papers. Every report card I'd earned from preschool through college Mom had neatly organized, chronologically, with great care. Underneath those were poems from my middle school day camp days, friendship bracelets from high school, my first driver's permit, and certificates for national honors society induction. Loose photos from birthdays and family vacations mingled with band and choir concert mementos and candid shots from local hikes and backyard barbecues.

Wonder stole my breath as I dug more deeply into the box.

"I can't believe you kept all this." She really had cherished me and my life.

I overturned the box with desperate impatience and found photos from my parents' wedding, and from her parents' wedding. I didn't know much about any of my grandparents, but I knew they'd lived a tough life, raising kids in the Great Depression and getting by with very little. I couldn't help wondering if they were happy as I stared at their youthful faces, captured in black and white.

When had the miserable marriages of my lineage begun? "Was it with you?" I asked. Or had it started long before?

A small notebook slipped free from the pile of papers and photos, an Eiffel Tower on its cover. I lifted it for a closer look.

Inside, an image of Mom and Sébastien was stuck to the page with brittle, yellowed tape. The couple clung to one another outside a restaurant called Le Bistro, and the street sign behind them read Rue Pasteur.

I raised the book to my chest and smiled through the window at the moonlight beyond. I'd found a clue to their location. Maybe to *his* location. "Thank you, Mom."

I held a book club meeting on the following Friday night, eager to show off the redecorated place and hear what my friends had been up to these last few months. I feared no one would come but extended the invitation anyway in the name of bravery.

I created an elaborate charcuterie board and a vanilla tarte tatin that smelled like my best dreams. Beside those, I set out bottles of wine and water. There wasn't enough time to read a book, so I'd simply sent the invite as a way to reconnect. We could pick the book for next month as a group.

Alicia dithered in the kitchen while I paced nervously in the living room, keeping watch through my front window. "My god, everything looks so good," she called. "I'm starving, and I want to eat it all."

I laughed. "Eat, then," I said. "It's for you too."

"No. I'm waiting. I can't be caught with a mouthful of bruschetta or basil leaves in my teeth when everyone arrives."

Might not be a problem, I thought, dryly. Who knew if anyone would actually come?

The back door opened, and Ilona's voice echoed through the first floor. "I brought a cheese ball. Am I late?"

Alicia moaned loudly. "I love a good cheese ball. Bring it here."

I smiled. "Please help yourself and tell Alicia to eat too."

We settled in the living room a few minutes later, small plates of goodies in hand.

"How's the search for your dad going?" Alicia asked.

I'd called her the moment I found the new photo, and together we'd searched until after midnight for a lead on his whereabouts. As it turned out, there were dozens of towns in France with restaurants called Le Bistro on streets called Rue Pasteur.

"So-so." I frowned. "It's a slow process."

"You'll find him," she said. "I'm starting to think you can do anything. Just hang in there."

A car slowed on the street beyond my front lawn, and I wrenched the curtain wider. "I think that's Jeannie's car," I said. Then the vehicle backed up and pulled into the driveway. "It is!"

A moment later, she and three others climbed out.

Alicia clapped, then opened the front door to wave from my porch.

My chest tightened, and my eyes lightly stung. "They came."

"Of course they came," Alicia said. "Why wouldn't they?"

I batted away the burgeoning tears and pulled in a shaky breath. How did my life keep getting better when, on paper, everything looked worse? I'd lost my mother and ended a long-term marriage last summer. I'd inherited endless unpaid bills and back taxes. My husband had filed for bankruptcy. Yet I'd never felt so filled with peace and joy.

"Welcome," I called as the foursome piled into my home.

"Sophie!" They shouted my name with wide smiles and open arms, then passed me around, delivering warm hugs and a million words of affirmation.

I introduced the ladies to Ilona, and thirty minutes later we gathered at my dining room table. Alicia opened a second bottle of wine.

"We were so excited when you texted," Jeannie said. "We refused to have book club without you."

I grinned, speechless and overwhelmed with gratitude.

"These are delicious," Jeannie said. "Did you make these?" Something I couldn't name ignited in her expression.

The other ladies exchanged similar looks.

"I did," I said. "I'm a pastry chef at Chez Margot now. So my skills are improving all the time."

"You did it," Jeannie said. "You were unhappy, and you got out. Now look at you. You have this adorable little home in the cutest neighborhood I've ever seen. You're doing what you love. You look incredible, and I hear you're about to become a mother-in-law!"

I laughed. "That's true. They haven't set a date, but Camilla and Jeff are tying the knot."

We talked for hours before I walked my friends to Jeannie's car. As Alicia chatted with the others, Jeannie took my hand and held me back.

"Hey, this is probably nothing," she said, "but do you remember your old HOA president? Joyce Futes?"

"The angriest woman in Virginia?" I asked. "Why yes. How could I forget?"

Jeannie's button nose wrinkled. She glanced at Alicia and the others before turning her eyes back to me. "She's head of the PTA at my kids' school this year, and she's a real stickler for parents making big efforts for the many special events and activities. She has a way of quietly tearing down moms who buy cupcakes and treats instead of making them. She says everything should be customized for the occasion, and she belittles folks who just don't have time."

I pressed my lips together. "I've known a lot of people like that. I'm sorry you're experiencing it too."

Jeannie bit her lip, and for the briefest moment, I thought she might ask me to bake for her.

"Go on," I said, smile widening.

"Her oldest son plays high school football with one of Alicia's boys, and apparently he had a delivery job this summer for a company called the Invisible Baker."

My jaw dropped, and my gaze snapped to Alicia.

She was joking and laughing, obliviously, with the women at Jeannie's car.

"You know who that is." Jeannie said. Her words weren't a question.

My cheeks flared with heat, and my tongue seemed to swell. I didn't want to lie, but I wasn't ready to tell the truth, not even to Jeannie. Information spread too easily. This was a perfect example. "I mean—"

She waved a hand, expression satisfied, and nodded her head. "That's all I needed to know. Your secret is safe with me."

"Everything okay?" Alicia asked. Her smile faltered as she took in my expression.

"Yep!" Jeannie kissed my cheek and strode away. "Just getting her recipe for that cheese ball."

Alicia quirked a brow as Jeannie dropped behind the wheel and drove away.

Ilona watched from the porch as I headed back inside. "Hey! That was my cheese ball. Whoa," she said, quickly changing tones. "I was only teasing."

I blinked, and the earth tilted slightly beneath me. If Joyce figured out that overworked moms were hiring a personal baker, and the baker was me, a neighbor who'd recently left the community without notice, she'd tell everyone who'd listen. That news would undoubtedly get back to Robert, who'd immediately aim his proverbial gunfire at my company, and he'd do all he could to burn it down.

I walked to the dining room, unsure what Jeannie's news meant to me, or what it could amount to, if anything. Then I poured three glasses of wine before turning to Alicia and Ilona. "I'm not sure, but I think I might have a cataclysmic problem."

Chapter Twenty

Fall bloomed fully as I grew roots in my life and found my place among the tight-knit staff at Chez Margot. Most employees had been there for years, and I was honored to be part of the family. Lucas worked closely at my side until I felt comfortable on my own. Then he'd begun the long, nerve-racking process of writing a proposal for his small business loan.

Any bank would be remiss to decline his request, in my opinion, but perhaps I was biased. Time and personal experience with Lucas had slowly etched away my hard-as-granite stance against the male of the species. Maybe they weren't all villains, but they definitely weren't all like Lucas.

From a purely unemotional standpoint, the bank approving the loan seemed like a no-brainer. Chez Margot had an excellent, dedicated staff and a prime location, and the proposed menus were impeccable. If that wasn't enough, the restaurant had a large customer base passionate about their favorite French restaurateur.

Still, Lucas worried.

He had a vision for his business, and he wanted it so badly. So, it surprised no one when he called the entire staff in early one morning for a professional photo shoot. "To capture the personal side of life here," he said.

I arrived, sleep deprived as usual, but with my hair and makeup done, something I typically skipped when going to work. It had taken a single day in the kitchen to see that any and all attempts at looking cute would melt away long before my shift ended.

Pam, who typically staffed the front desk, met me at the welcome stand. "You look incredible," she said, tugging a blond section of hair over her shoulder.

"Thanks. I love your braids," I said.

She beamed. "Pigtails increase tips. It's been tested."

I grinned.

"It's so strange seeing the kitchen staff all dressed up," she said. She motioned to the men and women who, like me, were usually covered in grease and sweat but today were freshly showered and photo ready.

"Anyone in particular?"

A deep blush spread over her freckled cheeks.

"Like John?"

Pam gasped. "How did you know?"

"Mother's intuition?" I guessed.

She considered that a moment. "Do you think I have a chance?" she asked. "Or is it weird to crush on someone I work with?"

My traitorous gaze jumped to Lucas, and he immediately turned in my direction. "Nope, I think some of the most incredible romances probably began at work." I wasn't sure where I got that idea, but it pleased her, so I was thankful for the thought.

"Pam, Sophie," Lucas called. He waved us closer, and we hurried to join him.

Lucas introduced us to Emily, a local photographer, then let her take charge. After she took each of our photos individually, she staged small group photos around the kitchen and dining area, then stayed to take candid shots when we began our prep work for the day.

I was in the ladies' room when my phone alerted me to a new email. I washed up and took a quick peek on my way back to my station. The preview stopped me in my tracks.

Ancestry Seeker: Your results are in

"Oh, shit." I looked around, then hurried past the kitchen to the employee lounge.

I flopped onto the chair where Lucas once bandaged my fingers, and I opened the message.

My hands trembled as I scanned the form letter explaining how to read the results. Then I clicked a link that promised my personal details. Belatedly, I recalled my vow not to read the findings without Alicia, and I opened my video chat app.

She still hadn't forgiven me for sending the sample to the lab without her, and that wasn't interesting at all.

The call rang through without an answer. No surprise.

School was in session, and Alicia was thirty teens deep into second period by now. Our schedules wouldn't line up until late this afternoon, and I was physically incapable of waiting that long for information I should've had forty-six years ago.

I flipped back to my results page and devoured every word. My mood plummeted at the sight of one particular sentence.

No direct matches.

My shoulders sank as I stared in disappointment. I hadn't allowed myself to consider this possibility, choosing instead to hold on to hope. I didn't want this test to be as fruitless as every other attempt I'd made at finding my father.

Maybe I was meant to be alone.

"Sophie?" Lucas's voice came from the doorway. "Everything okay?"

I nodded, eyes stinging from the absolute letdown.

"I went to see how you were doing in the kitchen, and I saw you running this way."

I turned my phone screen to face Lucas as he entered the room.

He met me at the table and steadied my trembling hand with his. He read the screen, then met my eyes. "Ancestry test results?"

I sniffled. "Yeah."

He looked at the screen again, a bit longer this time. "You're French," he said brightly. "Why doesn't that surprise me?"

I laughed at his enthusiasm despite my mood. "I have no idea."

"It's because I believe all the most beautiful women are French."

I stared. Everything I'd felt about the test results whooshed from my mind. Did he just—?

Lucas winked, then strode confidently back to the door. "Let me know when you go back to the kitchen," he said. "Meanwhile, take your time."

I stared at the empty doorway for a long beat after he'd gone, then dragged my attention back to the ancestry charts.

A region in the South of France was highlighted on the map. Three of the small towns I'd found with a restaurant on the corner of a street named Rue Pasteur fell inside the shaded area. A thrill coursed through me. I'd been right! *Or very close.*

Unfortunately, I didn't have the time or money to trek across France, knocking on doors, in search of Sébastien Allard. But I loved this confirmation.

"I'm French," I whispered, allowing the notion to fully register. Before seeing the map with my DNA results, the fact that my biological father was French hadn't fully sunk in.

Holy shit! I am French!

I made immediate plans to spend my evening between bakes researching the Var area of France. I'd already learned that Var was part of the Provence-Alpes-Côte d'Azur region. The area was a provincial paradise that included the mountains, the sea, and the freaking French Riviera.

Excitement popped and fizzed in my stomach. I wanted to race home and look up everything about the small towns where my parents might've met. But for now, I had to get back to work.

Lucas stood at my station in the kitchen, mixing and prepping desserts in my absence. He smiled at my return. "All good?"

"Very good," I said, heating slightly at the memory of him casually calling me beautiful.

He stepped away to allow me access. "Things got busy, so I kept up with the pace."

"Thanks."

Lucas went on his rounds without further ado.

I worked on autopilot until the end of my shift. My busy mind focused on two things: how to prove Robert was hiding our money, and how I could get enough of that money to visit France.

In between those two things, a montage played out in my head. Alicia and I held old-fashioned, accordion-folded maps in our outstretched arms, trying to locate Rue Pasteur. Our floppy sun hats and long maxi dresses fluttered in a warm breeze. We entered cafés and shops on espadrille wedges and asked locals if they knew my father.

Every day, we wore ourselves out on the mission. Then we carried bottles of French wine to beautiful locations with panoramic views. We ate French bread and Brie and asked ourselves why we didn't take a trip like this much sooner. And we vowed not to leave France until we completed our quest.

I tried to stay in the vision long enough to see my biological father, but instinct kept pulling me back. I imagined knocking on doors and hearing the locks slide away, but before the person on the other side came into view, I lost the image.

The only photos I had of Sébastien Allard were taken a half century ago. I couldn't properly imagine what he might look like today. Thin and craggy? Robust and healthy? Portly and bald?

How did life treat him after the summer he met my mother?

I tossed my apron into the canvas laundry bag on my way out that afternoon and caught sight of a woman ogling the empty bakery display case. Pam wasn't at the welcome stand.

"Hello," I called, redirecting my path. "Can I help you?"

The woman straightened and glanced at my name tag before looking at my face. She wore a gray pantsuit with patent leather pumps and a matching bag tucked under one crooked arm. "You work here?"

"Yep."

"Tell me about the pastries," she said. "I hear amazing things about them all day, every day. I was practically forced to check them out."

I tipped my chin upward to maintain eye contact. She was easily a half foot taller than me in her heels. She exuded confidence that made the height difference seem double. "The pastries vary a little throughout the week," I said. "But usually we have éclairs, macarons, pains au chocolat, and madeleines. Occasionally there are mille-feuille or kouign-amann as well."

She crossed long legs at the ankles and pursed her glossy pink lips as I spoke. Her flawless skin and makeup made me feel dowdy and old, even on a day I'd come to work looking my best.

My time in the kitchen had long ago erased those efforts.

"When are the deliveries made?" she asked.

"Daily. If you stop in for coffee tomorrow morning, you'll have your pick." I pulled the car keys from my pocket and smiled. Something about her demeanor bothered me, and standing there beside her, sweaty and exhausted, was taking a toll on my self-esteem. "Nice to meet you."

"Virginia Bonnie Black," she said. "I didn't catch your name."

I made a low, strangled sound. I hadn't asked for her name, but now that I had it, I wished she'd take it back. And leave.

Virginia Bonnie Black was the human behind Virginia's Secrets, a wildly popular social media account. She'd built her following by exploring various local legends and state lore, then reporting her findings. She also dug into modern issues, small town news, and big events in our state. Her most popular posts often involved scandals. Followers ate it up with a spoon and licked the screen.

I was a follower. I'd counted myself as a fan until this moment.

The last thing the Invisible Baker needed was any interest from her.

She sighed, gaze locked on mine, and my brain misfired as I tried to recall her question.

"Sophie." I nearly collapsed with relief. All she wanted was my name. I immediately wished I'd given an alias.

She nodded, having already taken note of my name tag. "What do you do here?"

I took a tiny step backward. My fight-or-flight instinct prepared me to run.

Jeannie's warning that Joyce, from my old HOA, had beef with local moms who didn't make their own treats for school events blew back into my mind like a tornado.

"I'm the pastry chef," I said, knowing she'd catch me in the lie if I said otherwise.

"Interesting," she said. "But you don't make the pastries for the display?" Her brow furrowed. "Is that odd?"

"Not at all," I said, feigning casual confidence and hoping she didn't see through me. "Sometimes I work with pastry doughs, but the desserts I bake are created individually upon request. Each is decadent and intended for leisurely consumption at the end of a meal. The pastries sold from our case are delicious, but most importantly, they're made in bulk and designed as grab-and-go options. Very different," I assured.

"Right." Her expression grew bored as I spoke, and she turned for another look into the empty display. "So they aren't made here. Do you order them direct from the Invisible Baker?"

"Lucas does," I said. "He owns the restaurant."

"Okay, so who makes the deliveries?"

I bit my lip. I'd started using a standard delivery service when Alicia's son's schedule and mine made it impossible to keep up. The change seemed genius when I'd thought of it. A different driver picked up from my house every day. Their businesses, like mine, were independent. They didn't all convene at a certain location to clock in or out, which meant it was unlikely that they discussed their jobs or compared notes on deliveries.

Unfortunately, apps kept records, I realized far too late. Someone like Virginia could easily access the details I wanted to keep hidden. She wouldn't need a court order to get the information. She was Virginia's Secrets. She just had to ask the right driver.

Which meant I had to make sure she never knew whom to ask.

But how would I make the deliveries without a service?

She set her hands on her hips, impatient as I mentally imploded. "Should I ask someone else? If you don't know, that's fine."

"I guess I'm not sure," I said. The one thing I was certain of, however, was that when I finally came clean as the Invisible Baker, I wanted it to be on my terms. Not because I was ousted like a scheming criminal. All concerns about Robert's probable reaction aside, I owed Lucas a proper explanation and enough time to make him see I hated being deceitful. I'd made a desperate decision, and I would do it again under those circumstances. I wasn't ready to be seen at that time, and I'd needed to be sure I could trust him.

"Who usually signs for the delivery?" Virginia asked.

I screwed up my features in confusion. "Whoever's at the desk, I guess."

"Hmm." She scanned the dining area. "Where's Lucas? You said he places the orders?"

Lucas raised a hand from his position at a nearby table.

I'd been so overwhelmed I hadn't noticed him chatting with patrons. How long had he been within earshot?

Lucas made his way in our direction, a bright toothpaste-commercial smile fixed in place. "Hello, I'm Lucas. How can I help you?"

I puffed out my cheeks, thankful for the escape but unable to walk away.

Lucas coaxed Virginia Bonnie Black into soft giggles within moments, and I rubbed my tired eyes to stop them from rolling.

"Can I get you something to eat while we chat?" he asked, already pulling a menu from the stand. "I'm sorry you missed the pastries, but every dish is fantastic here. I promise. My treat."

Her lips curved into a quick cat-that-ate-the-canary smile. "How can I say no to a meal with a handsome stranger?"

"No one is a stranger here," he assured, then motioned her to join him as he led her to a table.

I tagged along, uninvited, and several feet behind. I paused alongside leafy potted plants and decorative brick columns as they made their way deep into the dining room. Then I hid behind the bar when they stopped.

Mason, the bartender, frowned down at me, and I shook my head erratically. He scanned the room, then smirked and nodded without making eye contact again.

I could stay.

Lucas effortlessly turned the conversation with Virginia to his plans for expansion. She gushed over the possibility of a new, upscale riverfront venue. For a moment, I wondered if he knew exactly who Virginia was as well.

Chapter Twenty-One

I gave up my post a few minutes later, satisfied I had nothing to fear, and cut through the kitchen and out the door nearest the front desk.

When I emerged, Camilla and Jeff were chatting with Pam at the welcome stand.

"Oh my goodness, hello!" I called, darting past Pam to hug my daughter and future son-in-law. "What are you guys doing here?"

"We were in the area looking at wedding venues, and I'm starving," Camilla said.

I held my smile in place. "It's a beautiful day. Let me find you a seat on the patio."

I led Camilla and Jeff to the patio, carefully avoiding Virginia. "Wedding venues, huh?" I asked, placing the menus on a table out of view from the inside.

Cami and Jeff stole meaningful looks at one another as they took their seats.

"We talked it over, and we both really want to get married near the river," she said. "Imagine wedding photos with the river behind us." She sighed.

"We both have such fond memories of the area," Jeff added. "I think it's brilliant."

I glanced over my shoulder at the stretch of green grass above the river, and flashes of Cami as a toddler, chasing ducks and throwing stones, curved a smile on my lips.

"Hey, there," Lucas's voice brought me back to the moment. He approached with a congenial smile and curious eyes. "Pam told me your daughter and future son-in-law were here. I had to come out and congratulate them."

I froze, desperate to know everything Virginia had said, but this wasn't the time. Instead, I made introductions. "Well, this is my precious daughter, Camilla," I explained. "And her fiancé, Jeff. This is my boss, Lucas."

"Welcome to Chez Margot," he said.

The men shook hands while Camilla made wide eyes at me.

I looked away.

"I thought I saw you leave," Lucas said.

Jeff rose to pull out another chair. "Sit," he told me. "I didn't realize you were off the clock. You, too, Lucas, if you have a minute. Join us."

Lucas shook his head. "Oh, no. I have too much to do, and that starts with bringing you some congratulatory wine and a nice charcuterie. When's the big day?"

"We're thinking early next spring," Camilla said.

I blanched. "That's only a few months from now."

"A perfect time to start something new," Lucas agreed.

"It's more than half a year," Camilla said, eyes fixed on me.

"Why the rush?"

She frowned, then forced her mouth into a tight smile. "Summer is too hot, and I want to be settled in a new home next fall, not stressing about the wedding."

"What about finishing college?" I looked to Jeff for some help, but the poor kid couldn't see me past the big red hearts in his eyes.

"I'm not quitting college," Cami said. Her voice was low with warning. "I am, however, getting married in the spring."

I locked my jaw to stop a flood of advice she didn't want and raised my eyes to Lucas, hoping for moral support.

He shifted forward, folding his hands on the table. "Do you know who the woman in the pantsuit is?" he asked. "The one asking about the Invisible Baker?"

Camilla inhaled sharply, then coughed roughly into one fist.

Jeff was on his feet in an instant.

"I'm fine," Camilla croaked.

Lucas set his dark eyes back on me. "Did you recognize her?"

"She told me her name," I said. "I knew who she was after that, but I didn't tell her. I hope she writes something nice about your planned expansion."

Camilla cleared her throat, still trying to recover. "Who is it?"

"Virginia Bonnie Black," I said.

Camilla's mouth formed a small O.

"I knew it," Lucas said. He drummed his thumbs against the table's edge and sucked his teeth. "She was more interested in where we get our daily pastries than in my black-tie dreams."

"What did you tell her?" Camilla asked.

I wanted that answer, too, possibly more than I needed air.

He squinted slightly, maybe weighing his words. "I told her I'd met the owner a number of times, and he was a very nice older gentleman who preferred anonymity."

"You met the owner of what?" Camilla asked, her gaze shifting quickly to me.

I frowned. "The Invisible Baker?" What he said made zero sense.

Lucas nodded. "She didn't seem satisfied, which was curious, so I asked her why it mattered. Where is the story?" He unfolded his hands, palms cupped skyward.

I forcibly stopped myself from launching across the table to tackle hug him. I had no idea why he'd lied, or if there was really an old man somewhere claiming my work as his own, but I didn't care. Lucas had saved my day, and I absolutely adored him for it.

Camilla visibly relaxed. "Where is the story?" she echoed.

Lucas shrugged. "I usually like her posts, but forcing a business owner, or anyone, really, to explain themselves seems a bit obnoxious. People still have a right to privacy in this country, I believe."

"Someone should tell her," Camilla muttered.

He grinned. "Yes, but in kinder terms, of course."

Lucas excused himself to bring us the charcuterie and wine.

Camilla and Jeff caught me up on the wedding plans, and I played my new mantra on repeat in my head.

Camilla is not me. Jeff is not Robert. Shut up and do not spoil their day.

Lucas joined us again as promised, and the conversation flowed smoothly, without further mention of Virginia or the Invisible Baker.

Camilla peppered him with questions about working with me.

I nearly drowned in pride when Lucas responded with unbridled enthusiasm.

"Everything I show her, she learns immediately," he said. "It's just like this." He snapped his fingers. "And she remembers. I never have to say anything twice. Except which way the doors swing."

I snorted a goofy laugh, and he smiled.

Camilla and Jeff traded odd looks.

"That's a long story," I said. "And Lucas is being too kind. He took a huge chance by letting me work here. I was lucky to catch on so easily, and you know I love to bake."

"Understatement of the century," Camilla said, lifting her glass to her lips.

Jeff chuckled, and I realized Camilla had shared my secret with him too. Of course she had. I didn't like the way the circle of people who knew my secret kept expanding. Alicia and I had been the only two who knew for years, aside from those who placed orders. I'd told Camilla and Ilona after Mom passed. Now Jeannie and Jeff knew. If I wasn't careful, Virginia's Secrets would soon know too. Which is to say the hundreds of thousands of her followers as well.

The pressure to reveal my secret was growing by the minute, and I hated it. Why did everyone need to know it was me? Why couldn't an anonymous person own a business that helped others without raising questions? I'd created the company as a shield. For busy moms. For my best friend. For me. If Robert had known about the Invisible Baker before, he'd have made me shut it down. If he knew about it now, he might take it from me in the divorce. I didn't know how, but I knew he'd try, and he rarely failed when he wanted something. And if he succeeded in convincing the court we were bankrupt, I'd need the second income stream to survive.

Stress flooded my bloodstream and lightened my head. My shirt was too tight and the air too thick. I felt as if I was under attack, though I sat at a lovely table in the autumn sun.

"Did you ever consider culinary school?" Lucas asked.

It took a moment to realize he was talking to me. I shook my head. "I didn't think of baking as a job until very recently," I confessed. But I liked the possibility of formal training. There was so much more I wanted to learn. "I think, if I had life to do over," I said thoughtfully, "I'd start baking professionally much sooner, and I'd open a storefront." *Instead of working in secret and dodging bullets from Virginia Bonnie Black.*

I imagined this alternate life, and I fell in love with the vision that rolled out before me. "I wouldn't have gotten married," I said, too harshly. "And I never would have given up all my dreams."

The table went quiet, and I recognized my faux pas.

Camilla's expression tightened, her energy deflated.

Jeff squirmed across the table, probably itching to reach for her, but was stopped by three feet of wrought iron.

Lucas appeared equally aggrieved.

I spluttered and backpedaled, but the damage was already done. "But I'm thankful for every choice that brought me to this moment," I added. "Being Camilla's mother and friend is the greatest joy of my life." I reached for her hands, but she pulled them off the table.

She offered a sad smile. "I get it," she said. "It's fine."

"It's not. I misspoke," I said. "I only mean that marrying young is a huge risk, and we never know if the person we marry is going to be the same a year later, or ten. If they let us down, we're just stuck. I don't want you to be stuck. Either of you," I added, jerking my gaze from Camilla to Jeff, then back.

Her lips drew into an impossibly deeper frown. "Nice, Mom."

Lucas excused himself, and I wished for the ground to open and swallow me.

I stared apologetically into my beautiful daughter's eyes, but I couldn't bring myself to say sorry. I wasn't sorry. Camilla was too important to me to pretend that marriage would guarantee happiness. Or that she definitely wouldn't become her husband's second mother, cook, cleaning service, mental load carrier, and potential kicking post. Because I didn't know that, and neither did she.

Camilla finished her wine quickly and made an excuse to leave within minutes. She offered me a limp, one-armed hug, then walked away with Jeff's hand in hers.

I'd messed up. My heart broke with the knowledge that I'd hurt her. I'd let the stress of the day interfere with my better judgment, and I'd been harsh when I should've bitten my tongue.

It was ironic, really. The amount of time I spent fearing Camilla would wind up just like her mother, only to open my mouth and realize I was becoming mine.

Chapter Twenty-Two

I dragged myself downstairs the next morning, exhausted from a long night of kicking myself for upsetting Camilla. I'd gotten carried away at the restaurant and let the thoughts in my head pour freely from my mouth. The things I said were absolutely not okay. I'd wrestled with my poor behavior until the first rays of dawn climbed my windowsill.

I wanted so much better for Camilla than the life I'd chosen at her age. If she and Jeff were truly in love, wouldn't they still be in love a few years from now? Why couldn't they agree to enjoy their young lives without the emotional and financial weight of a marriage? Why did they have to get married right this minute? What was the rush?

I rubbed my forehead over a cup of steaming coffee.

Pictures of my mother, Sébastien, and me covered the refrigerator now. I'd hung all my favorites as a reminder that my childhood wasn't always awful, even if Mom's marriage to Dad was consistently shit and built on a lie. Nonetheless, I could see now that Mom had shielded me from his anger, as much as possible in an eleven-hundred-square-foot cottage, and from the aftermath of her emotions by keeping me at arm's length. She and I had grown apart as a result, but Dad had never once laid his hands on me.

The long hours I spent outside with neighborhood kids after dinner and on weekends took on a new perspective as well. Dad was home during those hours. She'd managed him while encouraging me to get fresh air and sun. I'd made memories, racing other kids down the sidewalk and later playing truth or dare in nearby parks. Mom had battled Dad alone, then nursed her wounds privately.

It was harder to understand why we hadn't grown closer following Dad's death, but maybe by then I'd pulled away too. I'd buried myself in raising my daughter and managing my own bully.

I hadn't been perfect at the job either. One of my worst memories was when Camilla was in middle school. She needed help with her math homework, but I was running late with dinner. I suggested she ask Robert, who was playing on his phone, unhappily waiting for his meal. I assumed the time would pass more quickly for him if he had something to do, and she'd get the help she needed. Two birds, one stone.

Twenty minutes later Camilla ran past me, crying and screaming that she'd never ask him for help again. I later learned that he'd done everything he could to make the interaction awful for her, by talking in circles, never giving straight answers, and making each step as convoluted as possible, until she'd given up in distress and defeat.

She'd approached him with hope and trust. And he'd destroyed both because he didn't want to be bothered. That was the lesson she learned that day. Asking Robert for anything resulted in a punishment.

For Camilla, at least, as long as she asked nothing of him, he was kind. So she'd found a way to live in his world under his terms. And I became a single, married parent.

I hated that I couldn't change any of it now.

But I could apologize to Camilla and promise us both that I would do better. I thanked my stars daily for the relationship I had with her, and I wondered if the bond we shared came from my parenting. She'd endured my unhealthy marriage with her father, but she also saw me protect, guard, and prioritize her above all else. I hoped that as an adult she'd understand why I didn't leave the marriage sooner. I wished I'd understood Mom's reasoning before she died.

I finished my coffee and opened the mail I'd left on the counter after my evening walk.

Bills, bills, bills. I was barely making ends meet on my paychecks. The Invisible Baker was going strong, but the price of ingredients to make all the fancy French pastries ate up the profits faster than I liked. And I hadn't anticipated the time it took to fill all the orders. Before, when I baked one or two nights a week, I'd found the process therapeutic and enjoyable. I'd only considered the outgoing costs and incoming profits. Now, I had a job that consumed the first half of my days. When I calculated the per-hour rate, I wanted to cry.

Not to mention, I lived in fear of my kitchen sink since it had last exploded. YouTube tutorials helped me stop the leak, and I cleaned the mess thoroughly, but I wasn't convinced my fix would last.

Worse, the appearance of Virginia Bonnie Black had me reconsidering my side hustle completely, or at least taking a little time off.

I'd lost a lot of sleep trying to figure out what to do about her, and I'd still come up empty. If I stopped baking the same day Virginia came snooping, that would surely raise suspicions. But if she beat the delivery to the restaurant some morning, she could badger the driver into revealing the pickup location—i.e. my house.

So, how could I safely get the orders to the restaurant? I couldn't exactly show up with the pastries myself.

Why was everything so fucking complicated?

I dressed for work with the speed of a sloth, then trudged downstairs, keys in hand. At least I made a reliable paycheck from Chez Margot, and had the most patient boss on earth. As long as I showed up and made delicious pastries, I'd have the job as long as I wanted.

A steady beeping reached my ears from beyond the front door. A backup beeper on a delivery truck, perhaps? But I hadn't ordered anything, and it wasn't trash day. Maybe the truck was at Ilona's or another neighbor's house.

I stepped onto the porch and stared at the nonsensical scene before me.

A tow truck sat in my driveway, a few feet from my SUV's bumper, and a man with a clipboard stood beside it. He glanced briefly in my direction, grimaced, then turned away.

Confusion clouded my thoughts as I bumbled down the steps and across the lawn.

A handful of neighbors lingered on street corners with dogs on leashes or pretended to tie their shoes on nearby porches.

I focused on the man affixing giant metal chains to my car. "Excuse me," I called. "I didn't order a tow truck." My SUV ran fine. It was only a few years old, and my closest confidant aside from Alicia. No one was taking her anywhere on my watch, except me.

The man didn't respond, and a moment later the back end of my BMW rose several inches off the ground.

"Hey! Stop! What are you doing?" I screamed.

He finally huffed a sigh and turned to stare me down. A patch on the chest of his work shirt indicated his name was Al. He looked over his shoulder and offered a bland expression, clearly illustrating his irritation.

I imagined whacking him with my purse, then checked to see if any of the neighbors had their phones out. Thankfully no one was filming.

"Sorry," I said, as the gears of the machine quieted. "I think you've made a mistake. This is my SUV, and that's my house." I pointed over my shoulder, but he didn't track the movement with his eyes.

Instead, he continued to stare, bored, at me.

"There's nothing wrong with the vehicle," I vowed. "And you can see it's parked perfectly legally. So, you can put it down now."

Al turned away, apparently having heard enough. "'Fraid not," he said. The low tenor of his voice was rough, audibly affected by a decade or two of smoking. "I've got orders from the bank to bring this one in. Just doing my job."

I frowned, thrown for a prolonged beat by his comment. "What bank?"

He ripped a page off his clipboard and handed it to me. "You can collect your stuff from impound."

"But—"

He gripped the bill of his ball cap and tugged it down in goodbye.

My eyes jerked to the paper. The mass of words jumbled in my head.

My car was three years old, and we always paid off our auto loans within thirty-six months. Why would the bank order a repossession? The thought barely registered before the answer presented itself.

The groan that left my chest was zombie horror worthy.

"Robert," I seethed.

Apparently he hadn't made a payment since I'd asked for a divorce. A quarter year from owning the vehicle, and he'd just stopped making payments to spite me.

Why would he do anything half decent when he was such a piece of gum on my shoe?

This was more punishment for my naivete. Robert insisted we put everything we had in his name only. The reason? I didn't have an income, so adding me to the loans would only raise his interest rate. Thank goodness the banker who worked on our mortgage convinced him to add my name on the deed, to make things easier in the event of Robert's untimely death.

I tried very hard not to think that his immediate death would be quite timely. He was my daughter's father, after all.

The sound of a closing truck door jarred me back to the moment, and I gave chase. "Wait!"

"Look, lady," he said through the open window. "Everything you need to know is on that paper. I just make the collections."

I glanced at the sheet in my hand. "But—"

Al drove away while I struggled for something more to say, my white SUV rolling nose-down behind him.

"Damn it!"

A dog barked, and I remembered the neighbors.

"Sorry!" I called, waving to the onlookers that had doubled in number since my first appearance on the lawn.

I hurried back inside to call the restaurant and let them know I would be late. Then I called Camilla to ask for her help. She didn't answer the call.

I swallowed my humiliation and typed out a heartfelt apology for my behavior yesterday. Then I sent a follow-up, apologizing for not sending the message sooner.

I sent up silent prayers for her forgiveness, then ordered an Uber. I texted Alicia on my ride to work. She'd get the message at lunchtime and text back. I suspected she was busy in her classroom by now.

Work was busy, but somehow time still moved like molasses. I burned my hands and fingers repeatedly, too distracted by potential life catastrophes to catch the important details right in front of me—like the open oven door or still-hot pans. I did my best not to draw attention but failed miserably. Everyone in the kitchen asked if I was feeling okay at least once, and I was confident Lucas would see straight through me if he even glanced my way.

Of all my many concerns, the potential damage I'd caused to my relationship with Camilla was most terrifying. My stomach revolted at the thought of losing her. I wanted to curl up and cry. To scream out my regret. Whatever else happened, I could not survive losing Camilla. Having her hold me at a distance because I'd used my words to hurt her, the way my mom had hurt me, was the absolute worst thing I could think of. And I feared that was exactly what was happening.

Thankfully, our boss wasn't himself today either. Lucas stayed out of the kitchen. He greeted a few guests, and roamed the dining area once or twice, but otherwise remained in his office. I should've checked on him. Instead, I—selfishly—counted his distraction as a blessing. I wasn't keen on lying to him about the Invisible Baker, and it bothered me immensely that I hadn't told him the truth from the beginning.

Why had I suggested Lucas check out the Invisible Baker online, instead of giving him my business card and a handshake?

Originally, I'd told myself I had good reason. I wanted to keep the business to myself a little longer. In many ways, the Invisible Baker had saved me. At first, by providing hope. Later by providing purpose. More recently by providing a much-needed income. I hated the thought of dragging something so precious into the light where it could be burned. What if exposing myself meant customers would be afraid to order from me? Wasn't the shared secrecy a big reason for their trust? Without anonymity, what was my company good for?

Unfortunately, lying to myself felt just as bad as lying to Lucas.

The ugly truth had risen to the surface as I tossed and turned during the night. Everything I'd told myself was true, sure, but there was more to it than that. I'd realized around three o'clock this morning that I'd lied to Lucas because I was afraid of being seen. Decades in a toxic marriage, combined with the example my mother set, had hurt me in ways I was just beginning to understand. I believed if I was small enough, if no one noticed me, if I didn't draw any attention, nothing could go wrong. No one could get mad at me. No one would rant, taunt, or yell.

I'd thought the name I chose for my business was clever, when in fact it was my trauma speaking. I just hadn't understood until now.

Being invisible never saved me from anyone's wrath. Dad found me anytime he wanted. Mom's harsh words always hit their target. And Robert—I pushed his name and face from my mind. I hoped he got everything he deserved in this life. And a little more.

I hunted for Lucas at the end of my shift, chin up and shoulders back, determined to tell him my secret. Maybe I couldn't get my SUV back or fix the mess I'd made with Camilla, but I could make one thing right today. Except my boss was nowhere to be found.

Eventually, I left the restaurant and stood on the sidewalk, debating whether to walk home or order a ride. The weather was nice, but my feet were sore. And my bank account was nearly empty. I turned toward my neighborhood and put one foot in front of the other. With a little luck, Virginia wouldn't pop out of the bushes, mic in hand.

A weary sigh rolled from my chest. My life couldn't look more different today than it had only a few months ago. How did so much change so quickly? Why did this life feel more real than the other ever had?

More impossible still? I'd somehow landed on Virginia's Secrets' radar, when nothing about my baking business was of regional importance. I helped overworked women accomplish one more thing without dying, committing murder, or being ridiculed by the at-home PTA vipers who refused to just let other women live.

Why did we do that to one another?

Women know exactly how difficult it is to be a woman, yet we judge and berate each other for making different choices. And we do that knowing the daily female struggle. Stay home with the kids or earn a paycheck? Breastfeed or bottle? Public school or private?

Choose whatever feels right for you and your family.

Then be told you're wrong.

Sacrifice pay, sleep, or both to show up for the school bake sale. Bring something to contribute, but that's still not enough, because you didn't personally make it? Who made these rules? And when will we take a collective, critical look at our unfair standard practices before blaming the patriarchy?

When will we finally stand together?

A funny, self-righteous thought to have when my personal opinion about when my daughter should get married might break us apart.

Chapter Twenty-Three

A sharp wolf whistle drew my eyes to the street, and I spun in the direction of the sound. Instead of giving a misogynistic creep a piece of my feminist mind, I found Alicia smiling wildly from her car window, and I grinned.

She pulled up to the curb, and I turned back to meet her.

"What are you doing?" I called over the sounds of afternoon traffic.

Alicia pointed behind her. "Bill is following in his truck. You're borrowing it until we get your ride situation sorted. He'll ride to school and practice with CJ until then."

Emotion gripped my chest as I searched the busy street for him. "No," I protested. "He can't do that."

The familiar old pickup pulled into the space behind her. A moment later, her middle son hopped out. Bill approached me in long, confident strides. "Hey, Auntie Soph."

I covered my mouth and batted back tears. I met him halfway and pulled him into a bone-crushing hug. "Thank you."

His deep teenage chuckle rumbled against me. "It's no big deal."

He was so incredibly wrong.

My tears fell, and I held him longer. Soon, his lanky arms returned the embrace.

It felt so unfathomably good to be loved. That Alicia's family would prioritize my needs was both humbling and immensely fulfilling. In keeping with my endless self-epiphanies these days, I understood this wasn't new. I'd just never let my walls down like this before. I'd carried everything on my shoulders when I didn't need to.

The same walls I thought protected me from pain had kept out the good things too.

I released Bill on a chuckle and wiped my tears. "Sorry."

His expression was surprisingly hard. "Uncle Robert is an asshole," he whispered.

Alicia slung an arm over his shoulder and tipped him closer. "Agreed," she said. "Uncle Robert is an absolute asshole."

Bill gave me his keys, looking as if he might just run home.

Alicia passed him her fob. "Why don't you take my car home? Sophie can give me a ride."

He looked at me, then at his mom's new Bronco, and lit up like those Friday night lights he loved so much. "Sweet!"

No one had to ask him twice.

He waved over his shoulder as he hurried away.

Alicia smiled at me. "He's a good kid."

"He's the best," I croaked. "Just like his mom."

We climbed into Bill's pickup, and I urged the engine to life.

Alicia and I drove to the impound lot to collect my personal items from the SUV. According to the paperwork provided by the tow truck driver, and the added fees charged by the lot, I couldn't afford to liberate my car anytime this side of the next millennium.

"Don't worry about it," Alicia said, consoling me as we returned to Bill's truck. "Even if you had the money, you probably couldn't spring the BMW anyway. It's still in Robert's name."

I buckled up with a groan. "Every time I forget he's out there trying to ruin my life, bam! He snatches something else away."

"At least this should be the end of it," she said. "The only other thing you have is your mom's house, and she left it to you fair and square."

I hoped she was right, but few things were fair when Robert was involved. The way our divorce was going, I worried he might force me to sell the house to pay off our alleged joint debts.

"I need to prove he's lying about the money," I said. That was the real problem. "How can I do that?"

"Any word from the forensic accountant?" she asked.

"No." I shook my head. "They won't be in touch for ninety days, unless they find something. Otherwise, I'll get a quarterly report updating me on what they've done so far."

"Well then, it's only a matter of time. Robert's smart, but he's arrogant, and that leads to mistakes. He knows you're smart, too, and savvy, which is why he's got you running in circles. He knows that if he doesn't keep you panicked and distracted, you'll figure out what he's doing with the money."

I barked a humorless laugh. "The view from where you're standing must be a lot different than mine, because it feels like he just wants revenge. I think he's trying to prove he still can control me, even though I'm no longer living under his thumb."

I felt her gaze on my cheek but kept my eyes on the road.

"I'm sorry you feel that way," she said softly. "I hate what he's done to you, but I am so fiercely proud of what you're doing every day for yourself."

I glanced in her direction.

We rode in silence for several blocks.

I wanted to tell her about my plans to confess to Lucas. He deserved to know I was the Invisible Baker. But letting go of old trauma was hard, and when I opened my mouth, I couldn't find the words.

"Something's broken in Robert," Alicia said. "He can't make real connections with anyone. He seems to think people are either out to get something from him, or they exist so he can get something from them."

My heart ached at her words. She saw Robert clearly, something I should've let myself do much sooner. I knew now that no amount of my unconditional love or servitude would've earned me his love, affection, or even incrementally better treatment. He saw me as a tool to use for his benefit. Camilla was that and more. She kept me tied to him while also promoting the image of family man to burnish his professional image. A double win. But we were both just cogs in the Serve Robert machine.

I pulled into Alicia's driveway. "There has to be a way to take him down."

She nodded and opened the passenger door. "If you think of it, let me know. Oh, hey, I almost forgot!" She turned wide eyes to me. "How'd you get the pastries to the restaurant this morning?"

We'd brainstormed possible solutions last night but repeatedly found a flaw in our ideas. I was at a loss until I came up with a plan over coffee with my neighbor.

My lips quirked into a grin. "Ilona."

Alicia cackled. "Bless that woman. I need details."

"She took the pastries in an Uber to that coffee shop overlooking the river. Then she took a Lyft to the park at the end of the block across from the restaurant and walked the rest of the way to cover her tracks. After she made the delivery, she stayed downtown until eleven, shopping, then met a friend for lunch who gave her a ride home."

"That's so genius," Alicia said.

"She said she felt like a secret agent, but I hate that it took up her entire morning. She can't do that every day."

Alicia considered that for a bit. "So what's the plan? Will you have to stop taking orders for a while?"

"Maybe," I said. "Or I could come clean." I held my breath the moment the words were out. What would Alicia think after helping me keep the secret for so long? Would it feel like betrayal? Would she think I was overreacting or getting ahead of myself?

"Let me know," she said. "Whatever you decide will be the right thing to do, and I've got your back regardless."

She stepped onto the driveway and turned to wave goodbye.

My heart had officially reached capacity. If my feelings on every topic got any bigger, I was sure it would bust. "Tell Bill I owe him big time for the truck," I called. "I'll figure out a new ride as soon as I can."

A burning hatred for Robert's financial lies led me to drive past my old house on the way home. Everything looked the same from the outside, but nothing was the same beyond the front door.

I parked the pickup on the corner and stared at the property. Hard to believe I'd lived there longer than I'd lived anywhere else. I'd left Mom's house at eighteen but spent twenty years in the giant mausoleum across the street from me now, the place where my soul had slowly died.

A truck with a local landscaping company logo drove past, and the driver lifted a hand in my direction.

It took a moment for me to realize he probably thought I was another contractor. Bill's truck didn't look like anything a resident would drive.

The idea hit with a bolt, and I cut the engine.

I climbed out and scurried to the front door. Robert was unlikely to be home in the middle of the afternoon, which meant I had time to look for evidence of his lies. If he was home, I'd use the opportunity to give him a piece of my mind.

No one answered when I rang the bell, so I decided to let myself in. My key no longer fit into the lock.

I gasped. "Asshole!"

I marched around the side of the house.

The utility door near the back patio swung easily inward. "Sucker."

I'd told Robert a thousand times that the lock wasn't properly aligned, and nine times out of ten it didn't latch. I never thought his refusal to listen would benefit me one day.

Lazy men for the win, I thought, slipping inside and pulling the door closed tightly behind me, and thanking my lucky stars Robert was too cheap to pay for a security system.

My heart pounded as I peeked out the front windows, on the lookout for lookie-loos and nosy Nellies.

Then I turned to examine my former home.

Why was it so unnecessarily big? It'd been years since I'd had a psychology class, but I was sure Sigmund Freud would have a field day with that question.

I moved through our home, astonished at how little it felt like mine, despite the fact I'd only been gone a few months. I didn't miss it. I was lucky to be free. Though Alicia would say that was all my doing. My perseverance. My courage. With a little more of that, maybe I'd finally shake Robert's continued grasp on me.

His office door stood open at the end of the first-floor hallway, and I crept inside. I felt like a criminal, though the place was legally half mine, and I'd been alone inside the room a thousand times. Stacks of file folders on his desk contained details related to his clients. A pile of unopened bills filled a tray.

Why pay the utilities when letting the accounts go to collections would further support his ruse?

I pulled a pen from the cup on his desktop and used it to open, then riffle through, his drawers. My prints were probably everywhere in the house, but I couldn't shake the feeling I shouldn't be there, and I didn't want to leave any evidence behind.

I pocketed the pen when I came up empty.

No smoking gun here.

But maybe he anticipated I'd come poking around. That was the only reason to change the locks, wasn't it?

I moved into the hallway and gave the office one last look to be sure nothing, save the pen in my pocket, was out of place. Then I closed my eyes and waited for a bolt of brilliance to strike.

"Oh!" My eyes opened on a burst of excitement.

I climbed the steps at double speed and raced to the primary suite.

Robert had a hidey-hole in the floorboards where he kept his porn. Too smart to leave a digital footprint, he still subscribed to magazines like his father before him. He had them sent to a PO box. Then he brought them home, and he had no idea I knew all about it. I'd found the loose board years ago while cleaning and had been devastated by what was inside.

❧

I stopped short when I crossed the threshold of my former bedroom. "Oh my god." Robert had rearranged the furniture and hung a massive white screen on the wall where my bookshelves once stood. A projector hung from the ceiling above our bed. "You turned our bedroom into a theater?" And watched movies from bed? How lazy was he?

I guffawed my way across the room, only to perform a triple take as I passed my walk-in closet. A belligerent gasp ripped from my throat as I caught sight of the weight bench. "No fucking way." I changed my trajectory and slapped my palm against the light switch, then glared as the complete home gym appeared before me. "Unbelievable."

Robert had made our primary suite into a private man quarters. A bedroom with a theater, gym, bathroom, and porn.

I shut off the light and forced myself away. If I stewed instead of returning to my mission, I'd burn the whole place down.

Across the room, I knelt beside the window and peeled back the corner of our area rug. I tested the floor by knocking until I found the loose board and checked underneath.

I rolled my eyes at the young, airbrushed body on this month's cover. I said a silent prayer for her health, and the well-being of every woman who bought into this idea of perfection. And I wished for karmic justice on the men who still objectified us.

I removed the magazines and placed them in careful stacks along the wall. For a moment, I feared I'd wasted my time. Then the small white corner of a document came into view. And just like that, hidden beneath Robert's copies of *Hustler*, I hit the jackpot.

Elation soared as I sifted through the paperwork, growing infinitely happier by the second. "Holy shit!"

Banking statements in his name revealed multiple six-figure balances. Stacks of paper bonds, stock dividend records, and a folder full of papers with the name of an LLC I didn't recognize completed the booty. Apparently I wasn't the only one with a business on the side. Somehow I suspected Robert's company made far more money than the Invisible Baker. I spread the documents on the floor and used my phone to take pictures of each.

When I began repacking the secret compartment, the title to a boat slipped free.

I blinked when the owner's name registered. "How long have I owned a boat?"

A low, familiar rumble rose from beneath me, and I stilled to pinpoint the noise.

The garage door.

Robert was home!

Chapter Twenty-Four

"Shit!" I returned everything except the boat title to the hole and stacked the magazines on top. I smoothed the rug over the replaced floorboard and tucked the title into my purse. Then I made a run for the bedroom door.

Robert's voice rose up the staircase, followed by a booming laugh. "That's the plan," he said. "Move it all to Bitcoin." His voice sounded airy and fake. I recognized it instantly as his telephone voice.

I froze, teeth gritted and panic rising. At least he was on the phone, not coming home with a client, or worse, another woman. Maybe he would change clothes and leave. Then I remembered he had no reason to leave—our suite had everything he needed to stay forever.

He whistled his way along the hall outside our bedroom.

Hide and wait him out? Or come clean?

I turned the light off and ran into the bathroom. If he saw me, he'd be livid. He'd probably accuse me of something terrible to keep the spotlight off himself. Fear tightened my throat and rib cage.

A swath of light slid beneath the bathroom door. He'd turned on the bedroom light. Soon Robert's whistles changed to humming. He shuffled across the plush carpet and the bathroom doorknob turned.

I imagined throwing myself through the large window onto the ground below.

His phone rang. The door didn't open.

"Hey, what's up? I just got home," he said.

Two calls in five minutes? Whistling. Humming. Laughter. How was his life this much fun, when mine was on the brink of explosion?

"No, no, no," he said. "I'm a married man." His false laughter raked fire down my spine.

I caught sight of my grimace in the bathroom mirror and rearranged my features. It didn't matter what Robert did, but I hated that he was still married. *To me.*

"Of course," he continued. "I'm going to catch a quick shower before I head out, but I'll be there. Oh, I'm sure," he said. "I'll catch you on the green."

My hands balled into fists. I needed a plan. Now.

"All right. Be there soon," he said. His voice grew louder as he moved toward the bathroom door. I had nowhere to hide.

I was busted, and I needed a plan before he had me arrested for trespassing, or some other complete bullshit. Who knew what he'd make up, given a golden opportunity like this one?

My mind rewound his phone conversation, and the worst plan imaginable took form.

Like it or not, Robert was still a married man.

I stripped out of my work clothes and used them to cover my handbag, then hopped onto the countertop in my bra and panties. I tried my best to imagine I was actually wearing a bikini, and was on a beach—or literally anywhere other than my former bathroom.

I struck a pose as he entered, aligning the length of my body with the vanity's cold marble edge and propping my head on one palm. I hated the massive ten-foot countertop he'd insisted the builder install. I'd never expected it would come in handy.

Robert flipped on the light and stopped short at the sight of me.

I sucked in a breath, forcing air into my lungs. "Hello, Robert," I said, faux breathlessly. I let my eyelids droop into what I hoped was a come-hither stare. "I was thinking of you," I said, counting on his self-obsession to make the lie easily acceptable. "It's lonely at Mom's house, and seeing you in court, so confident and self-assured, I can't get you off my mind."

He stared at my breasts as I spoke, then ran his gaze farther along my body. "Sophie."

"I thought if I came over, maybe we could talk." I made a wide swipe across my lips with my tongue and caught some fuzz, probably from the inside of my work shirt.

Robert crossed the threshold in my direction, pupils dilated. "You shouldn't be here."

I swung my legs over the counter's edge and sat tall. "I know, and I'm so sorry," I blurted. I didn't think my acting skills were good enough to cover the fact I hated him. Even wearing only a bra and panties.

He loosened his tie. "This is . . . naughty."

"Oh." I grimaced. Once again I'd underestimated his ego. The thrill of tricking him was quickly snuffed by the reality of my predicament. I couldn't keep up the facade of wanting him. Even if I forced the words through gritted teeth, I wouldn't be able to stop myself from vomiting if he touched me.

"Did you come to apologize?"

"Uhm." I was out of words and in a new predicament now.

His gaze flickered to mine, then back to my body. "Are you here to beg forgiveness?" he asked. "Or did you come for a punishment?"

I bit the insides of my cheeks to avoid laughing at his ridiculousness. Was he truly so daft? Or was this what looking at those magazines had done to him? Too many years spent imagining those women posed just for him.

Gross.

Robert released his tie with the whip of one arm. "Fuck, Soph. Where was this version of you before?"

If I lifted either foot quickly enough, I could kick him in the crotch before he knew what happened. I leaned back as he stepped closer, craning for another look at the bag and boat title hidden beneath my clothes.

His next step brought him against my knees, thoroughly eliminating my view of anything else.

"We should talk first," I said, attempting to buy some time. "Or maybe you want to take a shower while I wait in the bedroom?"

He dug meaty fingers into my ass and hauled me to the edge of the counter with a dark chuckle.

I squealed at the sudden movement, and he laughed.

"That's my girl," he cooed. "Always so on edge. But I like this new you. Needy and brave."

I made a disgusted, throaty noise. "I am not needy."

He pulled back, scanning me with a smirk. "No?"

"No. And this isn't a new me. It's *me* me." I scooted back on the counter, putting a few inches of space between us before he tried to touch me again.

Something familiar passed in his eyes at my disagreement and rejection. "You changed your hair," he said. "It looks incredible. I've been telling you to cover your grays for years. I'm glad you finally listened."

My mouth opened in outrage, but he pressed ahead.

"And from the looks of those lacy white panties, you got a new look down below too. Who knew a little time away could make you so hot?"

I pressed my knees together, hating that he could tell I'd gotten a Brazilian wax. That wasn't for him to know. But thanks to laundry day and my smallest, least favorite panties, it was easily noticeable.

Fueled by his own evil, he added, "And you lost a little weight. You're making improvements all around."

I burst into loud, fake tears, and he jumped back.

"What the hell?"

"You think I'm fat," I said. "You thought I needed to lose weight." I pushed him out of my way and launched off the counter, then crouched to gather my things. "Wah!" I cried. "You hate me! You don't want me! I'm ugly and gross!"

"I do want you!" he hollered. "Where are you going?"

I darted down the steps at full speed, flashing thong-exposed butt cheeks past windows on my way to the first floor. "Wah!"

"Sophie! For crying out loud! What is wrong with you? Crazy nutjob!"

I raced into the garage and yanked my shirt and pants on, covering myself and running to Bill's truck. I dove behind the wheel and raced home as fast as my conscience would let me.

Everything I needed to prove Robert was a big fat liar rode shotgun at my side.

I alternated between desperate relief and nausea as I navigated the traffic. How had I ever found Robert attractive or interesting? Why did I think his cruelty was acceptable?

I shuddered at the memories, then grew angry.

Robert had quietly bullied me all our married life, and now that I'd grown strong enough to leave, he'd found new ways to mistreat me. Namely by hiding money. At least now I knew where. Stocks, bonds, and a company he'd never mentioned. All more attempts to prove I was inconsequential. That everything we had belonged to him.

My grip tightened on the steering wheel. It was too late in the day to reach my attorney. First thing tomorrow I'd call and tell her everything. Then I'd send the photos. And what had he said about Bitcoin, before walking into the bedroom?

I didn't know anything about digital currency, but I would add it to my nightly research. Hopefully I'd have better luck with that than I had looking for my biological father in France. I certainly couldn't do worse.

I glanced at my purse, puzzling over the boat title in my name. I only vaguely recalled Robert's interest in buying a boat. I had no recollection of signing paperwork for one, but those things were easy enough to do online these days, I supposed. When we were younger, Robert talked about buying assets in my name to increase my credit score. Was the boat meant as a gift before I'd asked for a divorce?

Robert was so assured about our finances that I never got involved. As a result, I'd never realized how little I knew about any of it until now.

Thankfully, tomorrow was my day off, and the timing couldn't be better. *First stop,* I thought, *is the DMV, or wherever people get titles to boats verified.* If the title was legit, then Robert had apparently paid thirty-four thousand dollars for it, likely as a way of draining funds from one of our bank accounts before the court started monitoring them. Lucky for me, selling the boat would be a great way to get that money back.

My mood improved instantly. I'd catch up on bills, invest in my growing business, and help Camilla with her wedding plans. *Right after I buy a reliable used car and return Bill's truck.*

I just had to find the boat and place the ad to sell it. I hoped that Robert moored the vessel at a marina rather than hiding it a storage unit somewhere. I could call around after I talked to the DMV.

My nerves relaxed as my plan came together and I put miles between Robert and myself. I fished my phone from my bag and tapped the Do Not Disturb feature in case he tried calling. I needed a little more time to think and unwind. I'd send the photos I'd taken to my forensic accountant the minute I got home. I had no idea if they'd found anything yet, but tonight's discovery should help pick up the pace.

Thinking of the evidence of various funds in his hidey-hole ignited my anger once more, and I pounded my palms against the steering wheel at a red light. "Fucking Robert!" I screamed, enjoying the rush that came with blowing off some steam.

Beside me, a white-haired woman in the passenger seat of a Volkswagen clutched her pearls and gaped.

I opened my mouth to apologize, but laughter poured out instead.

I was driving a beat-up old pickup truck and screaming profanity. I'd broken into my old house and snooped through my husband's things. Then I'd stripped and pretended I stopped by for sex!

Who am I?

The light changed, and I motored into my neighborhood, mind brimming with more thoughts than I could manage. I wished it was morning so I could get started finding and selling the boat, contacting my attorney and the accountant. I'd never be able to sleep tonight. Not now.

Then I recalled the Invisible Baker.

I pulled into my drive and hung my head a moment. I snuffed the engine and reached for my phone to check for new orders. A berry cheesecake. A tiramisu. A party tray of mini vanilla cupcakes and mini salted caramel macarons. And a request for three dozen chocolate chip cookies using the recipe on the bag of chocolate with no added care, to appear authentic.

That last order was definitely from a tired, possibly bullied mom. I made a mental note to apply a heavy discount.

I gave the new orders another scan, thankful I wouldn't be up all night baking. Then I noticed something I'd missed at first glance. Chez Margot hadn't placed an order.

Had Lucas decided it was better to avoid Virginia's attention by not ordering? I couldn't blame him. I felt exactly the same way. Was Virginia the reason he'd been so distracted at work today?

I climbed out and rushed across the lawn toward my door. The sooner I finished baking, the sooner I could toss and turn until dawn.

The crunch of tires on the driveway behind me tightened every muscle in my body. I sent up seventy rapid-fire prayers that Robert hadn't followed me home to demand a real explanation for my appearance tonight. Or worse, to confront me about the missing boat title.

I forced myself to peek over one shoulder as I turned my key in the lock. I still had time to go inside and shut him out, if necessary. I only had to cross the threshold to be safe.

The broad male figure moving in my direction sent my spiraling thoughts into a standstill. All the frazzled ends inside of me fixed onto a single word.

“Lucas?”

Chapter Twenty-Five

I blinked to clear my head and focus my eyes. I wasn't hallucinating. My boss, and barely suppressed man crush, was at my house.

This entire day wasn't real. It couldn't be.

muI would wake up and tell Alicia about the completely bananas dream I'd had.

On the lawn before me, Lucas stepped forward, running a hand through his mussed hair, and my thoughts quieted again. "Hey, I know I shouldn't just show up on your doorstep, but—" He frowned. "Did you just pinch yourself?"

"Nope." I turned away, focusing on unlocking the door. "It's nice to see you. Come on in." I jumped inside and dropped my purse behind the door. Then I turned to face him with what was probably a maniacal smile.

He dragged his gaze over me as he climbed the porch steps. "Are you okay?"

"Good as a goose." I nodded, determinedly not reacting to the stupidest thing I'd ever said. "How about you?" I scanned the street over his shoulder, wondering if any of the onlookers from this morning were peeking through their windows now.

"Great as a snake," he answered, with a furrowed brow. "You seem a little shaken."

"Not at all," I promised. "I just need a minute to—" I waved one arm in a circle, then pointed at my couch. "You know what? Have a seat. Please. Make yourself at home. I'll get us something to drink. Do you want coffee?"

"I don't think you should have any more coffee," he said.

I ran for the kitchen. I needed time to collect my thoughts and lower my heart rate, but of course, that was impossible. This was the absolute worst time for Lucas to show up on my doorstep.

Raisin passed me on my way through the dining room, then sat in front of his bowls.

I pressed a palm to my chest. I was in the middle of a breakdown. Did the cat not care? If I had a heart attack, who would feed him?

I pulled a bottle of water from my fridge and chugged it.

"I really don't need anything," Lucas called. "I won't stay long."

Slowly, my pulse fell back in the direction of normal, and I set the water aside.

Raisin bit my leg.

"Ow!" I bent to pet his head and redirect his frustration but something else grabbed my attention.

All around me, stacks of pink bakery boxes covered every flat surface. "Shit!"

"Sophie?" Lucas called. "Are you sure this isn't a bad time? I can come back. Or we can talk tomorrow. I didn't mean to blindside you like this. I had good news and I wanted to share it."

I flung myself in the direction of the nearest boxes and heaved them into my arms. I ferried the stacks to the open pantry and tossed them onto the floor inside. "Almost done!" I spun back for another stack, then another, until the boxes toppled and collided over one another in an ugly heap.

"Really," Lucas said, his voice scarily closer. "No coffee for me."

I yanked the pantry door shut, and the whiteboard on my refrigerator came into view. A list of upcoming orders for the Invisible Baker written in pink marker filled the space. "Ugh!" I whipped the magnetic board off and turned it face down on top of the fridge. Then I smacked my laptop shut, hiding the customized Invisible Baker wallpaper. Good grief!

Lucas was in the doorway when I turned to see if the coast was clear. His gaze drifted around the room, to the laptop, then me. "Do you know your shirt is inside out?"

My lips pressed tight, and I nodded remorsefully. "I had a stain and didn't want anyone to see it."

His expression turned bland. "Whose truck are you driving?"

"Alicia's son's."

"Why?"

My last nerve screamed audibly before dying, and I pulled two glasses from the drying rack. "I'm having a glass of wine. Would you like a glass of wine?"

He didn't respond, so I poured two glasses of merlot. He accepted when I passed one to him.

"Are those your parents?" he asked, motioning to the photos taped to the refrigerator, a few inches below where my whiteboard had recently hung.

"Mm-hmm," I said, willing my racing heart to settle again. "They met in France when my mom was on a college trip. She never said where, specifically, but she gave me a few photos. Well, she gave me one, and I found a few others. His name is Bastien Allard."

Lucas's brows rose. "He didn't raise you?"

I shook my head. "He didn't know about me."

"A shame," he said, stepping close and looking more carefully at the image. "They seem happy."

His words were a kick to the heart, because he was right. They appeared young and in love.

"I've tried finding him, but I haven't had any luck," I said. That truth suddenly felt like one more failure in an epic pile of failures. "Let's sit in the living room."

I led him back in the direction he'd come. I was deeply grateful he hadn't seen the place a few months ago. Tonight, I realized I'd achieved a level of boho chic I didn't know I loved until all the details were in place.

We took seats on opposite ends of the couch, a foot and a half of space between us. Then I told him about my SUV's recent, public repossession thanks to Robert.

"Ah," he said. "That helps explain your strong feelings against marriage."

I toed off my shoes and pulled my feet onto the cushion beneath me. I'd briefly forgotten he'd witnessed my comments to Camilla on the subject at lunch the day before. I took a long, slow pull on my wine and savored the robust flavors of cedar and clove. "She's not speaking to me because of that outburst. We've never been in a fight, and I don't know how to manage this," I admitted.

Lucas stole a few looks at me before setting his glass aside without taking a sip. He bent forward, resting both elbows on his thighs. "You've seemed on edge lately. I guess you have more on your shoulders than I realized."

I nodded and sipped again.

"You could've told me," he said. "We're friends, aren't we?"

I took another drink and let my head fall back against the couch. This was my chance to tell him about my secret small business and the big fat omission of that information on the day he hired me. Now that the opportunity arrived, however, I still wasn't ready.

"How about you?" I asked. "I barely saw you at work. You were in your office all day, but when I went to see you, you were gone. Is everything okay?"

He stared at me, jaw clenching and releasing. "I was looking into something."

I took another sip as silence stretched between us. He didn't elaborate.

The wine warmed my stomach and eased my tension.

I turned my focus to the handsome man seated one cushion away. It seemed so strange to see him there, in my space, at my home. He was a work person. Those people only existed when I went to the restaurant. Yet here he was.

Why was he here?

Did he already tell me?

Lucas cleared his throat. "I'm sorry about your ex-husband," he said. "It's too bad he's making things more difficult for you than they already are."

"That's Robert," I said. "Always reminding me I made the right decision." I set my empty glass on the coffee table, and Lucas passed me his.

"I have a long drive," he said. "You look like you need this more than I do."

I accepted and raised the glass slightly in cheers. "I'm guessing you didn't come here to talk about my problems."

"No." He chuckled and clasped his hands where they hung loosely between his knees. "But we can. If you want."

I considered him a long moment. I wanted to tell him everything, and I wanted him to share his life and concerns with me as well. Would he, if I asked? "What were you looking into?"

His brows rose. Then his expression pinched. He seemed to debate something before finally speaking again. "Virginia Bonnie Black," he said.

I froze. "And?"

"I don't understand her interest in the Invisible Baker," he said. "So I looked that up too."

Is that why he was here? *He found out I lied, and he came to fire me, quietly,* I thought. A kindness, so I could preserve my dignity. Maybe he even planned to keep my secret, but he couldn't trust me anymore, so he had to let me go. "And?" I asked again.

Lucas watched me closely, still debating something, it seemed. "I think it's a good story, but it's not hers to tell," he said.

I sucked in a short, shaky breath. "You think it's the older man's place to tell," I said. "The one you told her about?"

He rubbed long fingers against his right eye, then dropped his hand back to his lap. "I guess," he said. "I stopped by tonight because I have a business opportunity."

I wanted to talk more about the Invisible Baker. Perhaps long enough for me to collect my nerve and confess, but a business opportunity with Lucas wasn't something I could easily ignore. "Tell me more."

Lucas picked invisible lint from his pant leg, looking more nervous than I'd ever seen him. "I've secured the loan I need to expand the menu and change my business's evening model. A new position comes with that change."

I sat up straighter and let his words sink in. "You got the loan."

He nodded, and the edges of his mouth slanted upward. "Yeah."

A burst of excitement rocketed through me, and I leaned forward, careful not to spill my wine as I set it on the coffee table. "That's amazing! Congratulations!" I scooted over and my arms went around his shoulders in an instant embrace. This was the kind of news I needed. Good things still happened to kind people. "You deserve this," I said, giving one final squeeze before setting him free.

No wonder he'd been so distracted today. His dream was coming true.

Lucas's expression was cautious but slightly amused.

"Too much?" I asked, sitting back on my side of the sofa. "I've recently learned that I'm a hugger," I said, smile growing. "I hug everyone these days, and I've had a rough one, so I think I needed this news as much as you."

He smiled back, and we stared at one another for several long moments.

The air grew warm. This thing between us felt cozy and nice. Not the angsty nervousness of romance books, but the comfortable connection of two people sharing a wavelength. I relaxed more fully as

I basked in the moment. And I allowed myself the time to examine his handsome face.

Lucas and I didn't spend as much time together at work these days. I'd found my comfort zone in the kitchen, and he'd been busy making his dreams come true. But when we stole a few minutes to chat, I always left with a smile. His kindness and patience meant everything to me. I had no doubt I'd grown as a baker under his tutelage. I'd become confident and made a dozen new friends with the kitchen staff. He had no idea how much he'd brought to my new life.

"I'm glad I could help," he said. "I'm elated, and I can't wait to get started on the changes." His lips parted, and I suspected he wanted to say more, but he looked quickly away.

"What?" I asked.

"I was thinking you remind me of Margot."

I grinned. Her photo sat atop the welcome desk. I knew for a fact we looked nothing alike.

"Not in appearance," he clarified, as if reading my mind. "In spirit, maybe. You have compassion and enthusiasm. It's contagious. And appreciated. People need more joy in their lives."

"First of all, I am honored to be compared to Margot," I said. "Your love and devotion to her is proof she was an incredible soul. Secondly, if you had any idea how much energy I've spent trying to be small and go unnoticed, you'd understand how great it feels to be appreciated and not ridiculed for my excitement. So, thank you."

Lucas met my eye with a hard stare. "Am I awful for saying I kind of hate that guy?"

"That would be the general consensus," I said. "You're in good company."

I swiveled on the cushion to face him. For a moment I considered telling him about what I'd found under the floorboard tonight, but he'd come here for a reason, and that wasn't it.

I supposed the subject of a failed marriage might be hard for him when he'd do anything to have his wife back. I'd never had a loving relationship like his with Margot, so it was impossible to relate. From his position, though, I imagined he thought the split was heartbreaking for me. "This is for the best," I said. "Robert and I haven't been married in any sense of the word for years, and we were never partners, so the loss is mainly just frustrating. I'm not even sure we were ever really friends. This divorce is long overdue. I don't want you to feel bad for me."

"Okay," he said. "I just want you to be happy."

"Careful, or I'll hug you again."

Lucas laughed.

"Enough about me," I said. "You were telling me about the restaurant."

He angled toward me, matching my posture. "I need a professional plater to elevate the dining experience for patrons. I know you're a baker, and an excellent one, but I also know you learn quickly, and you light up when a new skill clicks for you. You thrive in the restaurant's kitchen, and you're creative."

I leaned forward as he spoke, drawn in by his delight.

"I think," he continued, "that if you're open to trying something new—and that's up to you, of course, there's no pressure . . ." He ran his palms over the tops of his thighs and took a deep breath. "You could be magnificent at plating food, and if you're interested in learning those skills, I would love it if you'd fulfill that role for my restaurant."

I processed his request slowly, knocked utterly off-balance for the tenth time in a single day. "Tell me more," I said, unwilling to squash his excitement. He deserved to be heard, even if my answer was going to be no. I baked pastries. I didn't plate food, whatever that meant, and I didn't have time to learn a new skill set. Nor did I have the desire.

Lucas bounced his palms against his knees. "Plating food is an art, and those skilled in the craft are in high demand. The new position at Chez Margot comes with a significant pay increase from pastry chef. Training is paid for and includes meals and travel. You'd receive your usual salary for the days we have classes, and I'll be with you the whole time, because I'm taking a few sessions in preparation for the evening changes as well."

"You?" I asked. Was he inviting me on a business trip? With him?

"I've run the café successfully as it is for many years, but I've never managed a place like the one in my visions. I need to be prepared for new challenges."

"I see." I plucked a stray fiber from the cushion's seam. "Are the classes given through the local community college? Or are they at the country club?" I teased.

His cheeks reddened, and for a moment, I wondered if we really were headed to a country club. "The classes will require travel and several days off work."

Traveling alone with Lucas? That could be interesting. "Who will manage the restaurant and make the desserts?"

"John will shift to manager mode. He has previous experience in the role, and he understands the ins and outs of everything I do. I'll cut the dessert offerings to a single option while we're away and train the staff to make it, so anyone can fulfill the order, temporarily."

My eyes narrowed. "How long are the classes?"

"Three weeks."

My jaw dropped.

He raised both palms to protest. "Don't answer yet. It's a big decision. Lots of moving parts, and plenty for you to sleep on. Not to mention the timing is terrible. Your daughter is planning a wedding. You're in the middle of a divorce. It's especially difficult for you to get away right now." He pursed his lips. "And the school is in France."

My eyes bulged, and I had to lean back against the couch to avoid rolling off it. "France?" I repeated. "Like the country across the sea? How much will that cost?"

"It was included in my business loan proposal," he said. "If I want to compete with other restaurants at the caliber I'm reaching for, I have to do things right. That means training from the best in the business.

And that means a trip home." His expression softened on the final word. "It's beautiful this time of year. You'd love it, I'm sure."

"No doubt."

Lucas dusted his palms, then stood abruptly. "I'm going to go now. I apologize again for stopping by unannounced and dropping all of this in your lap like a bomb. I wanted you to have as much time as possible to consider the offer." He lifted a hand in goodbye, then turned for the door.

I hustled after him, tangling my legs beneath me, then fumbling for my footing as I hurried to the porch.

He was in the yard before I reached the top step.

"Lucas! Wait!"

He stilled for a prolonged beat before turning to look up at me in the failing evening light.

"Where in France?" I asked.

"Oh." Something in the small word sounded like disappointment, and I wondered briefly what that might mean. "Nice."

Nice. In the French Riviera, the region where my mom met Sébastien Allard.

"When?"

"Right after your next court date," he said. "You requested time off. It's on the calendar." He waved and climbed back into his car.

I watched him drive away, in awe of how my night had turned itself around so completely.

I was going to France!

Chapter Twenty-Six

I woke to a series of pings and beeps from my phone. I squinted at the nearby clock, hating the offending daylight. I hadn't crawled into bed until after midnight. Then I'd struggled to settle my mind. This was my day off, my day to sleep in.

My phone dinged again, pulling my eyes open. When did I shut them? And what was that sound?

"Stop," I whined, taking a swipe at the persistent device. "What are you even trying to tell me?" These weren't my usual alerts or an alarm. I pulled the phone off my nightstand and cursed whichever app had lost its mind.

A stack of notifications filled my lock screen. I recognized the seven new-order icons. That was a lot, especially overnight. Probably a local group or school with a bake sale or fundraiser. The other notifications were from people tagging the Invisible Baker's account on social media. Those must've been the unfamiliar sounds.

All remnants of fatigue vanished as my brain kicked into gear.

No one ever tagged my business. My customers didn't talk about where they got their goods. That was the whole point. First rule of fight club, and all that. So what the heck was happening?

The sense of doom that came next sat me upright. I hoped I hadn't received a complaint. I baked so often at night, exhausted from my long days. What if I'd ruined something and never knew it? What if I mistook salt for sugar, or swapped baking soda for baking powder? The finished products looked beautiful and smelled delicious, but what if something was fundamentally wrong, and I'd delivered it to a customer?

I tapped the screen and scrolled in search of the problem, and it was worse than I'd imagined.

All the tags on my account stemmed from a video posted by Virginia's Secrets.

"Dear lord in the morning," I whispered. I pressed one palm to my heart and tapped Play with the other. Then I braced for whatever came next.

Virginia stood in a kitchen, flour on one cheek, and her hair in a snit. A child cried in the background, and everything visible behind her was in disarray. "Ever feel as if you can't possibly do it all?" she asked the camera. "Then one of your kids gets off the bus with a note saying they need thirty-six gluten-free cupcakes by eight a.m.?" With a defeated sigh, she turned to lift the toddler from their seat. "The last time this happened, you bought the treats on your way to school, causing you both to be late. Then you caught hell from your boss, and your kid came home with a note from another mom implying your effort wasn't good enough? Because the parents who really care about their kids make their baked goods at home. Those parents don't buy preservative-laden sweets from a store. Like you." She made a disgusted face. Then a child, clearly dressed for soccer practice, ran in holding their shoes and asking for help, because they were late.

I lowered the hand from my chest. I didn't hate where this was going. I'd anticipated a witch hunt, but she'd accurately captured the reason I created the business in the first place. Moms could be judgmental and sometimes downright mean to one another. And for what? Weren't we all just doing the best we could? Who were these women that had enough time on their hands to care what other moms did or didn't do? I barely knew what *I* was doing when Camilla was young, and I'd stayed home with only one child! The whole thing burned my biscuits every time I thought about it.

The image of Virginia and her chaotic household blurred. "Did you also know that if you live within delivery distance of one small town, you don't have to deal with that nonsense anymore?" Virginia asked.

My lips pinched. "Here we go."

The next scene revealed Virginia in a cute sweater set and capris. Her hair and makeup were done, the kids were playing nicely, and her home was clean. She lifted a palm, and my logo appeared above it. "Just hire the Invisible Baker, and let them handle the baking for you. No questions asked, all requests accepted, and they'll never say a word to anyone. It says so right there on the home page of the company's website."

Links to my site and social media accounts appeared along the bottom of the screen.

My heart fluttered, and a thrill raised goose bumps on my arms. She didn't bash me or demand my identity be revealed.

"If you don't need enough pastries for a classroom, you can still enjoy the delicious treats at one popular riverfront restaurant. Chez Margot has taken the private baking company out of the shadows and put it in a display case. I'm not sure how this helps busy moms, but it definitely helps locals and commuters with a craving for something sweet. I'm guessing the orders help the company, too, and whoever is behind the veil deserves a raise. Because these macarons?" She lifted a treat into view and made a show of enjoying a bite. "Worth every penny."

I zoned out as she segued into her "like, follow, and share for more" requests, and I watched the numbers on all those icons increase in real time, along with a growing amount of comments.

In the hours since the video was posted, it'd been shared by hundreds of viewers and liked nearly two thousand times.

I set my phone aside to process what this meant.

When Virginia didn't return to the restaurant, I'd assumed she changed her mind about pursuing the story. But someone had clearly made the trip to Chez Margot for that macaron. I didn't have any recent orders for those outside the restaurant.

Thankfully, Lucas gave her the story about an older man being the company's owner, I thought. Maybe that was enough to dissuade any further interest. My stomach sank a little at the thought. The state of Virginia didn't allow anonymously owned LLCs, and I'd registered the business in my name. My contact information was directly connected to the company, and anyone with enough motivation to check the state's business page would easily find me.

I could only hope it didn't come to that.

At least my customer records would be safe, even if I was outed. Every customer except Chez Margot. I couldn't deny that one, but Lucas wasn't trying to hide the affiliation. He'd put a sign with the company's name in the bakery display. I groaned. No wonder he hadn't placed another order after Virginia came snooping. He probably didn't want the drama and nonsense that came with an online personality's interest.

If only I'd done the same. Maybe if I'd temporarily closed the online shop, she would've left things alone.

I dragged myself out of bed with an ugly snort and headed downstairs for coffee. Who was I kidding? Closing up the day she came hunting would've surely fueled her fire.

Raisin raced past me on the stairs, and I grabbed the handrail for balance.

"Lunatic!" I called. "If I break my neck, who will feed you?"

At least he didn't stop to bite me. I had to count my blessings where I could find them.

A free trip to France, for example.

I stuffed the thought into a mental lockbox and wrapped the container in chains. I wanted to go, but the reveal of my lie could result in a withdrawal of his offer. I couldn't think about that before I had at least one cup of coffee.

My phone dinged as I padded across the first floor toward the kitchen. Another order for the Invisible Baker.

I'd have to work all day to fill the orders, and I'd have to turn away additional orders to catch up. The influx was a result of Virginia's video, and if her views and responses kept growing, my orders might as well.

Until I learned to duplicate myself, or stop time while I worked, I had no hope of keeping up with demand. *Champagne problems,* I thought. But the issue remained nonetheless.

I fed Raisin, then made a cup of coffee and carried it onto the patio.

Dew clung to the blades of grass, and a chill lingered in the air. My second season in this house, and a new era in my life. Nature's fanfare felt poetic. A rainbow of autumn leaves. Pumpkins and mums on doorsteps. Little ghosts and goblins soon flooding the streets on Halloween night.

I couldn't wait. I craved every change, big and small. New traditions. New memories. I wanted it all. But only if I could share the moments with my daughter.

I sent my eleventh text since our botched lunch, begging for her to talk to me. Then I sent up the usual prayer to go with it. *Please let me fix this. Let me heal us.*

I needed a plan to deal with the obstacles in my path. My phone buzzed, and I smiled. Instead of an answer to prayer, I received another order. I guessed I'd start there.

If I wanted to help as many customers as possible, I had to streamline. A number of favorite seasonal desserts came to mind. Mini pumpkin pies, baked apple fritters, and cinnamon-spiced coffee cakes, for starters. Limiting available options would allow me to bake in bulk, satisfying more than one request at a time. Buying only ingredients for the set options would save me time and money as well.

I opened the notes app on my phone and started a list. An incoming call from Cami interrupted the process.

I looked at the ceiling, hoping my mom could see this, and that she'd help me do better with my daughter than she had with me. "Cami," I answered. "I'm so sorry for the things I said. I promise I'll do better."

"I know," she said. Her voice was soft and remorseful. "It's okay."

I shook my head, though she couldn't see me. "It's not okay. Stealing your joy is never okay. I let my old wounds cause you fresh pain, and that's not acceptable. Ever."

She released a long breath, and I held mine, wondering what she might say next. "I understand, Mama. I know you're hurting and frustrated with Dad. You're going through so much right now. I get that, and we support each other when we struggle, remember?"

My heart swelled at the sweet memory.

The first time I'd said those words to her, she was still learning to tie her shoes. The accidental knots she'd created made it impossible to take off her sneakers. We were late for something, and she lashed out in anger. I didn't blame her. I understood her screams and tears had nothing to do with me and everything to do with her situation. Then I'd told her we never get mad if we can be compassionate instead.

"I remember," I said, emotion thick in my throat.

My baby girl had grown up to be a kind and compassionate woman.

What happened to a mother-daughter relationship when the daughter didn't need parenting anymore? I couldn't begin to guess. I wasn't sure I'd ever been parented. But I knew unequivocally, I didn't deserve my precious daughter.

Camilla sighed, and instinct told me something bad was coming next.

"What is it?" I asked.

"Can I make a confession? No judgment?"

"Always."

"I talked to Dad last night, and I lost my shit a little," she said. "So you weren't the only one saying things that were probably better kept to yourself."

I bristled, nonsensically, at the thought of her speaking to Robert, though he was her dad. And I hated that he'd upset her. But I bit my tongue and waited, letting her talk while I listened.

"I called to tell him about all the amazing venues we checked out by the river. Then he told me about filing for bankruptcy."

"Oh, hon." Guilt rolled over me when I realized I hadn't told her. I tried not to speak of Robert in her presence, because I never had anything nice to say. But I should've thought about how his nonsense would impact her life, too, and I hadn't. "I'm so sorry I didn't tell you."

"It's okay," she said. "That was his story to tell, and he never said a word. Not when we met you for dinner and announced our engagement. And not after he had time to think about it. So I've been planning this elaborate dream wedding, knowing Dad will want to make a spectacle and invite everyone he knows, so they can see what a great guy he is—" Her voice cracked, and she groaned.

"Go on," I encouraged. "I'm just here to listen." She certainly wouldn't hear me telling anyone to speak kindly about Robert anytime soon.

"The worst part is how sad it makes me," she said. "I realized how much I really want a big, romantic ceremony with all the sweet little details. Now I have to settle for good enough and pay for it with my salary as a college student and part-time yoga instructor." She gave a humorless laugh. "It sucks."

"I'm so sorry." Wow. I was saying that a lot lately. I wished I didn't have to, but every apology was more than necessary. Though this one, admittedly, wasn't mine to give.

"Please don't tell me to wait five years until I can afford the hoopla," she said. "That's not what I need right now."

"I wasn't going to say anything like that." Though it was a solid option.

I wished we were together so I could hold her, but I was thankful we'd closed the emotional gap between us. I'd never say anything to push her away again. "I can't help thinking that this is a little bit my fault too," I admitted. "If I hadn't filed for divorce, nothing would have changed."

"Mom," she chided. "That's not true."

I was almost certain it was true, but I let it go. The fact was that I did file for divorce, and Robert was claiming bankruptcy. Now Camilla wouldn't get the wedding of her dreams, and I had to buy a bus pass.

"I love you," she said.

"I love you too. Thanks for accepting my apology."

"Always," she said. "I have to go. Can we talk soon?"

"Of course," I said. "I'm off work today. If you have time later, stop by and we'll figure out the big wedding," I promised. Though I had no idea how.

"You know," she said. "If I take a year or two off from college, I can apply the tuition money to the wedding. Then I can get student loans after I'm married and finish school later, when I'm ready."

My heart spasmed, and I covered my mouth with one hand, thankful she couldn't see me. I wasn't convinced Robert had left any money in her tuition account, but that was the smaller problem. She needed that degree to support herself one day. "Honey, I—"

"I know, Mom," she said, cutting me off. "Let's talk more soon."

We disconnected, and I hung my head.

"Fuck."

I made a cup of coffee. Then I sent photos of the paperwork from Robert's hidey-hole to my forensic accountant and left a message with my attorney to discuss the findings. I wrestled with conflicting emotions as I prepped one of the cookie orders that had come in during the night. I was deeply thankful for the reconciliation with my daughter, and horrified at the possibility of her leaving school to fund the wedding. Being married without a degree to support herself, should things go south, was far worse than just getting married too young. But there wasn't much I could do about any of it, and I didn't want to risk overstepping again.

I turned my attention to things I could control and disabled the ordering function on my website. Then I posted two new graphics. A hot-pink-and-white banner thanked customers for their orders and advised all visitors that I'd reopen as soon as I'd had a chance to catch up. A second sign, in the shape of an orange-and-tan cupcake, announced a fall menu coming soon.

I was just starting a third round of order fulfillments when my phone buzzed again. I smiled when I saw it was Camilla. A peek at the clock told me I'd been working far longer than I'd realized.

Cami: Wedding dress shopping?

Cami: Last-minute appointment at Southern Charm!

I groaned. Shopping for gowns at Southern Charm was a tradition for local brides. The store worked with brides by appointment only, and getting in usually took several weeks. I understood Camilla's enthusiasm, though I didn't share it.

I'd always made a conscious effort to prioritize my daughter, so she never felt unimportant, but today I had a hard time accepting her last-minute request. Aside from receiving more online orders than I wanted to think about and finding the boat I apparently owned, I still needed to tell Lucas about my company and let him know I was all in for training in France, if he still wanted me. I didn't know anything about plating food, but how could anyone pass up an offer like his?

I tapped my thumbs against the sides of my phone, debating briefly before doing what I had to do.

Me: Exciting! Count me in! Just say when

Cami: Two!

I let my eyes fall shut. I didn't want Cami to get married yet, and I definitely didn't want her quitting school to pay for it. The whole situation felt like watching a slow-motion train crash. I saw the prospects for her future shrinking without that degree and her currently wide-open life being funneled into a narrow tube, fastened tightly with a wedding band. And there wasn't anything I could do to stop it.

So I swallowed my complaints, and I drank my coffee.

Another message arrived a moment later.

Cami: Bring Auntie Alicia!

I smiled. Luckily it was the weekend and her favorite auntie didn't have school.

Me: I'll call her now

Cami: TY! I love you, Mama!

Me: I love you too sweet girl

I forwarded the exchange to Alicia, then went back to work on my order. When the cookies finished baking, I showered and prepped myself for dress shopping. I decided to walk instead of driving to the shop. Heavens knew I needed the fresh air to clear my mind before facing my baby in a wedding gown.

I called the local DMV on my way and was instructed to contact the Department of Wildlife Resources regarding the boat. That seemed strange, but I did as I was told. Within minutes, a representative from the DWR confirmed the title I'd found was authentic. The twenty-three-foot-long sport boat, valued at thirty-four thousand dollars, was mine. Technically, only seventeen thousand of that was mine, but at the moment, any amount of money would change my life.

Alicia called as I stopped to lean against a brick building and absorb the information.

"Hello?"

"Where are you?" she asked. "I'm outside. You aren't answering."

It took a moment for her words to make sense. "You stopped at my house?"

"I wanted to pick you up. I didn't think you'd have left yet."

That was so nice, and she was right. I would still be at home if I hadn't chosen walking over driving. "I'm on First Street," I said, smiling at her gesture. "I'm getting in some steps. Plus I need to multitask."

Alicia growled. "I'm trying to get a few extra minutes with you before your little girl expects you to be excited for her," she said. "Stop moving. I'll be there in like five minutes."

I turned and walked back the way I came so I could see her approach, and continued our conversation. "I am excited for her," I said. "I wish we all shared her blind optimism about love."

"That's what I'm talking about," Alicia said. I could hear her turn signal ticking in the background. "You need to stop that. Even when you don't say those kinds of words, your face does."

"I said I was excited for her."

"And you probably looked as if you sucked a lemon, because that's how you look anytime anyone says anything about love or marriage. I saw you scowl at a billboard for an upcoming bridal fair last week, and your death glare at the radio whenever a ballad plays is terrifying. If you slip and steal her joy today, she'll build a wall to protect herself from feeling that way again, and that's exactly what you spent her whole life defending against."

I stopped walking when Alicia's Bronco appeared in the distance. "I really am working on it." I'd recently decided late one night to accept the notion Camilla would find happiness as a wife. If I kept that mindset, I could also experience the associated joyful moments by her side. Share her good times. See her smiling and carefree. Then, when she realized her mistake, I'd be there as emotional support, a friend, and confidant, to help her through the fallout. A win for everyone. Except Jeff, because I couldn't promise I wouldn't poison him when he broke her heart.

Alicia pulled up to the curb, and I climbed into her ride. "Tell me about the multitasking," she said.

I told her about my calls to the DMV and DWR. Then I backtracked to recount the details of my night. About how I'd basically broken into my old home though the side door Robert refused to fix, riffled through his desk, found my primary suite redecorated as a man cave, then the title for a thirty-four-thousand-dollar boat, in my name, hidden with Robert's porn and documentation of the money we absolutely still had. I died a little inside as I described my reckless means of escape and then finished with how Camilla and I had a great talk this morning. "We did more than just make up," I explained. "We came to an acceptance and understanding. I think we're going to be okay, and I'm not worried we'll end up like my mom and me anymore. Camilla and I are stronger, healthier. Better."

"Holy shit," she said. "That's a lot. Why didn't you call me? Before you say it was late, or something equally ridiculous, this is the kind of news you wake up your best friend for."

"I know." And in the past, I would've called. For decades I reached out to Alicia when I felt too overwhelmed to sort my tangled thoughts without help. Lately, I enjoyed working through things on my own. "I feel as if I'm putting out little fires all the time. I barely get through one crisis and something else goes wrong. Oh." Virginia's post and all my new orders came to mind, and I brought up the clip on my phone.

"Oh?" she asked. "What oh?"

"This," I said, pressing Play. "Just listen. Keep your eyes on the road so we make it to the dress shop."

Alicia's face contorted at the sound of Virginia's voice. Her expression eased as the clip ended. "Okay," she said. "That could've been much worse. So what's the plan? You're going to be overrun with business after this."

"I'm closed to new orders now." I explained the updates on my website. Then I unloaded my biggest news last—Lucas offering me a free trip to France. Specifically to the region where my mom met my biological dad. A man I hadn't been able to locate from this side of the Atlantic.

"No way!" She whipped off her sunglasses and hit my arm with them. "I can't believe you didn't call me!"

I pressed my lips together and shrugged while she found a parking space outside Southern Charm and cut the engine.

"Oh my god." She unfastened her seat belt and slumped against the seat. "This is so huge. How is it real?"

"I don't know," I said. "Which is why I didn't call. I needed thinking time, and it felt like speaking it aloud might make it disappear."

She rolled her head to face me. "It makes me sad that I'm just hearing about all of this. You always call."

"I know. I'm sorry."

Alicia offered a sad smile. "Don't be. I like that you're confident enough to know you can handle whatever comes on your own, and I love that you know you can fill me in later, when you're ready."

A breath of relief swept through me, as did a rush of pride. "I still need you. Don't start thinking I don't."

I wanted her insight on everything. I wanted to dissect every detail of our lives over wine and laughs. I just didn't need her to make decisions for me anymore. I could weigh her advice without relying on it. And that was monumental.

"Holy hell," she whispered, replacing her sunglasses and dropping her keys into her purse. "You're going to France!"

Chapter Twenty-Seven

Southern Charm Bridal Salon was the oldest wedding-gown shop in the area. Owned by a well-known and respected family for four generations, every southern Virginia bride aspired to buy her dress from this specific store.

I hadn't been inside for decades, but I remembered the experience all too well.

"Wow," Alicia said, stepping inside with an expression of hazy nostalgia. "This brings back memories."

She'd joined me on the hunt for my perfect dress. I might've drop-kicked my mother into the river without Alicia present.

Soft classical music drifted from hidden speakers, drawing us into the vaulted foyer. Rows of chandeliers hung from exposed beams in the high, arched ceiling overhead. Enormous windows on two sides invited massive amounts of natural light.

Passersby slowed to enjoy the displays and occasional bride-to-be on a pedestal up front. Shoppers admired views of the river and rear patio in the back.

I'd found my wedding gown here, as had my mother before me. She'd complained about the prices the entire time I shopped. When I asked her to stop, she justified her behavior by saying her mother had done the same to her, and she could finally understand why. I'd vowed in that moment to let my daughter, if I had one, choose the dress she wanted.

I'd married Robert in a discounted gown I didn't love, because Mom wouldn't spend more on the one I wanted. I'd walked the aisle at a church he chose for the aesthetics, because neither of our families went to church regularly enough to lay claim on any specific one. His mother had coordinated the details, taking liberties anywhere she chose, because she and Robert's father were paying more than half the costs. Traditionally, the bride's family paid for the ceremony, but we simply couldn't afford the tastes and demands of the Biancos. So, they stepped in with their wallets and walked all over my family in the process.

Day one of more than eight thousand similar days to follow. "Did you just roll your eyes?" Alicia said, crossing her arms and lowering her brows.

"No."

"Yes, you did. I saw it. What did we just talk about?"

I wrinkled my nose.

"Stop that."

"I'm sorry!" I laughed. "That was an apology face."

"Mama!" Camilla called. "Auntie Alicia!" She sprinted toward us in four-inch white satin heels, then pulled us into a group hug. She'd rolled her jeans up her calves, presumably for a better look at the heels. Her cropped green sweater brought out the flecks of hazel in her brown eyes. "I was so excited I couldn't wait for my appointment, so I came early," she said. "Isn't it amazing that they could fit us in today? I just called yesterday and poof! They had a cancellation! We're taking pictures of everything I try on to send to my bridesmaids as soon as I ask them." She covered her mouth and made wild eyes over the tops of her fingers. "I want to send flowers or some kind of cute gift when I ask. I can't decide what to choose. Why are there so many decisions?"

I smiled, warmed by her joy, and certain things between us would never be too bad to sort out.

A woman wearing a black pencil skirt and cream blouse appeared, and Camilla stepped away. "Luckily, we're here to help," the lady said. "We will be your decision helpers today." She smiled at Alicia and me.

"This is Patti," Camilla said. "Patti, this is my mom, Sophie, and my aunt, Alicia."

Alicia and I took turns shaking Patti's hand.

She smiled warmly. "Camilla was just giving me a rundown on her dream wedding," she said. "We, here at Southern Charm, are prepared to do everything in our power to make those dreams a reality for her. I'm sure you are too."

My smile tightened, but I told her how much I appreciated that instead of asking her to drop the thinly veiled sales tactics.

Alicia nodded approvingly when I glanced in her direction. Then she raised one thumb covertly.

We followed Patti across a sea of high-polished wooden floors, and past the bay of windows overlooking the river, to a large, private rotunda with a rack of wedding gowns on each side. Two overstuffed armchairs and a velvet settee centered the space before a platform with umpteen mirrors and a single fitting room.

Camilla fizzed beside me, hands clasped to her chest. "We've already picked a few things out."

I scanned the racks and laughed. At least a half dozen garment bags burdened each rack. "I see."

"And I'm obsessed with these shoes," she added, lifting one satin heel from the ground, then the other. "The dress has to match these amazing works of art."

"Those will go with anything here," Patti assured.

Alicia pinched me discreetly, and I straightened my face.

"They're perfect," I told Camilla.

Patti motioned to the central settee. "Sit. I'll help the bride into a few gowns, and we can pinpoint her style from there."

We obeyed and were handed mimosas as our reward.

Patti followed Camilla behind the pink curtain, and I downed half my drink.

"This is even fancier than I remember," Alicia said. "Remember my wedding dress? My mama's gown from the nineteen seventies. It was atrocious, even with the alterations I could afford. The cheapest tag on anything in this place is fifteen hundred."

I choked on my second sip and coughed violently into one hand. "Dollars?"

She pointed a finger at me. "Sophie Grace, stop making that face."

"I'm choking!" I told her.

Once the store added sales tax to the purchase, the price would reach nearly two grand, and that was only if Camilla chose a dress in the lowest price range. Darn our old Southern traditions. Not to mention, throughout Camilla's childhood I'd rebelliously spent Robert's money on her because I could, and I knew he hated it but wouldn't complain too much because a nicely dressed child reflected well on him. As a result, she knew what she liked and didn't like, and she knew quality.

My banking app probably wept the moment Camilla sent me the text asking to meet her here.

I finished a second mimosa before Camilla exited the fitting room in gown number one. She looked like an angel in white satin. The material hugged her youthful curves and draped elegantly along her décolletage. Sweet. Classic. Understated.

She smiled, but I saw uncertainty in her eyes. "What do you think?"

Patti loved it.

Alicia told her she looked like a page from a magazine.

I shrugged. "It's a beautiful dress, and you look incredible in it, but I wonder if this is the right one for you."

"Yeah," she said. "I agree. This would be perfect for the reception, when I want to dance and mingle without hauling around a massive gown, but—"

And there it was. Camilla didn't want to "haul a massive gown" around the reception, but she did want to make her big appearance in one at the back of the church.

Patti jumped into action. "Say no more. We'll focus on full skirts for now. How do you feel about embellishments?"

Camilla's shoulders relaxed as she followed Patti into the dressing room.

I set my empty glass on a little table at my side.

The next time Camilla emerged, she wore something shaped like a cupcake and grinned.

"Too full?" Camilla asked.

I gave the gown a look and grinned. If Alicia, Patti, and I formed a circle around Camilla and attempted to hold hands, ring-around-the-rosy style, we couldn't.

"A little," I told her.

Camilla laughed, and it opened something in my heart.

After that, I took photos of every gown and hated that I'd missed the first two. Alicia and I finished the pitcher of mimosas, and Camilla tried on dress after dress until sweat beaded on her brow.

"Last one," she said, trooping back inside the fitting room. "Tell me we can get something to eat after this," she called through the curtain. "We can review the gowns I've tried. I want your honest feedback."

"Sounds like fun," Alicia said, wiggling her empty flute.

"Agreed," I said. "Anything but French food. It's my day off. Don't make me go to work."

"I'm thinking tacos," Camilla said. "Or pizza."

I perked at the idea of having both. "How about the food trucks by the water? We can grab a table and enjoy the decent weather before temperatures drop."

Behind the curtain, everything fell silent. No more rustling of material or whispering voices.

Patti stepped into view and held the pink curtain aside so Camilla could follow.

Tears filled her eyes, and a heavy blush spread across her cheeks.

The gown was gorgeous. Layers of white chiffon crisscrossed over a corseted top, accentuating her trim waist and delicate collarbones. I could imagine my mother's pearls on her neck, the "something old" portion of her good-luck charms. Chains of organza flower petals fell in ultrafeminine loops from her shoulders. The skirt was full without bulk or structure, just layers and layers of the most weightless-looking fabric I'd ever seen stretching out behind her. The whole aesthetic was ethereal, as if she were part of a dream.

"Mama," she whispered.

My heart broke on that little word, and I knew. This was the dress. We couldn't leave here without it.

I nodded. "Perfection."

After long minutes of staring into the mirror while Patti, Alicia, and I fawned over her, Camilla changed into the clothes she'd arrived in and returned the dress to Patti. "I have to think about it," she told her. "And I'd better use the ladies' room before lunch." She pointed the latter comment in my direction.

I waited for her to leave the room, then rushed for a look at the price tag. Alicia kept pace at my side. "How much is this one?" I asked.

Patti returned the gown to the rack, then smiled knowingly as she revealed the tag.

I nearly vomited on the number printed there.

Alicia gripped my arm. "That says seventy-two hundred dollars."

"Yes," Patti confirmed. "It's a generous price for this designer. She tries to make her gowns accessible."

"To whom?" Alicia asked. "Bill Gates?"

Patti frowned. "This is at least a ten-thousand-dollar dress."

I covered my mouth as panic churned.

"The required deposit is only ten percent," Patti informed us. "The balance can be paid in monthly installments. We keep a credit card on file, and you pick the day of the month that's best for the withdrawal. Or we also have an excellent financier, if you prefer to work directly with a bank." She passed me a business card from the pocket of her skirt.

Alicia pulled her chin back sharply. "People take out loans for a dress?"

"Of course."

"Hold it for us," I said, tucking the card into my bag.

"This is the sample," Patti said. "I can order one in her size."

"I'll call with the deposit as soon as I can."

Patti removed the gown from the rack and nodded. "I'll write it up and have it ready for you. You won't regret this."

"Don't tell her," I said, tipping my head in the direction Camilla had gone. "I want it to be a surprise."

Now I *really* needed to get my hands on that boat.

After walking to and from an early dinner along the river and discussing wedding gowns at length, Camilla went to yoga with plans to hit up Robert for money afterward. She thought he might be her hero and buy the dress despite his claim of bankruptcy. Somehow I kept a straight face, knowing Robert would have to show the court where he'd found that kind of money, and giddy that, with a little luck, I could provide her with something he could not.

Aside from parental love, respect, and protection, all things without value to him, because unlike the dress, humanity lacked a price tag.

Sobered by the sun, Alicia and I made phone calls until we tracked down my boat at a yacht club ninety minutes away. Then, we made a road trip.

My day was nearly gone, the time arguably well spent, but mending relationships and making memories didn't help me fill my backlog of orders for the Invisible Baker or leave time to talk to Lucas. I had a confession to make, and I wanted to accept his offer in person. I also needed to get in touch with both my attorney and the forensic accountant about our next steps, now that I'd found proof of hidden funds.

"Here," Alicia said, motioning to the clubhouse. A quick stop inside confirmed the boat's location, and a young woman at the desk encouraged me to become a member. I let her know my husband was already handling that. She agreed to reach out to his company, and Alicia and I tracked down the boat in question in the marina. The vessel was larger than I'd imagined. And large black block letters along the back spelled **BIG & FAST**.

"I'm not touching that boat name," Alicia said. "It's too easy."

I bit back the childish urge to add *that's what she said*, and moved on.

Alicia took photos while I typed up a sales pitch for an ad. Neither of us knew the first thing about boats, especially not a high-end watercraft like the one before us, so I used the internet to locate buzzwords.

"I hope this sounds right," I said, seated on the dock and kicking my feet over the edge. I had every right to climb aboard, but I left that to Alicia. My stomach coiled at the thought of getting any closer.

"Why don't you write something like *imagine how big and fast people will think your penis is, if you own this boat*?" Alicia suggested.

"These ads charge by the word," I said. "I better stick to the facts."

I listed *BIG & FAST* on multiple boater sites before we left and had my first offer before bed, which I accepted.

Transferring the boat title and nearly forty thousand dollars digitally was unbelievably simple. I cheered for modern technology as things finalized in a matter of minutes.

I called Southern Charm the next day from my afternoon break and placed the order for Camilla's wedding dress. Pride swelled in me as I read the banking numbers to Patti and scheduled the delivery. Camilla could set up fittings at her convenience, and typically the dress stayed at the shop, but I wanted her to receive my gift in a big white box with a pink ribbon and a cutesy note. I asked Patti to include a card that read: *For my beautiful daughter, You deserve the gown of your dreams on your wedding day.*

I imagined the shock and joy on her face when she received the gift, and I couldn't wait to answer her call after she opened the box.

Lucas didn't come to the restaurant during my shift, and I worried he was avoiding me. That maybe he'd researched the Invisible Baker a little more and confirmed it was me and I had lied. Or maybe he'd changed his mind about taking me to France and decided to offer the training to someone who'd been in his kitchen longer, like John, who was an incredible chef and much more familiar with French food.

I didn't know what to think, and I couldn't ask him, so I pressed the anxiety down and kept moving forward.

After work, I bought a compact sedan from a used car lot in walking distance, and let Alicia know Bill could have his truck back.

I had spent my half of the money from the sale of the boat in less than a day.

Easy come, easy go, I supposed.

I drove off the lot on a cloud of dopamine. I owned a car, purchased for me, by me, and I'd never felt as powerful or free.

Chapter Twenty-Eight

Lucas wasn't at work during my shift for the next few days, and I didn't know how to reach him without asking the staff manager for his number. I couldn't bring myself to do that, and the fear he was intentionally avoiding me pressed on my lungs. I wanted to accept his offer. I wanted to go to France. Most importantly, I wanted to confess my lie and my reasons. For the first time in a long time, I didn't want to hide.

In the meantime, I refocused on the things I could do until I saw him again, like meet with my attorney for pretrial preparations.

I parked my new-to-me sedan along the curb outside the law office and headed inside with my head held high. We hadn't spoken since the day I detailed my findings to her, and I hoped she had some good news for me.

The office was utilitarian with zero frills or pretense. The paralegal at the front desk welcomed me, and I sat in a plastic chair before a window overlooking the street.

My attorney came to meet me and walked me to her office several minutes later. "How've you been?" she asked, sweeping her brown hair into a knot atop her head. The move revealed blue and purple strands beneath, and I smiled.

"I could be better," I said. "But I'm also quite happy. Finalizing the divorce would be the frosting on my cake."

She nodded and motioned me to an armchair across from her desk. "I'm glad things are going well for you. I'm sorry you're having to put up with the added trouble of your husband's bankruptcy claim. I've printed and noted everything you sent me about the paperwork hidden at the marital home. We don't want to reveal our knowledge of any of that to opposing council, if possible."

I sat back with a frown. "How can we use it to prove he's lying if they don't know we know?" I asked.

She tapped her pen against a file folder, looking as frustrated as I felt. "The temporary orders which were put in place following the initial hearing require both of you to be mindful, respectful, and noninvasive of one another's personal space. No harassing, no stalking, that sort of thing. I'm afraid that breaking in, after he'd changed the locks—"

"Why was he allowed to change the locks?" I interrupted. "It's still half my house."

She lifted a palm. "I know, but regardless of how the judge will feel about the lock change, you knew the place was locked, and instead of reaching out to him or coming back another time, you found an alternate way inside. I can guarantee the judge will frown on that. Furthermore, you snooped through his private things. If the tables were turned, and I knew this had happened to you, I'd be in court making a stink."

My mouth opened, and I slumped. The idea of Robert in my private space, searching through my new home for something to use against me, made me sick.

"What he's doing is wrong," she said. "But two wrongs don't negate one another. Is there any chance he'll discover you were there?" she asked. "Security systems, hidden cameras? Loose-lipped neighbors? Anything like that?"

Goose bumps cascaded over my skin at the memory of lying on the bathroom vanity in my underwear. "He knows," I said. "Do I have to give details?"

She hung her head. "Based on your expression, I'm going to pass and move on, unless there's anything else from that night you want to share."

I told her about the boat and its sale.

She grimaced.

"I have the receipt, and I opened a savings account with half the money that's meant for him. Depositing it into one of our joint accounts would only set off his alarm bells, plus the court wants to split those accounts in half, and I've already taken my portion of the boat money." *And spent it,* I thought.

Jill made a note. "Any word from the forensic accountant?" she asked.

"No."

"Don't worry," she said. "I've worked with that team enough to know they'll take the information provided and use it to find exactly what you need."

We spent the next hour preparing for the divorce pretrial. She walked me through what to expect from the time I arrived at the courthouse until the moment things ended. She and Robert's attorney would do most of the talking, privately with the judge. They'd present all the issues we had and had not agreed upon through mediation and the things the judge might have to decide upon via a trial, unless we came to an agreement sooner.

She assured me that most divorce cases don't go to trial, and that many are settled on the day of trial before the trial even begins.

I held on to that hope with both hands.

"It's ironic," I said, standing to leave. "If you'd asked me when I first moved out, I would've said I didn't want anything. I just wanted to be free of him. Back then, I didn't have a job and would've struggled infinitely without at least some of the marital money. Now, I've shown myself I can make it on my own, but I intend to get half of everything, because it's half mine. We built that life together, each playing our specified roles, and regardless of anything he said or will say, my role was just as important as his."

My attorney smiled. "That's what I like to hear."

❧

I stopped by the restaurant that evening, hoping to catch Lucas. I took a leap of faith and prepared a grand gesture in case he was there. A half dozen of my best pains au chocolat, the pastry I'd used to introduce him to the Invisible Baker, sat inside a pink bakery box, clutched in my trembling hands. I wanted the gift to double as a revelation.

I hoped Lucas would appreciate the sweet reveal. Or at least, I hoped the offering would soften the blow of my deceit.

I tightened my grip on the petal-pink box as I opened the glass front door. The dinner crowd was thick as I made my way to the hostess stand to ask if Lucas was on shift.

A cluster of women in pink T-shirts filled the space near the desk.

I contemplated searching for him myself, but frayed nerves held me in place.

The group before me chattered as they waited for the hostess to return. Someone suggested a photo, and they moved to stand before the empty display case with a *The Invisible Baker* sign on top.

My mind boggled when they turned, revealing the print on their matching shirts.

NOT ALL HEROES WEAR CAPES.
SOME BAKE.

Time slowed as I read the words again.

The hostess, Pam, appeared in the distance, hustling in our direction, until her eyes met mine. Then she stopped short, pulled a phone from her pocket, and hurried away.

My phone rang a heartbeat later.

The pink-shirted group turned toward me at the sound. Their eyes widened.

I balanced the box against my hip and answered the call, panic tightening my throat.

"Sophie," Pam whispered. "They know. We all know."

My mouth opened, then shut.

Should I run? Feign confusion? Spill the truth to these strangers before speaking with Lucas?

No, I couldn't do that.

One of the gaping women raised her phone, and I winced in response. But she didn't record me; she turned away and tapped the screen. Was she sending a text? Making a phone call?

My heart hammered and my pulse beat audibly in my ears as the others stared. They looked to my panicked face, then at the box in my hands on repeat. My skin heated to combustion, and my emotions launched straight from earth and into the atmosphere.

This was not how tonight was supposed to go. I'd planned to share my secret with a friend, whom I trusted to accept my confession without making me regret it.

The epiphany nearly derailed my panic. I trusted Lucas.

Not just abstractly, or in theory, but in practice, and completely.

As if somehow conjured by my thoughts, he appeared.

Virginia strolled along at his side.

The disappointment in his eyes nearly ruined me.

Virginia's expression lit up when she noticed me at the front desk. "Sophie, we were all just talking about you."

My good manners insisted I return her polite greeting, but words failed. I looked to Lucas for help, and he nodded. What did that mean? What should I do? Where was Alicia when I needed—

No, I thought. *I don't need someone else to handle my messes anymore.*

I could do this.

I had no idea how, but I would figure it out on my own.

Breathe, I reminded myself. Collapsing now would only cause a scene and ruin my perfect pastries.

"We hoped we'd run into you tonight," Virginia said. She motioned vaguely to the women in pink shirts. Her easy smile added confusion to my already rattled mind. Her morning post about my company was positive and informative. I'd assumed that would be the end of her interest in my story.

So why was she here?

"We stopped by earlier," she continued. "I thought I'd catch you around the same time we met before. Oh!" She pressed a hand to her chest. "I'm so sorry. You probably don't remember me. I'm Virginia Bonnie Black. We talked about the Invisible Baker," she said, as if that was something I could possibly forget.

She had me cornered with a camera on her phone and a captive audience, but she didn't call me out on my lie. She'd asked directly about the Invisible Baker, and I'd dodged her.

Why wasn't she burning me alive?

Virginia tipped her head at me from several feet away, where she'd stopped, presumably giving me room. "This isn't an ambush. I promise."

I darted my gaze around the foyer and dining room, where guests had taken notice of our interaction. If this wasn't an ambush, then what the hell did she call it?

"When I realized you were the woman behind the Invisible Baker," she continued, "I had to speak to you again. I couldn't help myself."

I caught Lucas's eyes and sighed. This wasn't the way I wanted to tell him, but I was done lying and hiding. I tented my brows in apology. I hoped he could see the regret in my expression. He deserved better than this. I sent up silent prayers that whatever came next wouldn't negatively impact his current business or plans for expansion. I couldn't bear to cause damage to his dreams or livelihood in any way. I couldn't live with that, and I had no idea how to fix things.

"How did you know?" I asked Virginia. Where had I gone wrong?

Her smile softened. "Occam's razor," she said, though her tone made the answer sound more like a question. "The simplest answer is usually the right one. Chez Margot hired a new pastry chef, who has everyone raving about desserts that were on the menu years before she showed up. Then they contracted a new company to provide grab-and-go pastries a few days later. It was suspicious."

My heart sank. She was right, and I was a failure at subterfuge.

"I asked around a little," she said, "and I learned you were new to town, following a recent move. I plugged your name into county auditor sites until I found two homes listed with your name. One is a few blocks away; the other is in an elite location a couple of towns over. Jealous of that zip code, by the way."

She spoke into the phone again, recording herself. "I talked to folks in the school pickup lines in your old district, and a whole lot of those parents seemed to know exactly who I was talking about when I mentioned the Invisible Baker. But they wouldn't say a word." Her eyes gleamed. "When I asked the same questions to parents in my home district, they looked at me as if I had two heads. The whole thing seemed very community coded. So I took to the internet." She lowered the phone and offered me a self-deprecating grin. "I plugged the LLC name into the state's business website and found all your contact information, but that's a less interesting story."

I laughed. "It is," I agreed.

A woman in pink approached with a business card from the bakery display case. "Will you sign this for me?"

I made a silly face. "What?"

Virginia raised her phone to film.

The woman passed me the card and a Sharpie. "We're all here because we appreciate you so much. Even if you can't completely save us from the judgy moms at our schools, the fact that you're out there, helping us and other moms get by, is everything."

I accepted the pen and card, then took longer, slower looks at their faces. I recognized two of the five.

"Your company restores our faith in people," another woman said. "And it reminds us that we all need to do better for one another."

My eyes blurred with sudden, unshed tears. I set the card on my box and signed the card as the first drops fell. I returned the card. "Thank you for saying that, but I was just trying to help." And make a little money doing what I loved.

I spotted Lucas watching from a distance. "I'm sorry I lied to you," I said.

He moved slowly forward, a heartbroken expression pinned to mine.

Virginia panned her phone from me to him and back, but I only cared about making amends with my new boss and friend.

"I wanted to tell you," I vowed. "I just—couldn't."

"I know," he said. "I understand."

Virginia rolled her eyes at her phone. "Sophie's boss tried to distract me with a story about a retired man baking for stressed-out moms. No one bought that, but good try," she teased.

Lucas blushed.

"You already knew?" I guessed.

Of course he did. Why else would he make up a story?

He ran a hand through his thick dark hair and averted his gaze.

"Why didn't you tell me?" I demanded. I'd been sick over my lie when he'd known all along.

"You didn't want me to know," he said. "And it wasn't any of my business. I knew you had your reasons. I stopped placing orders to give this time to simmer down, but"—he motioned to the group of women in pink, then to Virginia—"it didn't help. I'm sorry this is happening. You should've been able to choose when, or if, you made this public. I tried telling them that. I've spent the last few days trying to reason with the unreasonable."

"You were protecting me."

The sadness in his expression took on new meaning. He wasn't upset that I'd lied—he was sorry he hadn't been able to help me keep my secret.

He nodded, and I snapped my mouth shut, suddenly hyperaware of our audience.

I'd assumed he was extra busy lately making plans for France or the evening upgrades to his restaurant, but he'd spent at least a portion of that time communicating with Virginia Bonnie Black for me.

My heart fluttered with fresh appreciation, but whatever was between Lucas and me didn't need to be aired on social media or broadcast to his restaurant. This conversation had to wait. There was a more immediate issue in need of resolution.

I pulled in a deep, steadying breath, then turned on my heels and cut through the pink T-shirts to the bakery display. I made a show of setting my box aside and raising my *The Invisible Baker* sign in one hand.

"I was invisible for many years," I said, speaking directly to the camera, "as I think too many women are. I cooked, cleaned, cared for my daughter, and managed the emotions and mental load of everyone in my family. I did that for decades. And I did it alone." An exasperated laugh seeped from my core. It was all so ridiculous. How had society remained this way for so long? "The sadder thing is that my story is not an anomaly. So many of us suffer silently, giving all we have to those around us, trying desperately to make everyone happy all while diminishing and depleting our own happiness. And there's always someone out there ready to complain that it's not enough. That we haven't done enough." Around me, the women in pink nodded and whispered their agreement. Their solidarity gave me strength. "I was invisible for years, like too many other women, and no one ever, *ever* said thank you. But I'm done with that now."

I held the sign in front of me, and with the Sharpie I'd used to sign the business card, I drew a big X through the letters *I-n*, changing the words on the sign to spell *The Visible Baker*. I spun the revision to face Virginia, and I looked directly into her camera. "I'm visible now, and I see you too."

A round of applause rose throughout the restaurant, and I realized our audience had grown. The women in pink shirts, and others from the nearby dining room and kitchen, made their way closer, many wiping tears as they offered me hugs, handshakes, and words of thanks. The very words we all wanted but rarely received.

"You heard it here, folks." Virginia's voice carried to me from somewhere beyond the crowd. "Now that Sophie Bianco's not invisible anymore, she's sure to reach a lot more of her intended audience. I'm guessing this baker is one who won't mind if you want to say you've made it yourself."

"Pardon me," Lucas said, moving along the fringe of people to Virginia's side.

She moved the phone to include him in her selfie-style view.

"When I first hired Sophie," he said, "I asked her what she would've done differently if she could go back and make changes in her life."

For a moment, his expression fell, and I wondered if his words made him think of Margot. I hated that he'd lost the love of his life when so few people ever found theirs. I wanted joy for him. This kind and caring human who taught me it was safe to trust people with my secrets. A boss who showed me I was worth having on a team even when I didn't carry the entire load.

The restaurant seemed too quiet, everyone listening closely as he spoke.

"The specific change she mentioned to me that day, that I think is especially relevant now, is that she would never have been the Invisible Baker. In another life, where she was seen, she would've opened a storefront and sold directly to anyone and everyone in need of a little fresh-baked love."

I laughed nervously. Lucas made my dream sound better than I did.

Virginia turned the camera on me. "Is that still what you want?" she asked.

I nodded. Unwilling to lie, I whispered, "Yeah."

"Well, viewers," Virginia said, "if anyone can make that happen, it's you."

Slowly, restaurant staff and guests returned to their stations and tables.

I opened the box and offered each woman in pink a pastry. I passed the last treat to Lucas.

Virginia winked. “Another of Virginia’s Secrets revealed, and this one is truly delicious.”

Chapter Twenty-Nine

I waited outside Lucas's office the next morning, determined to say my piece.

He rounded the corner, then slowed at the sight of me. He was beautiful. Clean shaven, hair damp and lightly mussed. His lips opened in surprise, and kindness flowed from him like light from a lantern in the darkness. "Sophie. What are you doing here? This is your day off, isn't it?"

"I came to see you," I said, offering the pink pastry box in my hands.

He accepted with a coy smile. "The Invisible Baker."

"Can I come in?" I asked, motioning to his closed office door. "I think we need to talk."

Lucas nudged the door open with his foot, then motioned me inside. He took a seat at his desk and opened his palms, letting me know I had the floor.

I lowered anxiously into the chair across from him. Then I opened a vein and poured out my heart. Tears flowed unbidden as I explained the blanket of protection my little company had once provided me. The hope for escape and independence that came with every sale while I bided my time until I could leave Robert. Then the fear I had at losing it all, as if giving away my secret meant losing all I'd gained in its shadow. And how I knew now that wasn't true.

"I am so deeply sorry for lying to you," I said. "I'm so incredibly grateful to you for giving me a chance as your pastry chef. You trusted me. I kept something from you, but it was never a reflection of my lack of trust in you, or anything about you at all. I'd just been so afraid for so long. It was all I knew."

"And are you afraid now?" he asked.

A small, humorless laugh escaped me as I shook my head. I couldn't imagine fearing anything with Lucas near. "I'm glad to be here with you," I said. Without thinking, I added, "I've missed you. I've felt as if you were avoiding me, and I hated it."

Interest lifted his brows. "I was giving you space."

"For what?"

"For whatever you needed," he said. "After I realized you were keeping this secret"—he waved to the pink pastry box—"I knew there was something behind it. People are generally proud of their success, but you didn't want anyone to know. Then, as you opened up to me about your life before we met, I understood a little better. I decided to let you tell me when you were ready."

"But why have you been avoiding me?" I asked. He still hadn't explained that, had he?

Lucas looked briefly away. He laced and unlaced his fingers on the desktop. "After hearing your strong feelings about marriage, I didn't want our growing friendship to become a problem for you. So maybe I hid a little too."

I blinked, stunned and unsure for new reasons. Why would my feelings about marriage have anything to do with him? Unless he had feelings toward me, and he thought I was against all romantic relationships.

Was it possible my attraction to Lucas wasn't completely one sided?

"I had plenty of work to do in here," he said. "I should thank you. I'm caught up on paperwork for the first time since the restaurant opened, I think."

I bit my lip and smiled. "I want to go to France," I said. "If the offer stands."

A flash of pleasure passed over his handsome face. "Of course." He opened his desk drawer and produced an envelope. "This is everything you need for the trip. And a few of the preview photos taken for the restaurant's marketing materials. I thought you might like to have them."

The phone on his desk rang as I accepted the envelope, and he offered an apologetic look. "I'm sorry—I have to take this call."

I stood on wobbly legs, overwhelmed by relief and acceptance. "We're good?" I asked.

He nodded. "What if we agree to just say what's on our minds from now on, yes?"

"Yes," I agreed. Then I floated out on a cloud of hope and deep appreciation for another person in my life who accepted me for me.

I drove straight to Alicia's house from the restaurant and waited while she changed out of her work clothes and into her varsity-football-mom clothes. Then we went to the high school stadium to watch her sons play in their homecoming game. I provided the usual three dozen cupcakes, iced in the school's colors.

Seated in the stands, under the Friday night lights, I told her everything about my chat with Lucas. Then I pulled the envelope he'd given me from my purse.

"You didn't open it yet?" she asked.

I shook my head. "I didn't wait for you with the ancestry things. The least I could do is wait to show you my paperwork for France." I worked open the flap and slid the contents onto my lap.

Scents of popcorn and hot chocolate lifted through the air on a breeze. Shirtless teens with giant letters painted across their chests walked in packs with others wearing face paint in the same colors.

Cheerleaders shook their pom-poms and bounced around on the track outlining the field.

I scanned the pack of uniformed players, searching for CJ and Bill.

"Lucas likes you," Alicia said. "Are you ready to combust? That's the only thing he could've meant with that line about your growing friendship." She sang the last two words.

I smiled. "It feels awful to say, because I'm legally unavailable, but I really hope you're right."

She smirked, obviously satisfied with my brutally honest response. Then she turned her attention to the paperwork. "Okay, what do you have there?"

I fanned through the stack. "Airline and flight numbers. Hotel information."

"Please say you got the last available room," she said. "And there's only one bed."

I snorted. "I think that only happens in romance novels."

"Why can't this be a romance novel?"

"Robert puts a real damper on the plot," I said. My gaze drifted to the photo on my lap, and I released a little gasp.

Alicia hummed a long note, clearly seeing what I saw.

A professional photo of the restaurant's kitchen, taken for marketing purposes and featuring Lucas and me. We stood shoulder to shoulder at the prep station, each holding a finished dessert and smiling widely. My head was thrown back in laughter, and there was a smudge of flour on my nose. Lucas's eyes were on me. The look on his face stole my breath.

"Soph," Alicia said softly. "That's not the look of a man with a possible crush. That's the look of a man who's head over heels."

And that photo was instantly my favorite of all time.

On the day of the pretrial, I dressed in the same black ensemble I'd worn to my mother's funeral, though ending the marriage seemed more like an occasion for a bright-pink party gown.

Alicia and Ilona rode with me to the courthouse and promised they'd wait on a bench in the hallway for as long as it took. I told them there wasn't any reason to come. I had no idea how long a pretrial might last. They insisted this was what family did for one another. It didn't matter what occurred in the courtroom today—they had my back.

And plans for tacos and margaritas immediately following.

Camilla insisted on coming as well, but she was running late.

My greatest hope was that Robert and I could settle on a fair division of assets so I'd finally be free of him.

The attorneys spoke with the judge privately before Robert and I entered the courtroom. We were sworn in, then seated. The facts of the case were stated. Then my attorney stood and declared my entitlement to half of all cash, retirement, investments, and assets, as well as a portion of Robert's paychecks in the form of spousal support for the next eighty-four months, based on the length of our marriage.

His attorney submitted a formal verbal agreement to our terms, then reminded everyone that we were flat broke.

The judge congratulated us on our willingness to come to reasonable decisions on our own and declared the paperwork would be written up for our signatures.

My heart rate increased, because it sounded like we might avoid a trial.

Jill shot me a sharp, knowing smile. She rose as Robert's attorney sat, and she pressed her palms to the table.

I braced for her to announce the findings from my forensic accountant. I hadn't heard from them yet, but maybe they'd called her directly. My hands balled into fists, fingernails biting into my palms as I waited. I let my eyes shut and sent up a prayer.

Please tell him to fuck completely off with that nonsense. Amen.

"Just a moment." Robert's lawyer spoke before mine.

My eyes opened and sought the source.

"Your Honor, if I may?" he asked.

The judge looked to my attorney, as if asking if she'd allow the interruption. It was her turn, after all.

Jill turned to me.

I raised my brows, because she was kidding, right? I had no idea what was happening.

She sat, then waved her outstretched arm. "Please."

Robert's attorney had passed his phone to Robert, whose initial shock grew into a grinch-worthy sneer. I was sure I heard the voice of Virginia's Secrets coming from the device. Robert nodded, and icicles prickled my skin.

The judge whacked her little hammer. "Mr. James. Do you or don't you have something to add?"

"I do, Your Honor. Regarding Ms. Bianco's finances," the attorney said. He lifted his chin and adjusted his jacket. "We ask that her full income be considered when determining the amount of support."

The judge squinted. "It's been established that Ms. Bianco is employed part-time, and her financial documentation will be included in all relevant discussions. If there's something more you mean to say, get on with it."

He cleared his throat. "It's come to my attention just now that she also owns a successful LLC registered in the state of Virginia, which she didn't include on her initial disclosure affidavits."

My attorney turned to me slowly.

I wanted to drop my head onto the desk and scream.

"Request for recess, Your Honor," Jill said. "I need to confer with my client."

Robert's attorney raised a hand and tutted loudly. "I would like to add that my client expects the full valuation of his wife's previously undisclosed business, its assets and income, be documented and divided equally as marital property in the final settlement."

His words landed like a slap. My ears rang and my head reared back.

The judge granted the request for recess.

My attorney moved me to a conference room and closed the door.

"Are you kidding me?" she asked, her voice a harsh whisper. "You own a company?"

"I can explain," I said.

Her eyes widened, and she pressed her lips into a thin white line. "Please," she said. "Otherwise, imagine how horribly embarrassing it would be for me to go in front of the judge and opposing counsel without all the information necessary to properly represent your case."

I took a seat at the little table and cringed, because of course, she was right. "When I filed for divorce, I rarely had more than one order a week. In the three years since launching the Invisible Baker, I never made enough money to necessitate filing taxes in our state. In fact, before I moved out, I usually lost money on my baking. But I paid for my supplies out of our household account. I bought the ingredients with the rest of our groceries, then put the money I earned from the baked goods aside for this very day. Or rather, the day I hired you.

"Recently, however, things have changed. My little start-up grew legs and finally started making money. Now Robert wants to take it from me." My voice cracked, and I pressed a palm to my chest. Of course he did. He took everything, and he ruined it.

My attorney exhaled a long, exhausted breath. "He's entitled to half," she said. "Just as you are."

Tears blurred my eyes and outrage clogged my throat. "That's not what's happening," I snapped. "He's keeping all that he thinks is his, and he's claiming half of what's mine too. He's cheating and stealing. He's reminding me that he's always in control. And he always wins." I wiped my wet cheeks and growled. "You can't let him do this." I'd worked too hard and come too far.

She nodded and shoved away from the table. "All right. No settlement today, then. We'll go to trial and hope the forensic accountants have something for us by then."

We returned to the courtroom and affirmed we would go to trial. Nothing could be finalized without a detailed report from the forensic accountant anyway. Jill assured me, yet again, that I could trust the company I'd hired, even if they hadn't been in contact since I paid their retainer. And she said nothing that happened in court today was a setback. Just a surprise.

I kicked myself internally as I went in search of my friends. It had never once crossed my mind to mention the Invisible Baker when I completed the paperwork to hire my attorney.

Maybe because none of this had seemed real until a few weeks ago. Not my ability to truly leave Robert behind. Or the possibility I could support myself financially. I definitely never imagined my cupcake endeavors could be seen as a real business entity by anyone other than myself. Certainly not something Robert would demand half of in our divorce settlement.

The white noise and voices of the courthouse muddled together as I shuffled along, feeling as if I were underwater. I made eye contact with Alicia a split second before I saw my daughter, running along the hallway toward her father.

"Daddy!" Camilla called. She threw her arms around Robert's neck.

I backed against the wall, confused by her enthusiasm and in need of support.

Alicia and Ilona rushed to my side.

"What's that about?" Alicia asked.

I had no idea, and I couldn't take my eyes off Camilla's unbridled joy. Though only a few yards away, it felt as if I were watching her through a looking glass. A world where she passed me by for Robert simply didn't exist. Yet there she was. With him. And happy.

"Hello to you too," he said, beaming proudly to onlookers. "What's all this about?"

"The dress!" she cried, releasing him to smile at his stupid face. "I received it today, and I can't believe you did this! I knew you would, but I'm still so—ah!" She lunged at him again, pulling him into another tight, adoring hug.

My hug.

Alicia gripped my arm. "Oh, my god. She thinks—"

A small choking sob escaped my throat. Of course Camilla assumed Robert paid for the gown. Why wouldn't she? How could I have afforded it? I'd always been financially dependent on my husband, and our daughter knew it.

"At first, I thought Jeff bought it," Camilla said, eyes sparkling. "He swore he didn't. Then I remembered you telling me you'd see what you could do to help, and I realized you found the money for my dress! I can't believe it! Thank you!"

Robert's initial confusion morphed into something dark as his gaze met mine. "Anything for my little girl," he said.

I watched in horror as he wrapped an arm around her back and led her toward a set of nearby chairs. I wanted to riot and break them apart. I wanted to tell everyone he was lying again. I bought that dress! I did that for her! But how could I say that much without saying the rest?

That I broke into our home and found a boat title with my name under the floorboards while he was away. Then I took it with me and sold our marital property without his knowledge or consent. And I used the money for her dress.

Alicia rubbed a palm against my shoulder blades. "This will be okay," she whispered.

Strange. I couldn't see how.

So I headed for the stairwell and walked away.

I didn't open the Invisible Baker website for new sales. The feelings of defeat that followed my pretrial weighed on me more heavily every day. In the week leading up to the trip to France, I obsessed over all the things that had gone wrong, and it was impossible to stop the continuous, ugly loop. Most days I felt as if I were sliding slowly down a mountain, into darkness, or back under the water.

I went to work. I came home and I slept.

I told my coworkers nothing was wrong, and I lied to Lucas when he asked, which only made me feel worse. We'd just promised not to keep things from one another, and I was already at it again. But I just couldn't bring myself to voice this defeat out loud.

Still, he checked in on me before and after every shift. He sent me a countdown widget for our trip, after we exchanged phone numbers in preparation for travel, and updates on the anticipated weather.

Somehow my halfhearted responses didn't reduce his enthusiasm.

Camilla sent texts, updating me on school, work, and wedding plans, too busy to notice I'd gone quiet. Alicia called every evening after dinner. I didn't answer, but I texted to let her know I was fine. Ilona brought breakfast most mornings. I thanked her, but I was rarely hungry.

Raisin seemed to sense my growing depression, and he stuck by my side when I was home. We binge-watched television and napped on the couch before going to bed early. He snuggled with me for comfort and groomed my ratty hair when I cried.

Sometimes I read Mom's notebooks and traced her messy scrawl with my fingertips. I'd spent a lifetime angry with her, not understanding that she'd been defeated, tired, and depressed. I never knew what that felt like until now. No wonder she drank and rarely left home. Forcing myself to shower before work was the worst part of my day.

I should've been excited about the free trip to France and the possibility of meeting my biological father, but instead, I hadn't even packed.

I had no interest in plating food. I loved baking, but if Robert got half my company, I didn't want the rest. Maybe that was petty, but he'd already taken everything from me, and if he took the Invisible Baker, too, it would be a hit I wouldn't come back from. The thought stripped me of hope.

He was winning. Again. Taking. Again. And I was powerless to stop him.

Again.

My phone rang as I stared at my living room ceiling.

I rolled onto my side on the couch, dislodging Raisin from my chest. My attorney's name and number centered the screen as I reached for the phone.

"Hi, Jill," I said, doing my best to sound bright and cheerful.

"Hey, I wanted to call and give you an update," she said. "I hate how pretrial ended, and I want you to know you won't lose your business."

I flopped onto my back again. Funny, I was just thinking about that.

I was always thinking about that.

"Your combined income between the restaurant and the LLC is still significantly less than Robert's income," she said. "Taking any part of the baking business would mean he'd have to pay you more in spousal support, which makes no logical or financial sense. The threat of taking half your company was a facade. Their real goal was to shake us and make you look dishonest before the judge, but don't worry. I've shut them down and cleared things up. He won't mention taking anything from you again."

My eyes shut, too tired to fight. "What if I agree to sign the paperwork before I leave on my trip instead of waiting for trial?" I asked. "I don't care if he keeps everything. The freedom of knowing it's finally over will be priceless."

The long silence that followed left me drifting. How could I still feel so tired?

"Sophie," my attorney said, gently, patiently.

I dragged my eyes open once more.

"I understand what you're feeling. Most of my clients reach a similar point at some time during the divorce process, and I'm going to tell you what I tell them: You hired me for a reason. This is what I do, and I'm very, very good. It might not look like it from where you are today, but things will be much better soon. You're almost there. And we're not about to hand your husband everything he wants just because he thinks he's entitled, or because he makes you feel some kind of way. He doesn't get to do that anymore."

I groaned.

“Go to France,” she said, her voice growing lighter. “Leave your problems in this country for a few weeks and throw yourself into something new. Let me handle this. If anything significant happens, I’ll reach out. Otherwise, trust that your life will still be here when you return, and trial will only be a week away. Don’t let Robert take the joy of this trip from you too.”

I reluctantly agreed to her request. Then I went back to sleep.

Chapter Thirty

The reality that I was going to France hit like a sledgehammer three days before departure. My countdown widget turned red, and something shifted inside me. Adrenaline replaced my sadness with panic. Whatever else had weighed me down, the only thing that suddenly mattered was that I had seventy-two hours before the trip of a lifetime, and I couldn't be lying around in bed!

I tore through my closet like a woman unhinged. I wasn't just going to France, as if that wasn't reason enough to freak out. I was traveling alone with Lucas. Possibly the man of my dreams incarnate, who looked as if he felt the same way—in photographs, anyway. And it was likely that Sébastien Allard once lived in the region where we were headed.

This was a cosmic storm of goodies. I needed a better wardrobe.

I visited a half dozen thrift stores in search of the perfect clothes, shoes, and accessories. Then I bought new underthings that made me feel young and sexy. Bras and panties Robert had never and would never see or touch.

I packed everything with care, including the photos of Sébastien and my mom, and the list of towns with restaurants on Rue Pasteur.

Lucas drove us to the airport. We chatted and laughed as if I hadn't been mopey and distant for days on end. I told him my pretrial hadn't gone well. He said a little time in France was probably just what I needed.

I couldn't disagree.

Renewed purpose etched away the bone-deep fatigue as I navigated the airports, security, and customs with Lucas. My habitual need to consider everyone else's comfort kicked in at full force, and I spent the day trying to stay hyperorganized and rushing each step of the way. Lucas did his best to slow me down, but he was no match for my desperation never to dillydally or hold anyone up. I checked my tickets repeatedly for the right gate numbers, even after we'd sat in front of them for an hour. Then I kept my phone in hand as I boarded the plane, careful not to somehow sit in the wrong seat. I hurried to stay out of everyone's way, practically throwing my carry-on overhead and diving out of the aisle.

Lucas moved at a more reasonable pace, unhurried but with confidence. He took his time straightening my bag in the compartment and waiting while I found both sides of my safety belt before joining me in our seats.

Apparently, traveling could be pleasant, even fun and interesting, when I wasn't burdened with the mental load of a man determined to ruin my good time. I did my best to relax into the easier pace and enjoy.

Lucas and I played travel word games on our phones and watched movies as we flew over the Atlantic. I confessed my dream of finding the Frenchman who gave me life. He offered to join me on every excursion for the cause.

I fell asleep with my head on his shoulder, feeling like anything was possible.

"Look," he said, nodding toward the window.

Outside the little window, an endless blue sea stretched to the horizon. Later, a new world of lights and landscapes awaited below.

"Welcome to France," he whispered.

And a rush of childlike wonder overtook everything else.

❧

We checked into our hotel, a charming, historic number overlooking the sea. The traditional stucco facade and bright, sunny colors made me smile upon arrival. The wrought iron balconies, unobstructed sea views, and rooftop terrace made me never want to leave. But Nice awaited just outside the door.

I changed quickly out of my travel clothes and into a long cotton dress and knit sweater. Then I met Lucas in the grand foyer for an afternoon of exploration. Classes began tomorrow, and jet-lagged though I was, I couldn't wait to explore. The winds off the water were strong, and the autumn air brisk. The promenade bustled with pedestrians, bikers, and more than a few in-line skaters.

Lucas nudged me as a couple on skates whipped past us at eighty miles an hour. "Have you ever?" he asked, watching the pair vanish into the distance.

I laughed. "If I had, I'm sure both my legs would still be broken. Have you?"

"No." His impish grin captivated me, and a little more of the exhaustion I'd felt before seemed to slip away.

We walked by buildings painted the same soft-pink color found inside oyster shells, a breathtaking blue sea on one side and distant green mountains on the other. The sun rose high in the sky as we wound along narrow streets and weaved through brightly colored shops, talking about everything from my lonely childhood and his loud, adventurous one to our first loves, first pets, and dreams for the future. I marveled at his honesty. And mine. With Lucas, there wasn't any judgment. I stopped frequently to admire views, buy snacks, and take selfies. My trusty companion never complained. It was, I realized wistfully, my definition of a perfect day.

"Penny for your thoughts?" Lucas asked as we climbed toward a hilltop garden.

"I'm really enjoying getting to know you," I admitted. "I appreciate your candor, and your perspectives. And today I feel very much like myself for the first time in a long while. The only other person I speak so freely with is Alicia, but she already knows everything about me anyway. I can't upset or surprise her."

"You think something you say would upset me?" he asked, slowing as we neared the top. "Is that why you sometimes seem to filter yourself?"

I widened my eyes at him and wiggled my head. "Well, yeah." Duh.

Lucas leaned against the railing of the garden. He motioned me to join him for the spectacular view of the sun setting over pebbled beaches. Vibrant streams of amber and apricot light reached across the water to us, catching fire in the shape of a shrinking red ball.

I'd never been so sorry to say goodbye to a single day.

Where had the time gone? How long had we walked? Was it truly all afternoon?

"You don't have to watch your words around me," Lucas said.

I felt his gaze on my cheek but couldn't pull my eyes from the impossible view.

I was in France.

My heart swelled and tears welled. How could this be my life? Twenty-three years of captivity in a gilded cage. And before the divorce was finalized, I was already living my dream.

"You know," Lucas said. "The only time I can't identify with what you're saying is when you speak so lowly of marriage. I know why you do. I might, too, if I was you, but for me," he said, "I think marriage is a wonderful gift and opportunity. To have a best friend by your side, a partner in good times and bad. Someone who knows every part of you and never judges, only encourages and supports. It's a miracle."

I bit the insides of my cheeks to stop a rebuttal. It was nice that he'd had a far different experience than mine. I didn't need to pooh-pooh it. "Sorry," I said instead. "I don't mean to downplay your joy. I'm working on my attitude, believe it or not," I teased. "My daughter is determined to marry, and I have to be on board."

"Would you truly never marry again?"

I studied his face, genuine and beseeching. Then I looked back at the smattering of tiny boats on the sea. "Maybe, if I found what you had," I admitted. It was what everyone wanted, wasn't it?

"Excellent." His voice was husky and approving in the dimming light. I imagined the picture of us once more, me laughing, him looking at me as if I was the only thing that mattered. "It's nice to know you still have hope," he said. "That bozo you married didn't take that from you too."

I laughed. "He did not. But don't get too excited," I teased. "I'm open to the possibility, but I assure you my trust issues are not. The walls they've built are much higher than this one." I patted the fence.

My attention returned to the boats in the distance. As they bobbed and dipped in the water, they rattled something loose in my brain. A memory of the front desk woman at the yacht club. Strange. She'd suggested I open a membership, and I had said my husband handled that. But why did she say she'd contact his company? Initially I assumed the yacht club membership was another perk of partnership, like the annual leasing of cars. But now I wasn't as sure. And was Robert's law firm the company she referenced? Or had she meant something else? A different company?

"You're right to protect yourself," Lucas said, continuing our earlier conversation. "I'm not condemning you for doing whatever it takes to heal. I just hope you'll find lots of joy in the process."

"I have joy," I said, turning to face him directly. "This is joy." I lifted my hands and my lips in a smile. "A week ago I could barely get off my couch, and look at me now! Look at this view!"

"It's stunning," he said softly, his eyes locked on mine.

I laughed. "What time is it in Virginia right now?"

He checked his watch. "Lunchtime, I guess."

I made a mental note to contact the yacht club when I got back to my room, just to satisfy my curiosity. Meanwhile, I chose happiness.

Lucas pulled his phone from his pocket and checked the screen with a frown.

"Everything okay?" I asked.

He tucked the phone away and smiled. "Tomorrow after class we'll take a road trip," he said. "I want to try a family-owned restaurant a few towns away. I'll rent a car."

"Wait. Where are we going?" My stomach knotted in anticipation. "A restaurant?"

"In Menton," he said, casting a look over one shoulder, and I hastened to catch up.

"Why Menton?"

"Remember the photo you showed me of your parents?" he asked, watching as I bounced back downhill at his side.

"On the fridge at my house?"

He nodded. "I think I found the restaurant. I thought you might let me buy you dinner, and we could see if it's the same place."

My heart thundered, and my stomach flipped for more than one reason. "That sounds like a date." I wrinkled my nose in jest. "I don't think that's allowed. Someone might report me to my boss."

He rolled his eyes and laughed. "Consider it research. Eating someplace off the beaten path will provide a little contrast from all the tourist-centric cafés near the water." He swung an arm in the direction of the pristine beauty of Nice below.

"Yeah, this is awful. I'm glad we're getting away."

He nudged me in the ribs for my sarcasm, and my arm rose on instinct to lock with his. Before I could pull away, he bent his elbow further and tugged me close.

"I wouldn't worry about your boss," he added quietly. "I'm confident he would approve."

We walked back to our hotel in twilight and companionable silence, arms intertwined, and my heart screaming like a schoolgirl.

I entered the big white classroom with Lucas by my side the next morning. Our matching white chef's hats and jackets were exactly the same, yet comically different. I hustled along beside him, avoiding curious stares from a handful of classmates in identical garb.

"I can't believe they got my size this wrong," I said. "I look ridiculous. Is this for a giant?"

He stifled a laugh. "This may be partially my fault," he said. "I originally thought John would attend the classes with me. I guess I forgot to change the uniform order when I updated the attendees."

"John?" I squeaked, sleeves flapping like a baby bird. "You mean the man with at least eight inches and a hundred pounds on me? That John?"

Lucas lost his sober expression and burst into laughter.

I shoved the sinking chef's hat back up my forehead so I could see.

When he nodded emphatically, I whacked him with the length of my sleeve.

"Then this is not partially your fault, you goofball," I whisper-screamed as he ran away. "This is all your fault."

The workstations were tall and sturdy, like the ones high school chemistry students stood behind, except these, like everything else in the cavernous culinary arts classroom, were white.

Everything, everywhere, was white.

Lucas watched as I shoved my sleeves up on repeat. "I think it's nice that we match," he said.

"We do not match. We look like a pair of marshmallows, but a giant smashed one of us into a puddle." I pinched the sides of my jacket and tugged them wide for emphasis.

Lucas sighed and reached for me.

I stilled, waiting to see what he'd do.

"Here," he said. "Stop that. You'll be covered in food if you don't roll up these sleeves." He took one of my arms between his hands and neatly rolled the stark-white material.

Electricity zigzagged through the air between us as he worked.

He made eye contact as he secured the fabric behind my crooked elbow. When he reached for my other arm with abundant caution, I suspected he felt the energy too. I hadn't been touched by a man other than Robert since I was still a kid, younger than Camilla. Everything about this felt different. I felt cared for, treasured. Precious.

The urge to grab onto him with both hands was powerful. To be held by this man. To be kissed—

Lucas finished rolling up my sleeve, then set me free.

I pulled in a short, shuddering breath and hoped he didn't notice.

A few minutes later, a dozen more students in well-fitting uniforms filed into the room like a wave, choosing their tables until no open spots remained.

I peeked at the newcomers' faces, eager to stop myself from staring at Lucas.

Were any of them from America? Did everyone speak English?

Oh, god. Was I supposed to speak French?

The crushing sensation that I was a complete impostor and likely to humiliate myself sat on my chest like an elephant.

"Why are you panicking?" Lucas asked, pulling my eyes to him. "Did something happen? How can I help?"

I made wide, wild eyes at him. "I think the real question is why you aren't freaking out," I said. "This is a professional culinary arts class *in France*. This is huge, and I don't know anything about cooking. I'm a baker."

He waved unworried hands. "We aren't cooking," he promised. "Only learning how we can make foods on plates look better."

"Okay, well, what if I can't do that? What if we both fail?"

His brows rose. "I'm not going to—"

I grabbed his arm. "What if I fall down?" Memories of wiping out in my kitchen, at the restaurant, and in my backyard flashed into mind. "I do that a lot more than I should."

"At our age, probably any amount of falling is too much," he agreed. "So we won't do that. Yes?"

"Yes." I bobbed my head. *Obviously.* "No falling."

"None."

I released a labored sigh. "You're right. We can do this. It's not hard. It's art." Creativity was my strong suit. Plus I'd researched food plating extensively leading up to the trip. I knew the technical terms and techniques, more than enough to prevent me from embarrassing myself.

"I forgot to ask you this morning," he said, interest furrowing his brow. "Were you able to reach the marina?"

My thoughts jumped to our morning together. We'd ordered real French press coffee from a café near the beach and shared a sliced baguette spread with butter and jam. I'd told him about the boat at the yacht club.

"I spoke with the woman I met at the yacht club last month, and she's looking into it and calling me back."

A tall, broad-shouldered man in a black ensemble, including a chef's coat and hat, entered the room, and the class went silent. He raised his arms above his head and spoke in French. Thankfully, he switched to English a split second later. "Welcome, students," he declared. "Call me Chef. Raise your hand if you're in crisis. Otherwise, we're covering a lot of material in a short amount of time, so let's save questions for the end of the day."

I kneaded my fingers in anticipation. I had dozens of questions already, and we hadn't even started.

"First we will plate scallops," Chef said. He lifted a plump circle of white flesh into the air for us to see. Then, without warning, he chucked it into the classroom.

I gasped.

Chef chuckled as someone at the table in front of me thrust up a hand and caught it.

The student examined the disk. "Plastic," he called.

Chef crossed his arms and nodded. "All the foods we'll use for the next few days, while we learn and practice techniques, are replicas. That means you can plate, rinse, and repeat the processes until you get the effect you're attempting. You can get your supplies out now. They're stored beneath the tabletops."

Lucas and I arranged the contents on our workstation. Sauces in plastic squeeze bottles. Small pots with jams and butters. Oils, purees, reductions, and emulsions. We lined up shakers of spices and seasonings beside bundles of fresh herbs and edible flowers. And finally, a plastic toy box of fake foods.

"Let's dig in!" Chef called, rubbing his palms together as he walked the aisles. "Often, when we plate, we use odd numbers. Let's start there."

I placed three plastic scallops on my plate. Lucas plated five.

"This is a popular technique that draws the eye around the surface, causing our brains to take in more details," Chef said. "Now, we use the sauces and liquids like edible paint. Plating food is art, and we are the artists."

I slid my eyes in Lucas's direction, expecting to share a commiserating grin. Instead, I found him too absorbed to notice me. All around the room, everyone else busily arranged scallops on their plates.

I eyeballed the other ingredients.

"If you aren't sure where to begin," Chef announced, drawing my eyes to him. "Try overturning a teacup on the plate before you add the food. Shake a seasoning, like pepper or paprika, over the cup. Now, remove the cup, and voilà, a perfect circle of color for your base."

A few students made soft sounds of *ooh* and *ahh*.

Chef returned to his place on the platform and worked methodically through countless ways to dress up a handful of scallops. Then a steak. Some chicken. And soup.

We dropped dollops of tomato reduction paste onto cheese soup, then dragged a skewer through the colors. I'd used a similar technique with frosting and knew the trick well.

Chef made the process seem magical.

Something in my gut insisted this lesson was nice, but plating was not for me. I did not share Chef's passion at all.

Chef spoke of edible flowers as if he'd invented them, but I'd used the same colorful buds to add interest, height, and texture to a number of specialty cakes every week for three years.

By lunchtime, I was mentally drained and out of motivation. I tried pretending all the food was pastry and imagined how I could translate the skills learned here to improve my business back home.

When Chef demonstrated the use of heavy, Dijon-based spreads on plates for flank steak, I imagined the mustard was caramel sauce, and the steak was a brownie.

His paprika was my cinnamon sugar.

Beside me, Lucas intently mimicked every move our teacher made. I couldn't help but think he'd brought the wrong staff member for training, and I needed to tell him sooner rather than later. I didn't want to plate for one more hour, let alone three more weeks, and a lifetime after that.

I also didn't want to disappoint him. Lucas had brought me all the way to France because he believed in me. Could I really let him down?

He smiled and nudged me, pleased with his plate. I beamed appropriately in response. His joys were my joys, because I cared about his well-being. Just as he cared for mine.

I refocused on my plate. I could be an excellent plater of food for Lucas in the evenings and run my baking company by day. Couldn't I? Why did it have to be one or the other?

"You okay?" he whispered. "Is he going too fast?"

"No." I shook my head. "I've got it." I upturned the bottle of pea puree and streaked the poison-green goo across a jet-black plate.

I just had to make it through this lesson. Then I had dinner plans with Lucas. Something major to look forward to, and only a few hours away.

When I might finally meet my biological dad.

Chapter Thirty-One

I was unprecedentedly nervous as we drove through the streets of France in our little rental car. Maybe it was the intimacy of sharing such a small space with him, or perhaps my jitters had more to do with the fact I would soon stand on the corner where my biological parents had stood so many decades before.

Tonight was the night I might meet Sébastien Allard.

"You doing okay?" Lucas asked, expertly piloting the car around a line of pedestrians attempting to herd children across the street. I was immeasurably thankful for him. He made driving through unfamiliar streets in a foreign country seem so easy and casual.

Then again, for Lucas, easy and casual were completely on brand.

"I'm okay," I said. Whatever happened or didn't happen tonight, I would be just fine.

I ran my clammy palms over the simple denim pants I'd chosen for our evening excursion. The cinched elastic waist had a wide red sash belt. I convinced myself, after trying on everything in my suitcase twice, that this was both casual, because denim, and nice, and because no buttons or zipper. Ultimately, I chose the most comfortable option in case I threw up or tried to run and fell down. If I couldn't be cute, I could at least be prepared.

My well-loved ice-blue turtleneck offered a small measure of comfort on a night of uncomfortable anticipation.

I relaxed a bit when we broke free from the congestion and chaos of Nice. The sun hung low in the sky, signaling the end of yet another beautiful day. I tracked silhouettes of birds through a cotton candy–pink sky and tried to imagine how dinner might end.

"You did great in class today," Lucas said, breaking the silence. "Did you enjoy the introduction to plating?"

"Yeah," I answered instinctively. "It was interesting."

He watched me for a prolonged moment before returning his eyes to the road. "I don't know what we'll find at the bistro," he said. "Maybe just a nice meal, but if you want to leave at any time, tell me. I won't hesitate to pay our bill and walk out or ask you to explain."

I looked away. The potential for the night to end poorly was astronomical, and he knew it. I appreciated the support, but somehow his acknowledgment inflated my anxiety.

"Sophie?" he nudged. "I don't always know what you're thinking. You have to let me know tonight so that I can help."

I rolled my head against the seat back, waiting to catch his eye. "Thank you for being so kind."

He frowned. "This is the bare minimum and absolute least I can do."

"Distract me."

He redirected the conversation to our classmates, and we dissected who we thought they were and the places they might call home. Chef hadn't wasted any time on icebreakers, so we had very few clues. Hypothesizing passed the time, and before I knew it, our destination came into view.

I removed the photograph from my handbag and raised it toward the restaurant on the corner, lining up the views. "Oh my gosh," I whispered. "I think this is really it."

Lucas parked, and we met on the sidewalk, then appraised the dark brick walls and large glass windows. The sign on the roof matched the one in the photo, though the one before me was nearly a half century older, more rusted, sun bleached, and worn.

"Before we go inside, would you like a photograph taken here?" Lucas asked. "Like the one with your mother?"

I nodded, speechless and eternally thankful for his thoughtfulness. I wouldn't have thought of it on my own and would've missed the opportunity.

"Chin up," he said, demonstrating the move, then smiling. "There." He took the photo with his phone, then forwarded it to me by text.

"Can we take a selfie with the two of us?" I asked. "Is that weird?" It seemed strange not to commemorate the fact we came together.

He slid by my side and swept an arm around my back. I leaned against him on instinct, comfortable and safe. We took turns capturing the memory with our phone cameras.

I closed my eyes and absorbed the moment, drinking in the crisp fall air and rich, buttery aromas wafting from the restaurant. *I made it, Mom,* I thought. *I found the spot where you had your last carefree summer. I wish you were here with me, but I also think you kind of are. Thank you for telling me about Sébastien and giving me this chance.*

"Ready?" Lucas asked, moving toward the door. "Deep breath."

I obeyed and followed him to the threshold.

"I didn't say it earlier, but you look very nice tonight," he said. "That shade of blue is your color."

My cheeks warmed. "Thank you. I'm glad you think so. I'm kind of a mess, in case you can't tell."

"I think you're doing great."

I led the way through a set of tall wooden doors with brass handles that opened onto a sea of vintage black and white octagonal tiles. A service counter centered the room, and tables lined the walls and windows. Overhead lighting shone through an array of old-fashioned bottles on shelves, casting rainbows over the space. We'd taken a step back in time.

Dozens of candid photos filled the space beside the door. The images all featured people standing outside the building just as Lucas and I had a moment before. I wished I had an instant camera, so I could add our photo to the collection as well. I opened my mouth to say as much, and then I saw him.

A small square photo near the collage's center featured Sébastien Allard. He looked just as he had in the photo with my mom, minus the apron. I raised my photograph to compare the two versions of him.

"That's him," Lucas said, confirming my suspicion.

In the photo a group of people in matching aprons stood at his side.

"He worked here," I whispered. Then, scanning the other photos, I saw him everywhere, and watched him age before my eyes. The group varied year to year, but Bastien was in every photo. His clothing and hair style changed most notably at first, then his posture and size. He grew tall and broad, gained facial hair, then lost it. Became thin again and eventually a little stooped.

I wouldn't have recognized him in the latter pictures if I hadn't noticed him in the first. But now, I thought I'd know the eyes anywhere. I thought they looked a little like my eyes.

A willowy woman in a black dress and shoes approached, greeting us in French.

I wanted to ask if she knew the people in the pictures, but I needed a moment to think.

Lucas responded congenially, speaking briefly in French before changing to English, for my benefit, as he had the entire trip so far.

She nodded and led us to a nearby table for two. "I'll be back with some glasses and water."

My heart pounded as I admired the dining area and chatting patrons, immediately in love with the energy all around us. The atmosphere reminded me of Chez Margot. Though the aesthetic was completely different, the feeling of connection between the staff and guests was obvious and strong. The man behind the bar called out to families as they entered or left.

I slid my gaze to Lucas, suddenly too timid to pose the questions I'd traveled from America to ask. Maybe he would do it for me. I could hide under the table and wait.

Lucas set one giant hand atop mine on the place mat. My eyes widened unintentionally at the unexpected touch.

"You're shaking," he said.

My bobbing knee stilled, and my vibrating frame went rigid. "Sorry. I can't believe he works here. We found him, but what if—" I couldn't say the words, couldn't bear to think them.

What if I was too late, and I'd lost him too?

Lucas offered my fingers a comforting squeeze, and every thought in my head focused tightly on his touch.

The hostess reappeared, and I pulled my hands onto my lap, suddenly terrified and wishing I hadn't come. If I didn't ask, I couldn't know he was gone. If I didn't meet him, he couldn't tell me he didn't want me.

An older woman strode alongside the hostess to our table, eyes homed in tightly on my face. She looked closer to my mom's age than mine, beautiful and lean with sleek silver hair. Her porcelain face showed evidence of laughter and a lifetime of smiles. Her smart brown eyes suggested she missed very little of what happened around her.

I envied her gray cashmere sweaterdress and knee boots. Why did I wear pants?

Lucas rose to greet her, hand extended.

I popped onto my feet a second later, unsure what was happening.

"I'm Mary Allard," she said. "I've taken the liberty of ordering a family dinner, and I hope you'll stay. I hear we might have a loved one in common."

My breath caught at the sound of her last name, and my knees buckled. My fear returned with a resounding whoosh. Logically, I had no reason to worry, but emotionally, my panic alarms had all sounded. The possibility of rejection crushed my lungs before Lucas finished making introductions.

The hostess poured glasses of water for each of us and left a carafe on the table.

Lucas and Mary took seats, and their eyes turned to me.

I drank greedily from my glass, then set it down with trembling hands. "I'm Sophie Bianco," I said, mouth parched despite the recent drink. "I'm looking for my father, Sébastien Allard." I set the photograph on the table, and Mary's eyes misted with tears.

She pulled the photo into her hands and smiled gently at the image. "I was Bastien's wife," she said. "We were married for forty-one years."

A ravine ran through me at her use of past tense.

"I'm very sorry to tell you we lost him last fall," she added. Her clarification was a punch to my heart, and my head lightened with the knowledge. Sébastien was gone too.

"I wish it wasn't true," she said, voice cracking as she spoke. "I miss him every moment of every day. We all do." She motioned to the restaurant. "He was beloved. And a very, very good man."

Mary explained that Lucas had been in touch before our arrival. The staff had alerted her to our reservation, and she'd been nervously awaiting the chance to share her story with me.

Lucas smiled softly when I looked to him. Then he rose and excused himself, promising to return before our meal arrived. As if he hadn't done enough already, he gave us the additional gift of privacy.

Mary watched him walk away, but I could only marvel at the woman before me.

Sébastien Allard's wife. *His widow,* I mentally corrected. Something about her presence made Bastien all the more real, even if he was gone. Before, he was just an image from a photograph and a person from my mother's past. Now, I sat here with his widow, and the thought raised gooseflesh on my arms.

"You have a good one there, too, I see," Mary said, nodding in the direction Lucas had gone.

I tracked him, belatedly, with my gaze, allowing what she'd said to register. "Oh, we're not—"

Her brow furrowed with confusion.

"We're . . ." I stalled again. What were we? Coworkers? Friends? Both were true, yet neither description felt like nearly enough.

Mary's answering smile was warm and kind. "Well, you'll figure that out in time," she said. "Right now, I'm so glad you're here. I've always wanted a daughter."

I blinked back tears as I told her everything about my own daughter, then a little about my mom.

"Bastien talked about your mother often when we were young, in the years before we dated," she said. "The pretty American girl who stole his heart and carried it back across the sea." Mary pressed a hand to her chest and looked toward the ceiling. She laughed. "Bastien had a flair for the dramatic, and a genuine zest for life. His passion was contagious. No one would deny it. He and I grew up together in this town, and all the girls wanted him. I was a few years younger and not on his radar until long after your mother had traveled home. I was just glad to be his friend. Then one day, seemingly out of the blue, he asked me if I wanted to go with him for a coffee. We were married six months later, and we stayed that way to his very last breath."

"That's beautiful," I said. "Forty-one years is a lifetime."

Her expression fell and a tear slid from her eye. "It wasn't nearly long enough. My mother said we made it work because a marriage built on friendship starts with a strong foundation." She shrugged. "Sometimes I think we just got lucky."

I thought of Camilla and Jeff. I'd pushed her to take more girl trips and do as much as she could without him, but she only wanted to make memories if he was in them. Anyone who'd met them could see Jeff felt the same way. They were the closest of friends, and building a life together made a lot more sense when I looked at it from that point of view.

Camilla had gotten love right, despite the awful examples she'd grown up with.

"You would've loved Bastien," Mary said, her brown eyes alight once more. "He was full of mischief, too, but in all the best ways." She laughed, then dropped a palm to her stomach. "Oh, and he loved to bake. One more of his many talents."

My gaze snapped to hers. "Bastien baked?"

She nodded. "Very well. And often. His mother taught him. Her father taught her. He probably baked for your mother. He couldn't stop himself, I'm sure."

Memories of my mother, working for hours in our kitchen, returned with a rush. She played the radio and sang, lost in her own world while she made the most magnificent creations.

Had she thought of him while she baked? When I stood on a chair beside her to reach the counter, was she sharing him with me?

"My mom taught me to bake," I said.

Mary smiled. "That's lovely. I'm sure she was an excellent mother."

I bit my tongue as old rants and negativity came to mind. I knew my mother better now. I understood her struggles more clearly. "She did the best she could," I said, and that was the truth of it. *And I think she missed him dearly.*

Mary nodded. "He would've loved knowing he had a daughter. We tried for children of our own, but that was never meant to be. We didn't pursue things, medically," she said. A blush crept over her fair skin. "We just enjoyed each other and cherished what we had. We believe that what is meant for us will find us."

"That's beautiful," I said.

Part of me wanted to tell her I was sorry she'd never known the joy of carrying a baby to term, of the pain and elation of delivery and of every other stage of a child's life. For me, those were the high points of my life, but Mary had other experiences, and I envied her those.

There was so much life to live. There wasn't enough time to live it.

Lucas returned as the waitstaff brought our meals, and I realized he'd been watching. Just as promised, he'd never left me alone.

The three of us spent the evening getting to know one another over loaves of fresh bread and bowls of pot-au-feu, a delicious meat-and-potatoes stew. Mary was the embodiment of grace, and when the time came to leave, I was reluctant to say goodbye.

"Promise me you'll stay in touch," she said, passing a business card into my hand. "My home number and personal email are on there. I'm on social media too. I like to keep up with my friends and family." She drew me to her for a long hug and air-kisses before turning to Lucas. "Bring her back to me soon."

He nodded. "I'll do my best."

I grinned as we walked back through the door. I hadn't found my birth father, but I'd found a woman eager to be my stepmother and friend.

I considered that a wonderful gift. One I would never take for granted.

Chapter Thirty-Two

Lucas and I walked the streets near the restaurant before returning to our car. I needed a little extra time to process and unwind. I'd lost my father without ever knowing him, but I was deeply thankful for the woman I'd found in his stead. And for all the stories of his life she'd so willingly shared.

I tipped my head for a better look at the moon and stars, glittering across an inky night sky. Soft music drifted from cafés, and a contented sigh left my body as I floated through the most surreal moment of my life.

"What?" Lucas asked, nudging my arm as we strolled in the direction of our rental car. "We don't have to go yet," he offered. "We can walk all night if you like. It's the perfect weather for it."

At the car I stood outside the passenger door and peered at him across the roof of the little vehicle. Everything about the moment felt profound. My time with Mary underscored the lessons I'd learned during these last few months. People died every day, and too few lived while they had the chance. I didn't want to spend any more of my limited days with people I didn't like or doing things I didn't love. "I don't want to plate food." The declaration came out before I'd had time to decide how to say it. The immediate relief pulled a smile across my lips.

His brows bunched. "What do you mean? You didn't have fun today?"

"I had fun with you today," I clarified. I didn't want to hurt or disappoint Lucas, but I knew this was the right choice for me. I needed to be brave and honor that. "I think I'd be good at plating, if I finished the course, but—"

Lucas pursed his lips and rested his forearms on the roof. "You want to bake," he said. "Of course you do. You're a baker. You should bake."

I laughed, in love with his words. I was a baker. And a pretty good one. "I'm truly sorry," I said. "I didn't mean to put you out. I really wanted this to work." I couldn't imagine what my change of mind cost him. I covered my mouth as the expenses piled in my head. *Time and money.*

"It's fine," he said. "I'll call John. I already know where I can get him a last-minute uniform." Lucas laughed. "I don't know why I thought you'd want to completely change jobs. I wasn't sure what might happen with the blogger, if your side business would be ruined, if you'd need the added income. I knew you'd do a great job at whatever you tried, so—"

"You were trying to help me." If the car wasn't standing between us, I'd have tackle hugged him.

"I might've had selfish reasons too," he said. "Don't think I'm a saint. I knew I'd have more fun in France with a beautiful, fun-loving friend than I would with John."

I tried hard not to focus on the fact he'd called me beautiful. "You're not mad?"

"Why would I be mad?" He unlocked the car, then folded himself behind the wheel.

I followed suit and buckled up beside him. "You flew me to France for three weeks of specialized culinary classes. Then I only took one before quitting," I said. "That's a big waste of money on your part, and an incredibly inconsiderate move on mine."

Lucas started the car and pulled smoothly onto the road. "This isn't a problem. This is life. Things change, and it's more important to follow your heart and seek your passion than to lie to yourself about what you want. I asked you to try this, and you did. I appreciate that. I also appreciate anyone who knows their own mind."

I watched him closely as he drove, but I detected no signs of a ruse, no indication of an emotional game afoot. Lucas truly wanted me to be happy. He wanted everyone to be happy. I believed now that good, kind men existed. And having one right beside me did complicated things to my heart.

Lucas and I parted ways again when my phone rang in the hotel lobby. I didn't recognize the number, but lifted a finger to Lucas, indicating I wanted to answer.

Lucas waved and moved onto the elevator, on his way to give John a call.

I pressed the Accept button on my screen and raised the phone to my ear. "Hello?"

"Mrs. Bianco?" a woman's voice asked.

I cringed at the sound of my last name. I would change that as soon as possible. "Yes. May I help you?"

"This is Karli from the Norfolk Yacht Club," she said. "I'm so sorry it's taken me this long to get back with you. We're planning a regatta next month and—" She cleared her throat. "Never mind. The important thing is that I finally had the time to look up that account for you, and I have the contact information your husband used when claiming the slip for your boat." She paused. "Did I get that right?" she asked. "You need contact information for your husband?"

I supposed that did seem odd. "That's correct," I said, improvising. "I'm doing our books and want to make sure things are aligned. You mentioned getting in touch with his company on the day I was there, and I need to be sure the right charges go to our corresponding businesses. So, just to clarify, the club membership isn't a personal one?"

"No, ma'am."

"Is it paid for by the law firm?"

They gave him a new Mercedes every year. Why not a yacht club membership?

"I'm not sure," she said. "The company name I have here is GraberCoCare."

"I see," I said. That didn't ring a bell. "Is there anything else?"

She read the address and phone number to me. The number belonged to his cell phone. I wrote the address down.

We disconnected and I took a seat in one of the plush lobby chairs.

I was sure I'd never heard the company name before, yet it seemed strangely familiar.

I plugged the address into my phone and an internet search linked it to a local UPS Store with rentable mailboxes. What kind of company didn't have a physical address? Something online? Something that didn't exist?

I'd barely finished the thought when I recalled the reason the company name seemed so familiar. I hadn't heard it before. I'd seen it on the paperwork in Robert's hidey-hole.

I looked it up on the state business website and learned the LLC was owned by a trust. I suspected it was also buried in a maze of legal loopholes the way only a trained attorney like Robert could manage.

Unfortunately for him, I'd hired a team of forensic accountants before all the money disappeared. I called them next.

"We've got him, Ms. Bianco," the team leader told me before I had the chance to share my news. "It took a little longer than we liked, but Robert was extremely thorough in his efforts, and there was a lot to unravel. We're still tying up some loose ends, but we'll have a full report ready for you next week."

"Does that mean you know about the LLC, the yacht club, and the UPS mailbox?" I asked, stunned by the man's victorious tone. Until now, I'd never made it past his voicemail or receptionist. If my attorney hadn't sworn by the company, I might've thought they'd taken my retainer and run.

"Yes, ma'am. I think you'll be surprised by all that we found, but I have to jump off right now, I'm late for an appointment, but I'll get back to you early next week. That's a promise."

Emotion overcame me as I considered the possibility. "You can prove he hid our money?"

The man paused before stating simply, "We can."

I tipped my head back and smiled at the ceiling. Now we could strike an agreement and settle out of court. I'd be free, and my marriage would finally be over.

I was in the gorgeous South of France, but suddenly I couldn't wait to go home.

I disconnected with the accountant and immediately called my attorney.

❧

I left France when John arrived, and I headed home to get my ducks in a row. Saying goodbye to Lucas was harder than I expected, though I'd see him again in a few weeks when the course ended. He drove me to the airport in the rental car and walked me to security.

When he lingered, I rose onto my tiptoes and kissed his cheek. That was allowed in Europe, wasn't it?

He blushed, and I smiled. Then I carried that sweet moment with me all the way home.

❧

Several important things happened within days of my return. First, and most shockingly, Robert was arrested. The forensic accountant gave me a heads-up the night before. As it turned out, the team I'd hired discovered evidence of Robert's financial crimes long before the night I'd called them from France. In fact, they'd run into an ongoing police investigation of money mismanagement at Robert's law firm the moment they started working for me. From there, they struggled to separate marital funds from gains acquired through illegal operations, which was the reason the team had been so hard to reach. Their hands and tongues were tied by the ongoing investigation, making it seem to me that they hadn't had any luck, when in fact, they'd hit a proverbial mother lode of criminal activity.

Thanks to the advance notice, Alicia called out sick and drove with me to Robert's office for the big arrest. We parked across the street to watch the authorities bodily remove him from the building in handcuffs. It was petty, but we brought a sign and popcorn to ensure he saw us.

I later learned that, as part of his greedy, miscreant behavior, Robert had purchased multiple large-ticket items in my name, and Camilla's, over the years. He used them to temporarily hide his pilfered money. He then sold the assets when he was ready and invested the money. A routine he followed compulsively.

The only downside was that because of the ongoing investigation, it would take months or more before I received funds from our marital estate. The divorce settled without a trial, however, and that was the real win.

Five months later, I still rarely stopped smiling.

"Sophie!" Alicia scolded. Her dark hair shone under the fluorescent kitchen lighting as she hurried in my direction. Her bright smile and little black dress made her look like the very young woman I'd met on campus all those years ago. How lucky were we to know a lifelong friendship like this one?

She opened and closed her hand, arm extended in the universal gesture for *gimme*. "Come on. Let's go. Stop fussing over those cookies. You don't even work here anymore. It's time to dance."

I untied my apron and pulled it away from my deep-purple satin dress.

I'd turned in my resignation at Chez Margot shortly after my divorce for a number of reasons. First and foremost, it was time to chase my dream. To keep choosing happiness.

Virginia's Secrets' coverage of my LLC had led to the launch of a crowdsourcing effort by her followers. I didn't know about it until she returned to deliver the news. Live. The video of my impassioned impromptu speech about women supporting women had gone viral while I was out of the country, and people from all around the world donated to help me reach my dream of opening a storefront. Something I'd done in grand, show-offy style one week ago today.

I did it scared, knowing all the ways new businesses fail. I did it knowing if I failed, my friends would still be right beside me, and I'd still be proud of myself for taking the leap and reaching for joy.

Because I didn't let fear or insecurity win, I'd baked my daughter's wedding cake in my very own commercial kitchen.

The bustle of a half dozen tipsy women echoed down the restaurant's hallway to our ears, and Alicia snickered. "They're coming!"

My book club arrived a moment later, cheeks pink from too many glasses of Lucas's free-flowing wine at the bar.

Lucas graciously offered Chez Margot to us for the rehearsal dinner venue. He'd used the opportunity to try out his new black-tie menu and atmosphere. And we'd packed the place with our nearest, dearest family members and friends.

Alicia's sons shared the role of DJ.

When Robert was arrested, Camilla was horrified, thinking he'd purchased her gown with stolen money. She was then thrilled to learn I'd sent the anonymous gift. I didn't tell her the money came from the boat, because she deserved to be happy, and not worried about the details. In the end, the authorities would figure out the money situation, untether the amounts that were legitimate and not, and the details would be clear. Until then, I chose to count my blessings and find peace where I could. I could always take out a personal loan if I needed to return the dress funds.

I fussed with the trays of pastries for tomorrow's wedding reception. They really were beautiful.

Ilona pushed her way through the group for a closer look at my work. "I thought those were ready when we brought them here from your store."

"They were," I said. "But there's always room for another detail or two."

"Not tonight," Alicia said, looping her arm with mine. "But I'm glad I heard you say that. I'll be prepared if you get any ideas about adding anything more to the cake."

I nodded soberly. "Wise." I'd already considered completely reworking the flower patterns and color scheme. My pinks were a little too red, and the green wasn't pulling its weight the way I knew it could.

"Cameron and the boys will get it over to the reception, so you don't have to think about anything other than making memories with your daughter."

"Thank you," I said. "And thank them again if I forget tonight."

Somewhere beyond the kitchen walls, a round of cheers grew into a roar.

We were missing something good, and I didn't want to miss another minute of anything in my life or Camilla's.

I opened my arms and moved our little group toward the party, herding them back through the swinging doors in the direction of the fun. "Okay," I said brightly. "Let's go."

Jeannie laughed and bounced against the others, a group picture of bliss.

Sylvia steadied her and smiled over one shoulder at me. "Your new life is so cute. I want it."

"Everyone wants it," Jeannie said.

"If it still comes with spending twenty-plus years married to Robert, I'll pass," Alicia said.

I laughed. "Touché."

"Oh!" Jeannie snapped her fingers. "Someone should write a book about it! I'd read the shit out of that."

The ladies nodded in agreement.

I grinned. It wasn't often that justice was served so abundantly in life, or that happiness prevailed so thoroughly despite unfortunate circumstances. And I would never downplay my mind-boggling good fortune.

My friends often said the life I had today was a result of that first, brave step I took last spring, when I walked away from my longtime bully and husband.

I preferred to think the life I had today was a result of all the love I put into the world boldly shining back on me. I believed in good karma, because I'd seen it in action.

I hoped my mom could see me now, and that she knew Camilla had chosen a better path than either of us had at her age. Camilla chose her own path. Finding a handsome, helpful best friend to go along for the journey was a really nice bonus.

As if on cue, Lucas rounded the corner into the hallway, and my book club ladies dispersed in a cloud of goofy giggles.

"Get her on the dance floor," Alicia called as she led the women away.

"On it," he returned.

"They're all drunk," I told him. "Your work here is done."

He opened his arms and smiled. "Your little girl's getting married tomorrow."

I stepped into his embrace with a deep, contented sigh.

Of all the things I never saw coming a year ago, Lucas topped the list. I probably would've guessed Robert's arrest before thinking the handsome restaurateur would give me hope for a different future—romantically speaking.

Things changed for us in France, though I hadn't realized how much until the dust on my divorce finally settled. Lucas walked beside me on my journey from frightened, newly separated, part-time pastry chef to confident, joyful, full-time businesswoman. From a woman who hated all men for the sins of one, and deplored marriage as an institution on principal, to one who deeply appreciated that anything was possible.

Mary's words often came to mind, because whatever Lucas and I had, wasn't it first built on friendship?

Lucas kissed the top of my head and rocked me gently in his arms. "Are you nervous for tomorrow?"

"Nope." I rested my cheek against his broad chest and inhaled the fresh, crisp scent of him. "I'm excited. Thank you again for letting us use the restaurant tonight." Holding the rehearsal dinner here made the day feel more personal and family oriented. I'd also saved a fortune on renting a venue, and the food was unequivocally fantastic.

"Anything for you or that precious girl of yours. Plus, you know how I like to party."

If party meant feed me and ply me with wine, then yes, he certainly did.

I laced my fingers with his, taking one more look into his soulful brown eyes before getting back to the event.

My thumb swiped across the backs of his fingers. The ring I always found there was gone. I worried instantly that he'd lost it. I liked knowing Lucas wore the band symbolically. An outward showing of his dedication and loyalty to Margot's memory and the relationship he'd cherished.

I raised our joined hands for a closer look. "Your ring is missing," I said.

"No," he said, touching his thumb to the naked patch of skin. "Not missing." His lips curved into a small, careful smile. "I spoke with Margot yesterday when I brought flowers to her grave. I told her I thought it was time I put her ring away, and she agreed. Long past time, maybe, but nonetheless."

My heart ached for him as I imagined his visit with her, and for the incredible, unfair loss they'd experienced. "I'm sorry," I whispered. "Are you okay?"

He chuckled and pulled me close. "Sophie," he said, voice low and gravelly in my ear. "I'm better than I have been in years. I'm with my best friend on the eve of her daughter's wedding, celebrating with her family and friends. And I think I'm falling in love."

I pulled back to search his eyes, skin tingling and proverbial butterflies in flight.

Lucas released my hands, moving his warm palms to cup my jaw instead. "I admire you, Soph. I am oh, so proud of you all the time. And I am head over heels in love."

Delighted, amazed, and speechless, I rose onto my tiptoes and kissed him. Because I loved him too. This time, the experience wasn't jangling nerves and skyrockets at midnight. It was rainy Sundays in jogging pants and holding hands on long walks through the snow. It was knowing Lucas saw me for exactly who I was, and he didn't want to change me. He, somehow, thought I was the coolest person he knew.

Make that make sense if love doesn't exist.

Another round of cheers echoed through the building, and I couldn't help thinking they were for Lucas and me.

He draped his arm across my shoulder and turned me toward the party. "How about a glass of wine?"

"Always trying to get me drunk," I teased.

The dining room came into view as we approached the foyer. Camilla and Jeff danced in a circle of family and friends. Easels on the bar held an enlarged photo of Mom and Sébastien beside another of tomorrow's bride and groom. My parents' photo carried a banner with the words *In loving memory*. Mary had brought the gift with her from France to congratulate and meet her unofficial granddaughter.

She sat with Ilona, smiling and watching as everyone danced. I wished my mom was here to see this, and maybe she was. I would be forever thankful Mary and Ilona could be here too.

Seeing so much joy on the faces of everyone I loved, in the same place, at the same time, I couldn't help wondering if I'd ever be happier than this. Considering I felt happy a lot lately, I supposed the answer was yes.

And as I passed the bakery display, bursting at the seams with my most colorful confections yet, I blew a kiss toward the big pink sign.

Now open!
The Visible Baker
111 Front Street
Because Everyone Deserves To Be Seen

About the Author

Julie Hatcher is an award-winning and bestselling author of mystery and romantic suspense. She has published more than fifty novels under multiple pen names since her debut in 2013.

Writing as Julie Anne Lindsey, Hatcher has earned many accolades for her work, including the 2020 National Readers' Choice Award for Romance Adventure and the 2019 Daphne du Maurier Award for Mystery/Suspense, among others.

When she's not creating new worlds or fostering the epic love of fictional characters, Julie can be found in Kent, Ohio, enjoying her blessed Midwestern life—and probably plotting murder with her shamelessly enabling friends. Today she hopes to make someone smile. But one day she plans to change the world.